NEFARIOUS NORTH

A Collection of Crime Short Stories

Edited by

Paul Archer

Library and Archives Canada Cataloging in Publication

Nefarious North: A Collection of Crime Short Stories : Canada; edited by Paul Archer.

Detective and Mystery stories, Canadian (English) 2,
Paul Archer

© Copyright in the collection 2013 by Karen Dryden

ISBN 978-0-9919465-0-1
eISBN 978-0-9919465-1-8

© Cover Art and Design by Deborah MacGillivray

Printed in the U.S.A.
Published in Canada

"The short stories you'll discover in this collection are enjoyable examples of the genre at its best. Due to the brevity imposed, writers are required to discover exactly the right word in a description, precise plot points, and quick but deep insights into characters. Mystery/crime short stories are my favourite. They always have a clever twist, a surprise ending, or a thrilling ride. The authors in this anthology accomplish all of this in spades. Safe crackers, ghosts, street criminals, crafty, nasty older ladies, hired or sympathetic killers, zombies, crooked cops, duplicitous friends or lovers, clones, fraudulent priests, agents of death and robbers abound in these delicious, brief, highly readable tales. The stories cover the gamut of passions: humour, grief, sadness, excitement and insanity. Each of them says something about the human condition, whether their voice is funny, crazy, serious or sarcastic. Readers will have fun with each and every one of these stories, which can be enjoyed on a bus or train or just before bed, because they're short and so very sweet."

— Catherine Astolfo,
Arthur Ellis Crime Short Story Award Winner 2012.

"Clever and intriguing cases of mistaken identity, endings with surprising twists, supernatural connections we can believe, vengeful spouses. The authors of Nefarious North brings us engaging stories that are brilliant gems—every one of them."

—D.J. McIntosh
National Bestselling Author

"This thrilling collection of short stories is sure to haunt you in the best possible way! Revenge-seeking ghosts, fed-up mothers-in-law, the voice of vigilante justice on Death Row, wives who decide to take matters into their own hands—or perhaps you'll just about kill for a cigarette? Unexpected twists and turns entertain, tease and shock, while the breadth of content ensures every reader will find a gem in this this treasure chest of macabre tales."

— Lisa de Nikolits, Author

PAUL ARCHER

Paul Archer is a veteran editor with more than 40 years experience in print media, including an early start with a weekly Muskoka newspaper and later, a 30-year stint at the Toronto Star, where he was an editor on a number of news desks. He was also an assistant city editor, deputy city editor and finally, a senior news editor when he retired.

He is a life-long mystery buff, cutting his teeth on the likes of Agatha Christie, Rex Stout, Dorothy Sayers, Colin Dexter, Ellery Queen, Ruth Rendell and P.D. James. Later on came other greats such as Peter Robinson, Ian Rankin, Elizabeth George, Michael Connelly, and Kate Atkinson. He also appreciates anything Stephen King writes. In between the full-length novels there was always time for short stories - British or U.S. anthologies.

He holds degrees in journalism and sociology and believes a proper short story has a big job to do: spark an intrigue that gets the reader interested right away, include well-developed characters, a few red herrings and a smart finish. It's a tall order.

He believes newspaper stories and short stories are a lot alike: you must artfully craft your words to pique the reader's interest using the least amount of space and time to tell your tale.

He and his wife live in Toronto along with Hamish, a wild Westie, and Binnie, a ferocious Bichon.

Table of Contents

Standard's Watch

Prelude to "The Standard Stories"

by Graham Freeman

Graham Freeman grew up in Yorkshire, UK and is a loyal supporter of Bradford City. He worked at an advertising agency, an Internet Service Provider, and an IT consultancy conglomerate before moving to Canada in 2004. Continuing to work in the IT industry, his pastimes include programming complex real-world simulations, cartography and horology, and listening to music by Kraftwerk, Orbital, and BT.

In 2008 he wrote his first play, which was staged in 2009 and was well received. His current Works In Progress include a Hollywood science-fiction screenplay, a psychological thriller novel, and the continuation of the Standard Stories *the first of which will be available in Spring 2014.*

He is co-founder and President of the Grand River Atheists, a Not For Profit organization incorporated in the province of Ontario. He currently lives in Guelph with his fiancé and three cats.

Ambrose Standard was 38 years old. He stood five feet, nine inches tall, and weighed 143 pounds. His straight, black hair was brushed backwards even though it was short enough never to fall into his eyes and disrupt his vision. He had a moustache, full but not bushy while the rest of his face was clean-shaven with the whiskers of a day's growth beginning to make themselves known.

At this moment, he was wearing a cap of the fashion sported by those who enjoy shooting partridges, or who fish with a rod and line whilst standing in the middle of a river. The cap was of a particular tartan; however in the darkness it was hard to discern which one. He wore a well fitted jacket and an overcoat that looked more expensive than it was. His white shirt was clean but had seen better days. It was laundered yesterday and pressed for a function in the evening that he did not attend. A cravat threatened to untie itself having previously been loosened in order to allow the unfastening of the shirt's top button. Small patches of mud were drying at the turn-ups on his trousers but his black leather shoes were tightly tied and spotlessly clean. The soles were repaired at Cobb's on Rutland Street just last week. On first or even second glance Ambrose Standard was the epitome of a completely forgettable figure. And that, dear reader, was not by any chance at all.

Upon this evening, Standard was kneeling in front of an Impenetrable safe, manufactured by the Impenetrable Security Company lately of Blackpool, Lancashire but more recently by Royal Appointment and thereby of London. The sparse room in which the safe stood contained a desk, three chairs and a bookcase. The bookcase was new; the books were most certainly not. The top of the desk was clean apart from a blotting pad and a short glass bottle two thirds full of dark blue ink. The desk drawers were closed but unlocked, having been picked open by Standard just minutes earlier. A window to his right displayed nothing but a scene of brickwork, to be expected of a room on the third floor, overlooking a forgotten alleyway. Behind him on the other side of the desk the only door of the room was closed. Standard studied the safe in front of him.

It was so dark of a green in colour that one could mistake it for a shade of grey. If one studied the safe closely one might just be able to make out where the body of the safe ended, and its door began. There was a single dial to the right of the door's center at which a silver handle was attached to the inner working of the safe's mechanism. Standard knew the Impenetrables well but this one had refused all attempts at opening it. Nothing in the desk hinted at a combination, and the blotter gave up no hints either. Working in the dark was nothing new to him, besides, carrying a lamp was risky. He could light a match, but that would leave clues for the Inspector who would no doubt attend the scene tomorrow, surrounded by a throng of bobbies eager to be part of the investigation. So darkness it was.

Standard crouched to his haunches and closed his eyes, out of habit more than anything, and once again placed the stethoscope's buds into his ears and held the other end with his right hand against the Impenetrable. He breathed in through his nose, held the breath while counting to four and slowly let the air escape from his mouth. Holding his breath thusly, he turned the dial clockwise ever so slowly.

Fifty-six, fifty-seven, fifty-eight — and there was the slight "snick" sound he knew was coming. He reversed the turn with his left hand, feeling the numbers pass by under his right thumb. The next snick could not be at a number higher than forty eight, it had to be lower than that. It was physically impossible to make tumblers of that size so close. But at fifty one, there was the snick.

Standard screwed his eyes up in a grimace and drew in an annoyed breath. He removed the stethoscope from the safe, and stood up. He frowned and absent-mindedly wiped at his moustache with his right hand. Finally, as though admitting some sort of truce with the safe, he took off the stethoscope completely and carefully placed the device into his overcoat pocket. He stared at the safe again. Outwardly it appeared like any other he had opened before. It should have been no more than two and a half minute's work for a craftsman such as himself. He dismissed the immediate thought he was somehow mistaken in the model number, or that this was anything but a regular Impenetrable. He discarded the idea he'd miscounted, or had misheard the snick. Four attempts were three more than he usually needed and he was absolutely sure he had counted each snick correctly.

Doubt began to settle as the possibilities dwindled. He went through the facts again, checking off each one on his fingers. This was a safe of the type he had opened many times before. It was not opening now. His tools were the same ones he had used last week at the Albion Bank in Smithfield. He had checked his tools earlier today before he set out. He had spun the dial twice before starting each attempt. Maybe he was losing his edge. Maybe he was getting too old for this game.

He sat gently against the desk and scanned the floor around the safe. All was clear; his equipment was in one pocket or another. There were no markings to show the safe had been moved recently. The carpeting was neither too clean nor too dirty to call attention to it. Everything was in its place. He could walk away right now and no-one would know. He'd have to relock the desk drawers, which was tiresome, but if he wanted to allow himself to fail for the first time it was something he'd have to attend to. Leave the scene as he found it, and just walk away. Where was the fun in that, he smiled slightly, rolling his eyes in the dark. He returned his gaze to the safe.

There was only a dim light from the window that overlooked the narrow alley, and the building next door was a dozen feet away at most. The dark brickwork did its best to keep the street lighting from reflecting in through the window, but enough made its way in so the room was not in complete darkness. Standard's eyes had adjusted to the dark but still nothing untoward was apparent about any part of this room. Something was most definitely out of the ordinary though, as evidenced by the safe remaining stubbornly closed. This was part infuriating, part entertaining. Standard's brain wanted him to get out, go home and live to plan another day.

His heart, though, was beating faster than it had for a long time. His fingertips tingled and he wanted to open the safe. Not, now, for what was in it - he wanted it open simply because it was closed. He could out think any safe and this one was just being temperamental, he mused.

He had been in this room for twenty minutes, near enough, so he had at least half an hour before there was any chance of someone passing by in the corridor. The room had one door, and one window. Exactly two ways to leave, he thought. He continued to stare at the safe.

He drew slow, deep breaths in an attempt to slow his heartbeat. Allowing himself to become panicky was not going to help at all. He had to be able to think straight, and act decisively. So thinking straight he started, once again, from first principles.

This was an Impenetrable safe, of the latest model. He knew from a source within the Impenetrable Security Company that the next model was not ready for manufacture until next year. The office in which he was standing was a common or garden side office of the Imperial Exporting Company, most recently occupied by Isaac Wellington, chief clerk of the Oriental Spices Division. The desk drawers held paperwork of value to nobody outside the spice trading industry. Nothing else about the desk was noteworthy. Other than the three chairs and the safe, the only thing in the room that might hold any clue was the bookcase.

He mentally removed the chairs from the list of possibilities after a brief pat down and some searching on his hands and knees. He was now sitting on the floor, staring at the safe. He glanced across to the bookcase. Each shelf was home to series of books, all as much identical as books can be. He surmised that the bookcase had been made for the specific purpose of housing these books, for that would be a fortuitous coincidence that one shelf held an exact complete series. All the books were in place, standing to attention as if on parade. Not a page out of order.

He returned his gaze to the safe. He had a little over ten minutes to open it before any watchman looked in. With a small *oof* he stood up. Perhaps, he thought, he *was* getting too old. Once again he approached the safe, and laid a hand upon its top. Cold. Just a safe, it could not think and so therefore could not out-think him. He would master this before he could count to six hundred, he was sure of it.

At that moment the whole world seemed to stop. Someone was outside the door. All thoughts of the safe evaporated as he ever so slowly turned and straightened, looking at the window and then back to the door. There was definitely someone outside the door. The muffled sound of Upper Thames Street was coming from the window now, whereas before it had been generally from the direction of the door. Someone's body was blocking the sounds of London's riverside nightlife. There was no crack in the door frame to let light through, so he had no idea whether it was one or many bodies. He held his breath, straining to hear the slightest sound. If someone sniffed, or dragged a shoe across carpet, he would hear it. This was not the clumsy night watchman, nor any Bobby who might have decided to check the insides of a locked office building. Things were most definitely wrong. First the safe, now an unannounced intruder. Present company excluded of course.

His options were extremely limited now. Leaving by the window would bring upon him a multitude of things to explain, like broken legs or a face cut by shattered glass. There was no way to scale the wall even if he could get the window open. The drainpipes ran down the corners of the building, and the windows had no ledges — nothing for him to gain purchase upon while dropping twenty five feet to the ground. The hard, unforgiving ground. He had reconnoitered the building days before, and discounted the windows as a means of entrance. As a means of egress, he would be caught for sure and maimed along with it.

His escape had to be through the door, which narrowed his choices even further. Either he opened the door, or it would be opened for him. Best keep the element of surprise for himself and not let whoever was out there get the better of him that way. He took half a step sideways so the desk was no longer between him and the door. He was about to weigh the idea of charging the door or creeping slowly towards it, when the door opened.

He had no idea what to expect, as to date he had never been interrupted on a job. There was only one figure in the doorway that much he could tell. Details were hard to discern through the bright light shed by a lamp held in the stranger's left hand. Standard squinted and raised a hand, as much to shield his eyes as to signal he was unarmed.

The stranger was not so unequipped. "I have a gun aimed at your head," said the figure.

There was a thunking click, and a wall-fitted electrical lamp illuminated the room. It had not occurred to Standard that electrical lighting was used in London offices anywhere but Westminster. The surprise of such a discovery was immediately quelled by the sight of the stranger's gun. It was indeed aimed at his head.

"Hello," said Standard, at a loss for anything else to say.

"You are Ambrose Standard," the stranger said. "You have, shall we say, an affinity for opening safes that do not belong to you but I shall wager that the safe behind you is the first to match your wits. I arranged for it to be...adjusted."

Standard opened his mouth, about to utter a witticism, before the better part of his brain closed it for him. Instead he smiled crookedly, and bowed ever so slightly. The gun remained pointed at his head.

"I watched you at work last week, in Smithfield," said the stranger. "Please, sit down. That chair over there will do," he continued, motioning with his head toward the chair nearest the window.

Standard moved to the chair, all the while staring at the gun. He sat carefully, not wanting to give a reason for the stranger to pull the trigger. The stranger was far enough away that to bring him down in a single leap would not suffice. Standard would have to take at least one step, and that would give the stranger more than enough time to shoot. Standard placed his hands on the arms of the chair and studied the stranger.

He was a couple of inches taller than Standard, though of slighter build. Older but not by more than a decade, he had hair that was almost grey but still had a hint of copper betraying what must have been at some point an exceedingly red mane. A bulbous nose and watery eyes made for an almost comical expression had he not been of a murderous disposition at this moment. His attire was that of a man of great means. He wore riding boots polished to a respectable shine, navy blue pantaloons embroidered tightly at the seams, a dark purple waistcoat across which a pocket watch chain dangled, and an over shirt with a superbly starched collar. Standard suspected the stranger had staff to attend to such details.

"You were not at your best that night," said the stranger. "You made one or two mistakes that would have had me on your tail, had I not already found you out."

Standard's initial shock of being caught was slowly being

replaced by a growing anger. First, who was this stranger, how had he watched him last week, and why on earth was he providing a commentary on last week's job?

"First, who are you, and wh..." started Standard, but the stranger cut him off.

"Oh do be quiet. I have the gun, I've caught the felon who has burglarized six financial establishments this month, and it is I who will hand you over to the police."

The stranger's face displayed no humour, no joy at having Standard in his sights. This was all an everyday situation for him, it seemed. Standard complied, wondering how this would play out.

"I make it my business to find interlopers such as yourself," the stranger said. "London would be such a finer place without an element of high crime. Businesses could run as intended, people would be happier, and money would end up where it was supposed to be."

The stranger moved toward the centre of the room, but was still out of leaping distance, Standard noticed.

"Are you going to kill me?" Standard asked.

"Not if I can help it," replied the stranger. "I'd rather you were made an example of. The police can have their day of glory, capturing such a nuisance and the dailies can write about you at length. The common man will no longer look to you with awe - they will instead see you for someone who gets his come-uppance at the hands of the judiciary. No doubt the courts will sentence you to hang, but that is no concern of mine."

"How did you find me?" Standard asked.

"I am a man of focussed purpose," said the stranger. "Deducing your methods, and analyzing the kind of person you are, took me a few days. After that it was simply discounting the suspects one by one until there remained only you." A faint smile appeared on the stranger's face at this. "There was a pattern to your crimes, and the longer you were left to your devices the more certain it was of your capture."

"The police would never have caught me," said Standard.

"Oh of that I am sure," chuckled the stranger coldly. "They

lack the wherewithal to find such a criminal as you. Please don't take it as a compliment when I say that you are much more of a criminal mind than the police could ever hope to capture."

"So they sought your employ to ensure my capture," said Standard.

"Not at all. I contacted them myself. It was obvious that left to their own devices they would be more of an embarrassment than they usually are in such cases. I waited until I was certain I had my man before I sent a telegram to the Inspector. He should be here by now, but his tardiness is to be expected I suppose."

Standard blinked at this. He was done for. The police would arrive, he would be taken to Guildhall and locked up until a judge would find him guilty and he would be hanged. This was a course of events that had but a single outcome once the police arrived. His only means of survival was to escape this stranger within the next few minutes, and that began by disarming him.

The stranger took a step backwards. "I can see you are contemplating escape. Your fingers are grasping the arm of the chair more tightly. It will not come to that. The police will have their day, mark you." With his left hand he took a pocket watch from his right waistcoat pocket, all the while keeping the gun pointed exactly at Standard's head.

The pocket watch seemed to shine with a glow from within. Small shadows were cast upon the stranger's chest. He opened the cover of the timepiece and the light grew stronger, bathing his features in a warm golden radiance. The moment his eyes left Standard to inspect the pocket watch Standard leapt from his chair toward the stranger, making a grasp for the bottle of ink upon the desk to his right. The bottle was in mid-air before the stranger thought to react, and hit the gun just as he pulled the trigger. There was a sharp crack, a flash from the revolver's hammer and a haze of oily smoke appeared as if from nowhere.

Standard had no idea if the bullet had hit him or not — he was intent on tackling the stranger, bullet wound or no.

Standard was a decent boxer, he enjoyed sparring with the younger prospects at a tavern in Maiden Lane and more often than not, was capable of giving as good as he got. This, however, was not boxing. Nor was it wrestling, another sporting pastime at which Standard excelled. The scuffle of two grown men fighting for control of a single revolver rarely ends when one has wrested the firearm from the other. These affairs reach a conclusion when one has caused the gun to be pointed at some body part or other of their opponent, and manages to squeeze the trigger somehow. Indeed, this was what the pair in the now brightly lit office was attempting.

The gun was buried in Standard's shoulder, but Standard had manoeuvred an index finger behind the trigger rendering it inert. He felt the stranger try to fire the gun, squeezing as hard as he could — the pain in Standard's finger caused him to cry out. It seemed like someone was attempting to remove his finger with a pair of blunt scissors. He pushed the gun towards the stranger with all his might and made a grasp for the barrel. He cried out again as a fiery heat seared his palm, but he steadfastly gripped the engraved metal cylinder and twisted up.

The stranger took a step back, trying to pull the gun from Standard's clenches. The sudden space between the two allowed Standard to use his weight to lunge against the stranger once more, but this time he had started from much closer and was already standing. The two started to topple to the floor, with Standard on top and the stranger beneath. The stranger bent his legs at the knees to minimize the impact, but the force of Standard's lunge caused him to lose all his wind and he was momentarily stunned. Standard took the opportunity to remove his now bleeding finger from the trigger guard and push farther up upon the barrel.

The end of the gun wavered under the chin of the stranger as Standard pushed harder.

The stranger started to kick, to no avail. Standard's weight was too much for the older man, and both his hands now had good purchase upon the gun. The stranger seemed to draw upon an inner energy in a final attempt to remove the gun from under his chin. In a sequence of events that Standard never understood at the time, the gun fired. At such close quarters, the firing of the gun felt to Standard like someone had smashed his face with a tea

-tray. All the world was bright then suddenly dark, loud then suddenly quiet. There was nothing except a profound silence. The office was spinning about him and he was not sure if he was still on the floor or was now standing. He could be on the ceiling looking down for all he knew, or hanging on the wall in the manner of a portrait of the Queen and her Consort.

The silence gave way quickly to a ringing that grew louder and louder until it was almost as loud as the gunfire itself. His eyes were open and as his vision cleared he discovered he was looking at his hands. They were against what looked like the spines of some books. Why were there books? And why were his hands covered in blood? They didn't seem to hurt, except for a dull pain in one index finger. He looked at what he thought was down, and saw his knees - they were on the floor. He was kneeling against a bookcase it seemed.

He shook his head and immediately regretted it. He closed his eyes and waited for the room to stop moving. After a few seconds he opened his eyes again. There was a book mere inches from his nose: Import Tonnages Soton 1843 Volume XIV. He blinked a few times and tentatively looked towards what he thought was the direction of the door. In one corner of the scene, which was still rippling at the edges, he thought he saw a hand. He turned his head around, ever so carefully, and saw the stranger on his back, motionless as much as Standard could make out.

Standard took a few deep breaths, but remained on his knees. He didn't quite feel up to standing. He tried to fix his gaze as best he could, on the body.

A growing pool of blood, black against the dark red of the carpet, was to the right of what remained of the stranger's head. The largest portion of his lower jaw was missing, as well as his nose, left cheek and left eye. From what Standard could tell, part of his left ear was gone too. The rest of the face was a bloody mush. Standard shuffled on his knees the yard or so toward the body.

Standard's attention was caught by the glow of the pocket watch, now loose on the floor though still attached to its chain. He made a grab for it, missed, and tried again. This time he managed to keep his fingers around it, and he yanked at it chain and all. It was cool to touch, though his eyes were telling him it should be warm, the glow was so calming. The watch face was intact; there was a smaller face within a larger one, ticking off the seconds.

Standard tasted blood, and spat on the carpet next to the stranger. He pressed his left hand to his face and rubbed. It came away with a smear of bright red suggesting his nose was bloody.

"Bastard," he muttered, the word hardly audible above the ringing.

He gingerly looked around for the gun and found it between his own legs. Picking it up he was amazed at how light it was. The gun's handle was wooden and polished, a fact hidden while the stranger had it pointed at Standard's head. He let out a loud sigh, and allowed the gun to drop to his side, though still grasped tightly.

A figure appeared at the door, followed by one then two or three more behind it. It was a shorter man in his twenties. He was gently bumped from behind as the mob of uniformed men behind him craned to take in the scene. Bobbies. They were the police, and the younger man wearing a dark suit that was all the rage these days was likely to be their Sergeant. No ... he was not in uniform, he was most probably an Inspector, thought Standard.

The shorter man said something. Standard looked confused, and the shorter man repeated his question. "Are you all right, man?" he asked.

"Er," Standard shook his head in a muddled fashion.

"I received your telegram and came at the exact time you said to."

Standard blinked away the tears of pain that were starting. His finger felt like it had been crushed to a pulp, and his head was in a vice grip of sorts.

The man in the suit moved out of the doorway and crouched beside the stranger.

"I see he put up a struggle. Are you all right?" he asked again. "I am Inspector Worth," he added.

Standard opened his mouth and some feeble noise escaped. He could not control his tongue, so he closed his mouth.

"Get this man some water," Worth ordered one of the Bobbies. "I am pleased to finally meet you," he said to Standard. "Your telegram has been the talk of the Division this evening, I can tell you."

Standard looked down at the stranger, then at the gun and watch in his own hands.

"You said to recognize you by the watch," said Worth. He looked down at the stranger. "So this is our fellow?"

Standard nodded. "Yes," he managed to croak.

A glass of water was thrust under his nose. He dropped the gun and took the glass. The water was warm. He took a small sip, washed it around in his mouth and spat it out to one side. He then gulped down the remainder of the water in one go. A hand took the glass from him.

"Come on," said Worth, "let's get you to my physician." He offered Standard a hand.

Standard looked up at Worth, then at the Bobbies now surrounding him and the stranger, then at the watch.

"I think that would be best," he said, slipping the watch into a trouser pocket. He took Worth's hand and felt a firm grip lift him to his feet. Worth was much stronger than he looked.

The pair of them began to head for the corridor when one of the Bobbies called after them.

"Mister Wainright. Your gun." The firearm was passed to Worth, who turned it over in his hands.

"Light," he acknowledged. "Easy to carry around I suppose," he said, offering it to Standard.

Standard took the gun, and slowly negotiated his way through the door and into the corridor

"Now that we've met, Wainright, and this thief will trouble bankers no more, perhaps you can tell me how you tracked him." The pair of them walked toward the stairs at the other end of the corridor.

Standard, now fully caught up with the Inspector's misunderstanding, played along.

"Perhaps that can wait until after your physician has seen to me," he said.

13

"Of course," said Worth. "He's in the carriage outside. Can you make the stairs by yourself?"

Standard nodded. "Oh yes," he said. Worth trotted ahead and started down the stairs two by two.

Standard stopped his hobbling, straightened up, and smiled. He could hear the Bobbies in the room behind him arguing about who was going to carry the faceless body. Obviously Standard's hearing was settling back to normal, as was his thinking.

He had made a choice not five minutes ago whether to move slowly to the door, or whether to charge toward it. Now he had another choice. From the corridor it was no difficult matter to find a corner office at the rear of the building and escape down a drain pipe. The safe would remain unopened, but he'd leave with his life more or less unchanged. Back to the planning of more nightly escapades, more break-ins, ego bruised but intact. He'd continue to pit his wits against inanimate security boxes, knowing he was the best in London, perhaps even Great Britain.

With a broad grin he strode purposefully to the top of the stairs and started down to the waiting carriage.

An Isolated Anger

by Heather Mac Archer

Heather Mac Archer draws on almost forty years of experience as an editor, reporter and feature writer. As a journalist, Heather worked on a number of Thomson Newspapers and The Ottawa Journal_*before landing at the* Toronto Star *for 29 years. She worked on various desks in the newsroom, but her favorite was as a sub editor on the City Desk, where the coverage of a number of notorious murder cases solidified her interest in the genre.*

She is currently working on two mysteries, both historical.

A life-long mystery book reader, Heather is passionate about murder, why people commit it, those who work to solve it and the idea of justice and redemption. She is a member of the International Sisters in Crime and Toronto Sisters in Crime.

She holds an undergraduate degree in Celtic Studies from St. Michael's College, University of Toronto and an M.A. in early medieval church history, University of Guelph.

She lives in Toronto with her husband.

Visit her at: www.heathermacarcher.com

May 22, 1922 Derbyshire

Ned Norton began the day the same way he did each morning. He dressed carefully, so as to not wake his wife, washed downstairs in the big blue enamel bowl while the kettle boiled, then stood thoughtfully over the stove as he stirred his porridge. He always made his lunch the night before and put it in his bucket so he only had to grab it from the icebox as he headed out the door. But first, he carefully washed out his porridge pot with the remains of the water from the kettle and a bit of hard soap, and cleared the table so as not to leave a trace of himself.

He donned his jacket, his cap and left his little cottage, which was one in a row of four identical homes, careful to latch the gate quietly. Alice, his wife, liked her sleep and he wouldn't have disturbed her for the world.

He was joined in his daily trek to work with the men from the three other cottages, men who worked, like himself, at the local cotton mill. There was newlywed Dick Mesley, who lived at the far end, widowed Roger Lambe, who lived next to Dick, and Peter Bartlen, who lived in the cottage at the other end, next to Ned and Alice. Peter was just a little older than the others and had a lovely plump wife and three adorable children. Dick Mesley and his wife desperately wanted children and in the evening, the occupants of the other cottages often heard their enthusiastic attempts at parenthood.

Ned's wife Alice snorted in derision and disgust when this happened and slammed all the windows shut, keeping out the light smell of the honeysuckle that wound around the kitchen window at the back and the earthy smells of the newly planted gardens in the front yards. Ned said little, just smiled a little to himself and wondered when their time would come.

All the men had fought in the Great War, all had received slight injuries and all had returned home to work in the cotton mill. It was expected of them, and they did it without questioning their fates. They knew, even as they donned their uniforms and took up arms that they would, if they survived, come home to the mill. It had a great hold over the men and women in the village and had put food on the table for generations.

The three other men had wed local girls, but Ned married a lively lady from London, a girl he'd met during a brief leave while dancing the night away at a London dance hall favored by young soldiers. What a night that had been. Ned had never experienced anything like it.

Alice was tiny, blonde and lively. Ned found himself caught up in her vivacity, completely ignoring the fact she treated her friends with derision, that she snapped at her parents and treated her only sibling, a sister, with complete disdain. She lied, too, but it was just little ones, Ned told himself. Nothing important. He was completely bowled over by the fact she made him feel like the only person in the room, even the universe when she turned those violet eyes on him.

She adored music and owned a gramophone and a pile of those new-fangled records that she'd put on when she was bored, dancing about the small cottage with abandon, a flower from their weedy garden tucked behind her ear. She wasn't much for house-work, and Ned was the one who took a soft cloth to surfaces when the rime of dirt became too much. She cooked, but it was poor fare, and Ned was always relieved and delighted when his ma, a widow now, invited them for dinner. Alice wasn't as pleased and she'd spend the evening making snide remarks about his ma's house and her habits. It was embarrassing and he wished mightily that Alice would stop. He didn't know what got into her some-times, but he always forgave her. She was so luminescent, so radi-ant and so very beautiful.

She spoke often of the two of them going back to London to live, Ned getting a job at a bank, or at one of the big busy shops on Oxford St. Talk like this scared Ned but he'd nod and say qui-etly, "Well, some day perhaps. We should wait a bit, save a bit of money, don't you think? Let's get ahead and be able to make a move with some real dosh behind us."

And the lovely Alice's porcelain forehead would pucker, her slim mouth would turn down and she'd ask petulantly, "How long? Just how long do we wait? I'll die in this place if we don't leave."

If Ned was lucky, that would be the end of that conversation and he'd join her in a dance, or they'd share a cigarette at the open back door (as long as the Mesleys weren't active), and per-haps make a cup of tea. That was on a good night after talk about London.

Other evenings it would be vastly different. Out of nowhere would come a black and overwhelming rage and Alice would turn into a woman he didn't know. He'd be forced to dodge blows from her tiny fists that rained down on his back and neck and he'd curl himself into a ball to avoid them.

Ned would never strike a woman. His dear father taught him this. But this would make her even angrier and she'd sometimes reach for something from the kitchen, a meat pounder, or a rolling pin (rarely used for domestic use) or a pot. She never uttered a sound during these sieges, but she'd be panting and pouring sweat when she was done, her carefully styled hair straggling around her face, her fine features screwed into an ugly sneer. At times like this, Ned wondered why he'd thought her beautiful, why he'd been fooled by her seemingly lovely face.

And hiding those bruises? Well, it was impossible, and he'd head off to work in the purplish morning light with his mates and hope they didn't see the damage inflicted by his wife. Of course people did notice and if everyone who'd heard his many explanations believed them, Ned would be the clumsiest, most inept and disastrously uncoordinated man in all of Derbyshire.

No. Everyone knew. It's just that Ned didn't know they knew.

And still Ned always forgave Alice.

This difficult situation had gone on for a good two years, Ned hiding his growing unhappiness. On this lovely late May morning as they strolled down the lane to the main intersection and the mill, Ned bore a deep red gouge along his left cheek. "Hit it on a hook in the kitchen last night," he mumbled to Dick, Peter and Roger. The men murmured their condolences, Roger saying he hoped Ned had washed it with carbolic as it could turn septic and that would be a damned shame.

"Oh yes, I washed it and put some Boots powder on it right away. Missed my footing, I did. Clumsy of me," he said as he drew his hand down the side of his cheek.

The others exchanged glances, even in the gloom, and young Dick rolled his eyes at Roger, who shook his head and put a finger to his lips. Peter kept his head down, embarrassed for his near neighbor.

The men didn't have a long walk to the mill. It sat at the end of their road, a square and imposing hulk against the skyline, its windows catching the rising sun, the sounds of the machinery starting up, the sound of the river that once fuelled the industry a constant reminder of their livelihoods. It was comforting to know the mill was there, their bread and butter, so close by. It had been there for one hundred and forty years and Ned's dad, and his dad before him had worked there. It was tradition. It was the only life he knew.

This day was different from other days as the annual well dressing would be held the following day and all the women and the children would be taking part in this long-standing tradition, also called 'well flowering.' It was a celebration, based on pagan times, so Ned's father told him, to give thanks for the purity of the village's water. Little villages all over the county took part in this festival. Visitors from elsewhere would also come and help celebrate.

Peter's children would be taking part with their school friends, but Peter's wife, Lavinia, had a dreadful early summer cold and couldn't, Peter told them. "She's in bed, with the eldest bringing her soup. Nose as red as beetroot, so it is. She's that sad to be missing it, but there's not much she can do about it." He laughed. "But she's a fit gal and she'll recover quick."

"Sorry to hear that," said young Dick. "My Elsie's going this morning to help decorate the well. She's got two baskets of petals gathered and some lady's mantle and lots of lilac flowers. Seems every bucket and bowl in the house is full. She's that excited, she is. It's her first time taking part." Dick's wife came from Devon, where this sort of activity wasn't a custom.

"My Annie used to love this time of year," mused Roger. The men said nothing, respectful of Roger's loss and his memories.

Ned was envious of Peter and Dick. Alice would no more decorate a well with flower petals than dance the Highland Fling on the village green. It was not just "pagan, it was a rural and backward activity that was boring, dull and stupid."

He was looking forward to events that evening which preceded the actual celebration of the well. The village men would get together at the pub and hoist a few jars, while the women were elsewhere celebrating the completion of the dressing.

Ned liked this part of it. He didn't drink much, just enough for his spirits to feel lifted, but he liked the good company. And he didn't care particularly if he left Alice alone tonight. It was tradition, and he was determined to be a part of it. He wouldn't be late and Alice could just put up with it. Ned was so tired of her behavior and her attitude toward village life – and him, especially after last night's catfight. He touched his cheek and felt a long streak on his cheek. It still stung.

They entered the gates of the mill and bid farewell as they headed off to their various jobs; Roger and Peter worked in maintenance, tending the thousands of parts that it took to make the fine threads of cotton, while Dick and Ned actually took part in the process, Dick working in the carding room, Ned in the cabling of the product.

Their days were long – twelve hours – and in the evening, all four would leave the mill covered in fine bits of fluff and lint, their jackets sometimes white, their hair fringed in cotton dust. Dick's wife laughed at this. "You look like an 80-year-old," she told him once. It was part of the job, just as a coalminer would return to the surface with his face as black as night.

No one questioned this. Except Alice. She hated the way the bits of fluff flew all over the house, covering the surfaces she never polished, gathering in balls on the floor under the furniture.

While the three other men went home through the front door, Ned was forced to go home through the narrow laneway that backed the cottages, returning through the garden where he shook off the worst of his job and hung his jacket on the line. Alice insisted on this.

Tonight was no different. Ned removed his shoes, and placed them in the little porch outside the back door. He sighed and gently opened the back door. He was met by the smell of strong spirits and the sight of his wife, a glass in her hand, dancing barefoot in the kitchen. An empty bottle of Old Tom's sat by the sink. She laughed at him.

"Back from the mines? We're out of this, by the way," she said, picking up the bottle. "Perhaps you'd get me more before you head off to partake of your pagan gathering?"

Ned stood in the kitchen, a quiet anger surging through him. His stomach knotted with it, his hands clenched, electricity ran along his spine. He was hungry and there was no dinner. He was tired, but there was no peace in his home. More surprisingly, as he stood there, he realized he'd never felt quite the way he felt just now; he was charged with an energy he couldn't discharge and he stood, rooted to the spot.

Something in his expression must have registered with Alice for she backed against the table and whimpered.

"Sorry about last night. It's worse than I thought. I won't do that again. I promise, Ned. Please. I won't. Would you be able to get your hands on more?"

Ned turned back to the door, quietly shut it and retrieved his shoes. He took his coat off the line. He burned with an emotion he'd never before experienced and wasn't sure if it was anger, humiliation, disappointment or fear. He needed to be as far away as he could from his own home right now and that felt exceedingly odd. He strode to the back gate and slammed it shut, looking up and down the lane. He remembered the times he'd gone over the top in the war, rifle raised, every fiber in his being alert to danger and the challenge of staying alive. This is how he felt now.

He turned down the lane toward the village green and headed for the Brown Mule. He marched quickly and ignored the postmaster, who shouted a cheery hello. He rudely brushed past a group of children, flush from their well-decorating exertions. They stopped and stood, shocked and disturbed by the angry man who usually seemed so quiet and kind. Now he seemed in an awful hurry.

Ned stopped abruptly in front of the pub, trying to calm himself, trying to steel himself for what he planned to do. He opened the door slowly, nodding to the proprietor, a balding man who'd known Ned from childhood.

"Greetings, Edward," called Eustace Grieves, the publican. "Bit early for the festivities, you are . . . what will it be?"

"I'll have a whisky, Eustace. It's been a long day. A long week, in fact."

"Oh? Hurt your face at the mill? I've heard there've been a spate of injuries there. Jim Tanton caught his hand in a ring spinner and he's out of work for a while. That will be hard on his family. But he'll mend. Nothing broken. And yourself? How'd you do that?"

"Silly accident, is all," Ned replied, taking the whisky from Eustace. "Nothing serious. And I'll heal fast, too."

"Still. Shouldn't be happening. Those new mill owners should be taking more care of the equipment. Looking after the workers better."

"It's not so bad. It's a living."

Eustace wiped down the counter then took up a cloth to polish glasses lined on a shelf behind him. He sniffed appreciatively as the homey smell of beef stew poured through the door from the Grieves' private quarters. He glanced back at Ned as his wife, Gladys, poked her head through the door with a bowl and spoon, offering it to him. Gladys looked askance at Ned, but Eustace shook his head and took the bowl.

"Care for some stew, Ned?" Gladys waited in the doorway and smiled brightly.

"You're welcome to join us, Ned," Eustace offered.

"No thanks, Mrs. Grieves. My appetite is off. But that's kind of you."

Gladys vanished and Eustace resumed polishing and eating, finishing the stew in record time. He rubbed his stomach and turned to Ned.

"Hoping this weather holds up for tomorrow. I hear a crowd will be coming from over Cutthorpe. Should be a good gathering. Your Alice taking part?"

Ned raised his head with such a look on his face Eustace stepped back.

"No. She's not. Another one, Eustace?" Ned held out his glass.

The publican filled the glass and excused himself, saying he'd be back in a moment. He took his bowl and spoon and held it up, indicating to Ned he was taking it back to his wife for washing up.

Eustace hurried through his parlor to the little kitchen at the back of the building.

"What's wrong with him?" Gladys hissed as Eustace entered the kitchen. She had the dishes soaking in the deep sink and she was sitting at the table, a lamp lit so she could read the local newspaper.

"God knows, but I'm willing to bet it's that wife of his."

"Do you think she did that to his face?"

"He didn't correct me when I asked if it was done at work, so I don't know."

"And I suppose he's knocking the whisky back on an empty stomach, too."

"He is. He's on his second. But I'll be watching him. I won't let him go too far. He's not a drinker at all. Ned's a good young man. Not like some of them."

There was a chorus of men's voices from the front of the building and Eustace hurried back to the pub. A fair-sized group of men had arrived and were shouting orders, pints, mostly. Ned tried to raise a hand for another whisky but Eustace ignored him until he'd filled the other orders. Shillings and pence clattered on the counter as fast as Eustace could put them in the money drawer and still Ned was holding up his empty glass.

"Another," he demanded loudly.

"It's on me, Ned," shouted someone, a worker Ned knew only slightly from the mill. The men cheered and Eustace tried to shake his head at the man. Still the fellow persisted and Eustace had no option but to pour another shot into Ned's glass.

From there on, the drinking became steady and the hum of voices became laughs and banter. Others ordered whisky or gin and Eustace was having trouble keeping track of what Ned was drinking for some of the men seemed to be taking delight in seeing the usually serious young man become increasingly drunk.

It was dark and still the men reveled in the celebrations. The pub had taken on a golden glow as Eustace lit the oil lamps. A small fire burned in the grate and now some voices were raised in song. Ned's head was pounding and he'd finally identified the swirling mass of emotion he'd been feeling earlier: It was rage—

sheer, pure and white hot. He rose unsteadily from his seat and waved away the shouts of "You're not going yet!" "Stay awhile yet, Neddie!" and "Another one for luck, boy!"

He stood outside the pub and stared at the night sky, the swirling stars, then the trees on the green that seemed to be swaying without a whisper of wind. He had a job to do, a soldiering type of job, something he thought he'd never have to do again. Ned moved unsteadily down the lane toward home, his surroundings a blur, the faint line of cottages a white spot in the dark night. He made his way down the tiny lane that ran along the back of the cottages, slipped his shoes off at the back gate and all but crawled up to his back door, quietly, so quietly it didn't make a noise as it swung wide. Ned left it open, creeping along the hall and upstairs. He was tired, so tired he wanted to curl up when he reached the top. But he kept on. And he did what he had to do. But he didn't stay. He crept down the stairs again, feeling a lot more sober, stumbled through the dark passage and out the door once more.

When he finally slept, it was just outside the gate, in the long tall grass along the lane. It was so welcoming, so soft, he'd sunk into it with a sigh, his heart and mind finally clear. He was feeling happier than he'd been in months. He didn't hear the other men returning to their homes, singing softly and laughing, slipping off shoes, collapsing on sofas, snoring, clattering out their back doors to use the privy at the bottom of their gardens. Young Dick had over-imbibed and even his retching noises at the end of the garden didn't stir Ned. Nor did the sound of Elsie's concerned voice, "Are you alright, Dickie? Are you sure?"

What finally woke Ned was a heart-breaking yell, a man's frantic cry and the sobs of small children. "Ma. Ma," the little voices loudly implored. "What's wrong da, what's wrong with ma. Wake her. Please." The voices cried harder, the man shouted for help.

Ned raised his head from the long grass and rolled over. He felt wretched and was terribly ill. When he finally got up he could hear shouts from all of the cottages. He heard Roger's voice added to Peter's, young Dick's, "Oh God," and Elsie's screams.

What was going on, he wondered. Then he remembered. It wasn't a dream at all. He'd actually done it. But why was Peter crying? Peter hated Alice. So did Roger. And Dick. And they were all raising a fuss.

He saw his own back door open, a disheveled Alice come out and stand, squinting down the yard to the lane. "Ned?" she called. "Ned! Where are you?"

Ned froze, his guts clenched and he dropped to his knees.

"Ned! Are you out there?" She was hysterical. "Ned, please come in. Someone has murdered Lavinia Bartlen. Oh God, it could have been any of us. It could have been me! Ned. You bastard. Where are you?"

Ned fainted.

Focus

by Steve Shrott

Steve Shrott has published over thirty-five short stories in print publications and e-zines. He has appeared in ten anthologies including two from Sisters in Crime–The Whole She-Bang, and Fishnets.

He was a winner in The Joe Konrath Short Story Contest. Steve has also crafted humorous material for well-known comedians, and speakers as well as written a 'how to' book on humor writing. Some of his jokes are in The Smithsonian Institute.

He has taught courses in humor and screenplay writing at various educational outlets such as The Learning Annex, Savvy Authors and The Romance Writers of America.

Cruz looked through the square in the back. He could see the world in a whole new way. It was clearer, more perfect.

It was the first camera he'd ever owned, even though his father had been a photographer. When someone told his dad, he had the "eye," Cruz would point at him and say, "no, two, daddy." His father would always laugh, then kneel down and tussle his hair. "You're right Cruzzy. Two. You're my little genius aren't you?"

Cruz wished he could have known his dad longer, but he died, a casualty of gang violence, before his fifth birthday.

Brushing back his long blond hair, Cruz ambled down the

front steps of the flophouse where he lived.

"Hey Jerkoff, where'd ya get that?"

Cruz turned and saw Officer Dan Alvirez's mean eyes glaring at him from the sidewalk.

I said, "Where'd ya you get it?"

"The camera?"

"No, your ugly face."

"Bought it."

"Sure you did."

"It's true."

"That's crap and you know it. Where the hell is a creep like you gonna get money?"

"Ask Daquon at the pawn shop. He'll tell ya. Gave it to me for three bucks. Film in it and everything."

The cop grabbed the camera, about to rip it out of his hands. Cruz could feel the strength, the power. He knew he should let it go. That would be the right thing to do. But he couldn't. He was tired of being pushed around, made to feel like some piece of shit. He had to stand up sometime.

He pulled back and the camera slipped out of the cop's hands. He glimpsed surprise, then fury, on Alvirez's face as he started running.

The officer gave chase, but Cruz had already bounded around the corner. After a few moments, the red-faced, puffing cop threw up his hands, leaned against the bus stop.

Cruz, still breathing hard, hid behind the remnants of the old burnt-down school. What's with that crazy cop? he wondered. The camera's mine. Bought it fair and square.

Cruz hated Alvirez. Before him, Sal Delucca had patrolled the area. He and Sal were friends. He would often pay Cruz for information he heard in the hood. Then Sal got transferred, god knows where, and Cruz had to find other ways to make money. Some of them not so nice.

After Sal left, the hood changed. Less friendly. Alvirez treated everyone as a suspect. He once hauled Cruz into an alley and punched him so hard, he coughed up blood. He claimed Cruz had stolen a watch, even though the owner of the jewellery store said it wasn't him. Cruz never told anyone about the punch, knew they wouldn't believe anything someone like him would say. Especially if it involved a cop.

Cruz walked the two blocks over to Fontaine Park. He took pictures of a robin hopping on the dewy grass, some yellow and red roses, and the old people eating lunch on a park bench.

On his way home, Cruz passed dark corners where nervous men made financial arrangements with ladies of the night and druggies complained about quality control to their dealers.

In one of the corners, he saw a fat man slip a large roll of bills to Alvirez.

Cruz thought a thousand different things, but his hands worked instinctively and took pictures with the camera. To Cruz, the click and whirr sounded as noisy as a body slamming onto the road from ten storeys up.

But the cop seemed not to notice, at least at first. Moments later, however, Cruz had doubts and raced down a side street.

Once on Decrue Ave., he felt safe and his run morphed into a walk. He neared Grossmans and decided to go in. The store had a musty smell to it, like everything in it was old, decaying. Cruz put his camera on the chipped glass counter and spoke to the horse-faced man behind it.

"How much to get film developed?"

Grossman shifted the camera over in his doughy hands. "Old camera. All digital now."

"Yeah," Cruz replied, not knowing what he meant.

The man looked at Cruz's ragged clothes, sizing him up. "Listen, business ain't so good. How much you got?"

Cruz checked his wallet with the broken zipper. "Six bucks."

Grossman thought a moment, tented his fingers, and then nodded.

Cruz walked home, the camera hanging by its strap around his neck. He climbed the stairs to the second floor.

As usual, Sergio, ten years Cruz's senior, sat on the step, reading a history book. Something about the Persian Wars. Sergio lifted his head, smiled at his friend. "Hey kid, what you got?"

"Camera."

28

"Gonna be a photog like your dad?"

"Maybe."

"Good. Give you something smart to do with your time. You need something smart to do with your time."

Cruz nodded.

"I gotta get me some smokes. Want somethin'?"

He shook his head.

Sergio picked up his book and headed downstairs. Cruz continued up to his room and opened the door with his key. Not that he needed it. Anyone could pick the lock in thirty seconds.

He moved through his tiny room and plopped exhausted onto the tattered mattress that lay on the floor. He removed the camera from around his neck and placed it beside his bed.

Cruz had a restless sleep, heard sounds, saw images he couldn't understand. When he awoke, he sensed something different.

He looked at the door, saw it was open a crack. Someone had been in his room. He had nothing of value, so he never worried about being robbed.

Then he noticed his one possession missing. His heart sank.

Who would take a crappy old camera?

Sergio came to mind, but he knew it couldn't be him. He had always been like an older brother. Besides, he'd once returned five dollars he found outside Gimley's Grocery Store to the manager.

He kicked the wall. "Shit." Then he heard something scrape along the ground, picked it up. A gold button. The kind you found on cop's shirts. A flurry of thoughts raced through his brain. Alvirez? But why?

Then it hit him. He must have seen me take the picture of the fat man passing him money. There must something wrong with that.

Cruz knew he had to find out what it was. The camera had little value to anyone else, but to him it meant something. Made him feel like his dad was still with him. Protecting him from all the bad stuff. He had to get it back.

He only worried that when Alvirez didn't find the film, he might try and hurt him.

He couldn't think about that now.

Cruz decided to hang around the corner where he'd seen Alvirez meet the fat man.

He spent two hours questioning whomever walked by. Some had seen the man, but didn't know him; others wouldn't talk.

Cruz, frustrated, took a break and ambled over to the ice cream store up the street. He didn't have money, but sometimes they let him have a taste.

"Could I try the orange cream?" Cruz asked the smiling woman wearing the pink hat with "Horgan's Ice Cream," embroidered on it. She looked him up and down, a hardness taking over the smile. "Do you have the money to buy an ice cream?"

Cruz, his face flushed, lumbered out. On the way home, he stopped at the photography store.

Grossman handed the developed pictures to Cruz, spoke in a quiet voice. "Lots of people come in with pics, mostly kids or ugly dogs. Nothing special. But these looked real good." The man tossed him a new role of film. "Take some more."

Outside the shop, Cruz examined the photos. They did look good.

Maybe he had the "eye," like his dad. A tear rolled down his cheek.

When he got home he saw his friend on the steps with the same book. Sergio looked at him, worry etched onto his face. "You got trouble, kid."

"Why?"

"Alvirez came by."

"What he say?"

"Wanted to know where you were. I told him I ain't your keeper. He said he'd be back tonight and you better be here."

Cruz sat down on the step. "Don't know what to do, Serge. I took a shot of this creep givin' cash to Alvirez. Next thing I know, Alvirez breaks into my place looking for it. Stole my camera, but didn't get the picture."

"What picture?"

Cruz grabbed the photos from his pocket, handed him the one showing the fat man passing money to Alverez.

Sergio stared at it, turned white.

"Know him?"

He nodded, silent for a moment, almost like he was afraid to speak. "Frank Delano."

"Who's he?"

"Wise Guy."

"How do you know?"

Sergio stood up, paced back and forth for a moment. "One of his men offed my uncle."

"Why?"

"He borrowed money from Delano for his barbershop. Wanted to spruce it up, figured it would bring in folks. Didn't work, then he couldn't pay Delano back. Couple of weeks later, police found his body in an alley."

Sergio wiped a fleck from his eye, moved close to Cruz. "You gotta stay away from him. He's a bad man. If Alvirez wants the picture, give it to him."

"Why would he be talking to Delano?"

Sergio shrugged.

That night Alvirez threw open Cruz's door and tromped in, face red, eyes bulging. "Here's your fucking camera." He threw Cruz's camera against the wall, pieces of yellowed plaster shooting off. "Give me the damn pictures."

Cruz grabbed the photos out of his shirt pocket, handed them to him.

Alvirez took out a gun, aimed it at Cruz.

"I gave you the pictures."

"The problem is you seen Delano give me cash. If someone comes around asking questions, you're gonna tell."

Cruz shook his head. "I won't."

"Only one way to know for sure." He moved close to Cruz, holding the gun in front of his chest.

Sweat smothered Cruz's forehead.

"After I shoot you, I'm going to have a talk with your pal, Sergio."

"W—w—what's the big deal with the pictures anyway?" Cruz said, moving around as if he were hopped up on coke.

Alvirez shrugged. "No reason not to tell you. You'll be dead in a minute." A smile spread across his face. "I do stuff for Delano, cover up some things sometimes. The captain is already suspicious. If he sees that picture, I'm dead meat." Alvirez threw up his hand. "For Christ Sake, stay put."

Cruz froze, any feeling of hope he'd had, crushed. Like a raccoon under a 4 by 4.

A shot exploded.

Cruz reeled, a stunned expression on his face, as the cop fell to the ground, blood spurting out of him.

Sergio bounded in with a smoking gun. "We gotta do some clean up, Cruz."

They waited till nightfall, then buried the body in the woods. Cruz told Sergio he'd never tell anyone. But he knew it wasn't over. There was more to come. And it would probably end badly. It always did when you tried to keep secrets.

Two days later, Sergio died in a hit and run. Cruz, holding his camera tight to his chest, went to the police station, to tell them what he knew. But no one would listen.

The next week, a new officer took over from Alvirez. He told Cruz he wanted to change things in the neighborhood, make it safer, better. Cruz didn't know if that would happen, or even if it was possible.

All he cared about right now was going to Fontaine Park and taking some pictures.

THE THREE GRACES

by Linda Cahill

Linda Cahill creates moody stories about crime and the redemptive power of love. Her experiences as a reporter covering police, criminal trials and demonstrations flavour her new mystery novel featuring Montreal police detective Michael Duluth, a man who can't commit to anyone except victims as he hides from his own criminal past. Themes of love and loss also recur in the two stories in this collection, The Warning *and* The Three Graces.

Linda lives in Toronto with her husband and family including Atlas a husky-shepherd. She is a member of Sisters in Crime International and Sisters in Crime Toronto and serves on the executive of the Toronto Chapter.

Linda is on Facebook, Google Plus and at www.lindacahill.ca

It was sing along time at Happy Hillside and the three old dears jostled for space on the overstuffed couch in front of the piano.

Gladys, large and ruddy, planted herself firmly between her sister Grace and their pal Rosie in the Great Room of their long-term care home, her elbows out and jabbing.

The other two were so tiny their feet didn't quite touch the dilapidated carpet.

"That <u>hurt</u>," said Grace, eighty-seven, giving Gladys a reproachful sisterly scowl through the thick lenses of her metal-rimmed glasses.

"*Ouch!*" said Rosie, a delicate eighty-nine, from the depths of a flowered pink and green cardigan. Nobody paid the old girls much attention as they squirmed away from the jabs.

Gladys, at eighty-three the youngest of the trio, just smiled as the music began. It was like the time she pushed that annoying Sheila off the merry go round and she broke her leg. Everyone said it was an accident; they were only ten after all. Or when she hid her sister's application to university and it almost cost her a scholarship. How satisfying to hear their parents criticizing the pretty sister for a change.

As the sun poured into Hillside's great room, the three united their wavery sopranos in "This Old House" one of their favourites. Pastor Bob, a seventy plus volunteer, loved gospel music and the packed hall of octogenarians reciprocated belting out the chorus: "Ain't gonna need this house no longer...I'm getting ready to meet the saints!" with gusto.

Nurse Daisy stood at the back sipping an Orangina from the adjacent cafe. She jumped as one of the residents sideswiped the back of her legs with his electric wheelchair. "Sorry Daisy," he said. "I'm late for Bridge." Before she could answer he was gone and in his place, her co-worker Renata sidled up nibbling an oatmeal cookie. "He's late for his Poker group," she said, "None of them play bridge."

"At least they aren't all laying claim to someone else's name," Daisy said.

"This morning I caught Rosie and Gladys helping themselves to Grace's fur coat and when I said, 'Rosie, where are you going dear? That's Grace's coat, not yours. Rosie said, *I'm* Grace."

"Gladys does the same," Renata laughed. "She won't take her meds; she doesn't even answer me unless I call her Grace."

Nurse Daisy smiled as they rode the elevator upstairs. But she was getting worried about her Graces.

Gladys and Grace had hit it off when Gladys first arrived from the suburban Irene Walters home to be reunited with her sister what was it? — two months ago? Soon Gladys and Grace were joined by a new arrival, Rosie, whose room was next door to Gladys's. Elbows and the occasional throwing of handfuls of cutlery aside, the three women had become inseparable.

Roaming the halls, they purloined glasses, clothes and shoes from residents too ill or demented to notice. These they hid in flower pots, the parrot cage by the elevator or tossed into the garbage bins. They also delighted in pushing wheelchair patients about the floor, whether the patients wanted to go or not. Everything was fine, if a bit chaotic, with the Graces until recently. When had it changed?

"Our floor." Renata was holding the elevator door for her. "Time to get lunch for the hordes."

"Right, thanks." That was it, lunch. The lunch period. The Graces all sat at the same table. And they had stopped getting along soon after Grace's son Murray had taken a job nearby and started visiting his mother and his Aunt Gladys every lunch hour. Daisy told herself she would keep an eye on them today.

Down in the Great Room, Gladys had stopped singing and was turning her head from side to side. She had dressed carefully in her best red sweater and brown elastic waist slacks today. And she was looking around for Murray.

But Murray wasn't here yet. She turned back to Pastor Bob and his out-of-tune piano but her mind was far away. She wasn't stupid, no matter what her sister said or her parents thought, just slow at letters. After leaving home, she moved to a different city. Working in a store while her sister went to university she rose to acting manager in footwear until an MBA was recruited. As if anyone could do a better job on ladies shoes. When the new hire tumbled over a box of Sorel boots left outside his door and was carted off with a concussion, she had stepped in graciously.

Now Gladys turned right around, looking everywhere for Murray and her two companions started shifting about as well. Noticing their restlessness, Pastor Bob tried to keep them focused by singing his finale directly at them. "We've got your mansions ready, Gladys, Rosie and Grace," he boomed, "So come right in!"

As everyone started singing about St. Peter touring the halls of heaven, Gladys pinched Grace, whose yelp was drowned out by the music, then looked at the door one more time.

There he was! Gladys heart beat a little faster as Murray entered the great room, so handsome, tall in his dark blue wool coat and striped scarf against the coolish day. He had gentle brown eyes; nothing like Grace's washed out blue. Gladys shouldered her companions aside and beetled over to him throwing her arms around his waist.

"Well hello there Gladys, having a good time," he disentangled himself gently. "Shall we all go up to lunch?"

Murray loved her, Gladys. She could tell by the way he smiled into her eyes when he came to visit. The way he held her glass for her to drink her vitamin supplement. Grace thought he came to see her but Gladys knew better, Murray loved her, Gladys, his true mother.

Murray wasn't himself at lunch. He looked tired and spent more time than usual with Grace, cutting her meat, feeding her like she was a hungry baby starling. Gladys glared at them both, seething until finally Murray escorted his mother to her room for a nap. Turning back to her own food, she noticed Nurse Daisy watching her. Immediately she started eating her caramel pudding, pretending not to see Daisy whispering to Renata one of the support workers.

Gladys had excellent hearing. And they were talking about Murray!

"So nice how he comes every day," Renata said.

"Yes, he charms them all, the way he tells them jokes, cuts their food..." Nurse Daisy paused glancing at Gladys who was pretending no interest.

"But they often fight after he leaves." Daisy had patched up a few scratched faces and bruised arms in the past few weeks. Tiny Grace with her mild blue eyes seemed to have borne the brunt, suffering a hair pulling that resulted in a wildly erratic heart beat for a couple of days. Murray had been anxious. Daisy had her suspicions about Grace's injuries. Now she motioned Renata into a quiet corner.

"I've been thinking we can break them up, get Gladys a nice room on the fifth floor," she whispered. Renata nodded, "That will make things more peaceful around here for sure."

Move her to the fifth floor? No way, Gladys thought. That was the lockup! Those bitches weren't going to break up her and Murray!

After lunch, the residents were free to rest or walk around before the afternoon's entertainment. Gladys formed a posse with Rosie and another woman, Catherine whose long white hair fell across her face and down her back matching her white knee socks and white skirt and went in search of Grace who wasn't in her room.

The bitch was hiding, Gladys fumed. Passing the nurses supply cart she resisted the temptation to grab diapers or hand sanitizer and dump them in the kitchen to annoy the cooks. She needed to focus. Gladys and her posse tried room after room, surprising residents having their naps. Finally they found her. She was cowering on Wilbur's bed, Wilbur who had just had a stroke. Tiny Grace had climbed onto Wilbur's bed and was lying by his side, her face tucked into the helpless man's neck, almost touching the oxygen tube snaking out his left nostril with her gray curls flowing over his pillow.

"There you are," Gladys said, her eyes bright with rage.

"Stupid Grace, you are not allowed in here," she said as the posse followed her into Wilbur's room, grinning and nodding their heads.

It was Grace's fault that she might be transferred away, away from Murray. It was time for Grace to pay.

Wilbur couldn't move but his eyes lit with fear as the posse ringed his bed.

"Get off!" Gladys grabbed Grace's little hand and pulled.

"No!" Grace clutched the bars on the side of Wilbur's bed. "No! Wilbur help me!"

"You have no right," Gladys shrieked.

"No," Grace shouted, raising her head, "No, Gladys, no, don't, Wilbur! Help me!"

Wilbur began to moan hoarsely and his eyes practically jumped out of his head.

"Bitch," Gladys screamed, "Bitch, you always get a man to help you. Not now." Still holding Grace with one hand, she slapped her across the face so hard that her head snapped back.

"You shouldn't be here!" Gladys screamed again then turning to Rosie and Catherine she said: "Let's get her!!"

Eyes gleaming with excitement, Rosie and Catherine joined in. Grace clutched the bedclothes as the other women grabbed her by the arm, hand and foot and pulled her weeping onto the floor which she hit with an audible thump, a groan and a clang where her head knocked into Wilbur's wheelchair. Grace tried to struggle up but Gladys thumped her and she crashed to the floor banging her head a second time.

"Bad Grace, you get everything, but not any more." Gladys pushed her foot against Grace's ribs. But Grace, suddenly even smaller than usual, didn't move. Her crumpled form lay between the foot rests of the wheelchair and the bedclothes she had dragged down with her. A stillness filled the room. The only sound was Wilbur's groans, the only movement the rolling of his eyes. Finally Rosie broke the spell, bending her head to chew at the sleeve of her sweater where she had spilled soup at lunch.

Gladys stared a minute more then pulled out the lighter she had taken from Wilbur's bedside table earlier in the day and tried to set fire to the sheets surrounding Grace on the floor. When the fire retardant fabric failed to catch she stuffed the lighter back into her pocket and went to her own room, trailed by the posse, and grabbed her handbag.

"You stay," she ordered and they stood looking at her for a minute. Gladys walked purposefully out of her room. Catherine wandered off but Rosie followed her leader. There was no one at the nurses' station, no staff in the dining area.

Gladys, with Rosie in pursuit, pulled open the unit door and proceeded to the lounge and foyer where the elevators waited. Like the others, she wore an anklet that prevented the elevator moving if she got on without an attendant. But there were stairs. Pretending an interest in Raymond the parrot, she loitered by the loveseats near his cage chatting with him and Rosie. At last a man burdened with tools and a small ladder exited the stairwell and stopped to adjust his load with the door still ajar. As he picked up his equipment she stepped lightly behind him and out the door.

He didn't even see her, she thought, hurrying down the stairs. Pushing the bar to the fire exit she stepped outside. At last, she was free. It had been so long since she had been outside she practically cried. Pausing for just a second to sniff the air she looked around then took off at a run. She was free and on a mission. She was going to Murray's house; she was going to see her baby again. Oh Murray, it had been so long.

Minutes later a panicked Renata burst in on Nurse Daisy writing charts at the nursing station.

"Gladys is gone!"

"Where?"

"She got out. A volunteer at the coffee kiosk phoned to say she saw her running across the grass toward the subway!"

"I'll go," Nurse Daisy hurried to the stairs at a fast clip. The lawns at Happy Hillside rolled gently down to a bus stop. Between the manicured grounds and the street lay a ravine with a river in flood.

As she exited the stairs, Nurse Daisy made a hard left past the parking lot and took off at a run following the most direct route to the road. Far ahead she saw a smear of red, Gladys in her favourite sweater. Gladys was running raggedly, handbag clutched to her chest. She had reached a narrow land bridge across the ravine but Daisy was gaining on her.

"Gladys," she called, "Gladys" finally Gladys stopped for a second and yelled back; "My name is Grace!" And continued on the path by the river. Nurse Daisy had paused for just a second during this exchange but seeing Gladys continue to dart ahead she poured it on for the finish, finally grabbing her just before she hit the sidewalk and the fast-moving traffic.

"You," she said out of breath, "are coming with me!"

"No, no," Gladys flailed at her, catching her across the face with her heavy handbag. "I want my baby back,"

"You don't have any babies Gladys," Nurse Daisy said calmly, eyes watering from the blow. "Here, let's sit down and rest awhile."

"Yes!" Gladys shrieked. "My name is Grace and she stole it and she stole my baby!" Gladys collapsed sobbing onto the sidewalk, head in her hands.

In the distance Nurse Daisy saw an EMS van hurtling down the street turning the corner toward the main entrance of Happy Hillside followed by two police cars. Damn. Surely no one called the police because of Gladys escape? It was a reportable incident, reportable to the Ministry of Health but not the police. But judging by the sirens someone had called 911. With a sinking heart Nurse Daisy thought of the reports, inquiries and blame assignation to follow. She crouched beside Gladys, patting her shoulder and holding her hand.

"Okay Grace, tell me all about it." Just then her phone buzzed. "Did you get Gladys?" It was Joyce, the residence administrator.

"Safe and sound," she panted breathing hard.

"Be careful. We have an issue."

Under the covers in her pretty new room in the locked ward, Gladys lay satisfied. They had given her injections and she had slept for awhile. Soon Murray would come. He would help her with her food and hold her hand and take her down to the great room for entertainment.

But Murray sat stunned as he sorted his mother's effects in her room on the second floor overlooking the ravine. They had called him at work. Told him what they knew. Numbly he came to see his mother, called the funeral home, made arrangements. Now he was back. There would be some sort of inquiry but meanwhile he only had until the end of the day to empty her room. Tomorrow it would belong to someone else whose family was grateful for a safe refuge in which to place their loved one.

The police had been called but the investigation was inconclusive. Grace had died from heart failure. There were a few oddities. Grace's face bore the imprint of a hand and Wilbur's lighter was on the floor. Suspicion fell on Gladys who had compounded things by doing a runner. Why would anyone, especially Gladys, hurt his mother like that?

Working his way through his mother's effects he found his baby pictures. No surprise. He had been a well-loved child and

Grace had pictures of him at every age. Strange there had been no other children. His parents professed to want more but no brothers or sisters arrived, not even one. Unsure what to do with the photos; he placed them in his briefcase. He would sort them at home. He was finding it desperately sad that his mother's life had ended so suddenly in another resident's room when she fell and banged her head.

He bundled up a few of Grace's books, and loaded them onto a dolly together with her radio and her TV. He would donate them to the home. The clothes he shoved into garbage bags and left on the floor. Let someone else throw them out. It was too painful for him to do it. Then Murray checked the desk Grace had brought into Happy Hillside with her. The main drawer was locked but he had a key. Inside he found her passport, a few out of date bank books and an old leather change purse. He held the soft blue leather in his hand and a tear tricked down his cheek. Grace had always carried that purse with her inside her handbag; she had never let him see inside. Now he held it gently and cracked open its enameled clasp. He was disappointed; He had expected jewels or at least money, something important. Instead, he found two faded documents. He pulled them out and opened them carefully. Baptismal certificates. Until the 1970s before government issued birth certificates became mandatory, these were acceptable proof of age and birthplace in some jurisdictions.

He opened one. It was his mother's, he supposed. But no, the name on it was Gladys Treadwell. This must be his aunt's birth certificate...why would his mother have Gladys' birth certificate? Anyway, the date was wrong; this was his mother's birth date. Then why was the name wrong?? Puzzled he opened the other, newer document. It was his own birth certificate. That made more sense. But what he read upset him even more.

Murray got permission to enter the locked wing and approached Gladys's room. Entering quietly he saw that the drapes were drawn and she appeared to be sleeping peacefully in the gloom. Moving quickly, he crossed the room and grabbed her by the shoulders, shaking her until she opened her eyes.

"I knew you would come," Gladys said with a smile.

"This says my mother's name was Grace," he said, holding out the yellowed baptismal certificate. "But my mother was born four years before the date this person was born."

"I'm Grace," Gladys said.

Murray let her go and folded up the hand written document with its old fashioned stamps. It was all there, mother's name, father's name, child's name, place of birth.

"Yes," he said, "you are, but you killed my mother."

"I'm your mother," Gladys said dreamily.

"Aunt Gladys?" he said again, still confused.

"I'm Grace," she said with a flash of her old spirit, "your Mother. When we were little she took my name because she liked it better.

"When I got pregnant she was already married and couldn't have children. So they took you away from me. And they gave you to her."

Suddenly things he never understood fell into place; his mother's discomfort with letting his young Aunt Gladys feed him, play with him. How Gladys's eyes would always light up when she saw him. He stood there, staring at the old woman in the bed. She reached out her hand and grabbed his arm.

"Everything's going to be fine now, Murray" she said as she clutched his sleeve. "You do see don't you, Murray?" She gave him a beatific smile.

"She can't separate us any more. At last, you're all mine."

THE IMPORTANT THING

by Tyner Gillies

Tyner Gillies, a Regular Member of the RCMP, has been telling himself bad jokes and writing them down since he was in grade school. Those bad jokes have somehow transformed into one published novel, The Watch, *and a first runner up finish in the 2010, Surrey International Writing Conference writing contest with his short story* What it Means to Bleed.*

Tyner lives and works in British Columbia's Fraser Valley, with a girl that is far too good for him, and two moderately evil cats.

Visit him at: tynergillies.com

"The most important thing," the sergeant in front of me said, "is to keep the rats from eating her."

"What?" I asked as I stopped and looked at him. The embankment beneath my boots was slick with mud from the constant rain, and I was trying to stay upright in the dark as I followed him down the narrow foot path towards our destination. My attention was focused on the ground, to lessen the likelihood I'd fall on my ass and soil my already soaked uniform, and I wasn't sure I'd heard him right. "What did you say?"

"The rats," he said over his shoulder as he negotiated the trail. "They keep trying to eat the body, and the homicide guys are all bent out of shape about it."

The smell of charred meat was thick in the air.

We reached the floor of the gully we'd been sliding into and the foot path carried on into the trees. I followed the sergeant through the dark, and arrived in a small clearing, only a few paces from one side to the other. Opposite where I stood was a tarp set up on tent poles, guarded by another shivering cop, his pale face slack from a night of standing in the rain. The greasy, charred smell was doubly thick in the clearing and I felt my stomach twist in a decidedly aggressive manner.

"Your relief is here," the sergeant said cheerfully, and clapped the shivering cop on the shoulder.

The drenched man nodded to me. "If you shine your light on them, they get scared and run into the bush," he said.

"What gets scared?"

"The rats. Big fuckers."

"Great," I said, that charred smell working its way further into my head.

"I'll leave you to it," the sergeant said, keeping his back to the clearing, and not getting any closer to the strung up tarp than he had to. He slapped my back and took off the way we'd come, nearly running up the trail in his haste to get away.

The shivering cop dug into his pockets and passed me two hand warmers. "You'll need these," he said. "And don't forget your flashlight."

He turned down the trail, his shape disappearing in the dark, and I was quickly very much alone. The tall, moss covered trees bore silent witness to my discomfort as I carefully avoided looking at the twisted, blackened shape beneath the roof of the tarp. I shifted my feet, the mud making sucking noises around my boots, as I tried to ignore the smell of the body that was still quietly steaming in the cool air.

There was no sound to penetrate the deep silence of the early October morning. There was no breeze to disturb the trees, and the closest houses were too far away for their sound or light, for their life, to reach this dead, blackened spot.

As I stood in the wet dark, waiting for it to get light enough for the forensic crew to return and start working, I heard a faint whisper behind me. I turned, a hot bloom spreading through my chest as I looked at the body; its jaw was moving slightly as it whispered, too quietly for me to hear. I had no interest in hearing what it had to say, of course, and I took two shuffling side steps, preparing to flee down the foot path.

In those two steps reason returned, and I realized the blackened corpse was not speaking, but being snacked upon by a rodent large enough to do a reasonable impression of a small dog. I drew the flashlight from the steel ring on my belt and flicked it on, and the bright, LED light hammered through the dark, throwing up hunched, glowering shadows. I saw two glowing orbs in the hard circle of light, and they regarded me for the space of a heartbeat, before they turned and flitted into the underbrush. I swept the beam of the light back and forth, chasing away two other pairs of eyes, and then let the beam rest on my steaming ward.

Despite my resolution to avoid looking at the body, I could not pull my eyes away and found myself taking a good, long look. If you didn't know what it was you'd have to study it for a while until it occurred to you. The limbs were so shrivelled and blackened they no longer resembled anything human, and the oddly white teeth leering out of the blackened, twisted skull gave the only significant clue to what it was. The small body, curled in on itself, was originally thought to be a child. It was not until the forensic team found the underwire of a bra seared into the corpse's flesh that they determined it was a woman.

I looked back up at the trees and thought the small clearing would be a lonely place to die. Then I looked at the body and hoped she was already dead when whoever dumped her there had set her on fire.

The next two hours were spent pulling my boots from the sucking mud and chasing the rats away from my grim faced companion. Eventually the forensic team showed up, and I was allowed to sneak away periodically to eat and answer nature's call.

The forensic people, three cops in blue jump-suits, went over every inch of the scene. They put small items into what looked like jewelry boxes, and bigger items into paper bags, all the while making copious amounts of notes in large, black notebooks. The rats weren't inclined to get too close with so many people there, and my job shifted to keeping the two legged rats out of the scene, instead of the four.

During the day my eyes were pulled back, again and again, to the horribly white teeth in the blackened orb of the body's head. It was the only thing I could see that evidenced her humanity, and that was the thing that terrified and fascinated me most.

The day wore on and night began to fall, the darkness coming all the more quickly under the cover of the trees and a cloudy sky. Just as it got too dark to work, the forensic team lifted my grinning friend from the ground and put her in a white body-bag.

"We need to hold the scene a while longer," the head of the forensic team, a middle aged sergeant with a neat mustache told me. "We still have to process the ground she was laying on." He looked at his watch. "It'll be a couple hours until your relief gets here. You gonna be all right?"

I nodded and rubbed a damp hand across my face. "Yeah. I'm already as wet as I'm going to get. A couple more hours won't hurt."

Very quickly they were gone and I was alone in the dark, again, with only the trees for company. I checked my watch every three or four minutes, waiting for my relief, dreaming of a hot shower to wash away the stink, and a few cold beers.

Suddenly, I caught movement out of the corner of my eye and turned back to where the body had been. Standing beside the tarp, looking down at the spot, was a pale young woman in a short black skirt and white tank top. I had no idea how she'd gotten past me, but hot anger made my heart spike; both at the fact I hadn't seen her, and that she was pissing about in my crime scene, and making me look like a stooge.

"What the fuck are you doing?" I shouted, as I shined my flashlight on her. "Get away from there. This is a crime scene!"

The young woman pushed her lank hair back over her ear and turned away from the sagging tarp to face me. She folded her arms like she was cold, but made no other movement, and only stood, staring at the ground near my feet with pale grey eyes.

"Are you fucking stupid?" I asked, stomping through the mud

towards her. "Get away from there."

Still, she didn't move, even when I was within arms reach of her. It was then I realized that she was standing in the pouring rain, but was not wet.

An awful feeling, like a rough, cold hand, gripped the base of my neck and I took a step backwards. The girl turned her grey eyes down further and pointed at the spot where the body had been. As her arm and finger extended she flickered, like the picture on an old television, and in that shift she turned from a still, placid figure, to a burning conflagration, her mouth locked open in a silent scream.

The shift was over in a moment, so quick I wasn't sure I had seen it, but the image of her bare, scorched scalp and blistering skin couldn't be shaken away.

I opened my eyes and looked at the girl again. She was still pointing to where the body had been, and was staring at my boots, unblinking, unmoving. There was no menace about her, but the sight of the burning figure still flickered as after-images in my vision, and I felt the muscles of my legs and back shake and rebel as I tried to move towards her.

I managed to seize hold of my own body and took three small, shaky steps forward. Her eyes never left my boots and her hand didn't waver.

"Was that you?" I asked, my voice sounding thin and mewling in my own ears. The girl, or what had once been a girl, I suppose, nodded once, her chin moving up and down slowly. She hadn't lowered her arm, and still pointed towards the ground where the body – her body – had been.

I took another short, quaking step forward, trying to divide my attention between the silent girl and the spot she was pointing to. I kept waiting for her flicker again, or for her to reach out one of her pale hands and latch onto me, but she didn't move and only kept pointing.

I followed the direction of her finger and saw a broad, flat log, the end of it just visible beneath the spread of the bramble bushes that ringed the clearing. It was almost full dark again, and I couldn't make out what she wanted me to see. I moved the flashlight from her face and shone the beam on the log.

My stomach flipped again as I finally saw what she as pointing at; several long scratches, and two broken fingernails, marred the weathered surface of the wood.

"You were alive when you burned," I said, turning from the log to face her again. She nodded again, just once, and lowered her arm.

I rubbed a hand across my eyes, suddenly convinced that this all must be an hallucination brought on by exhaustion. If I rubbed hard enough, I thought, I could wipe the image of this pale girl from my sight and the world would go back to normal. But when I opened my eyes again she was still there.

"What do you want?" I asked, dropping my hand from my face. "Why are you here?"

She turned and walked towards the edge of the clearing. As she stepped she flickered again, her long hair and clothing replaced by a charred scalp and scorched rags hanging from a twisted body. At the edge of the clearing she stopped and looked back, her grey eyes visible over her bony shoulder.

I stood on the opposite side of the clearing, near where her body had been, my boots steadily sinking into the muck as I watched her. The logical part of my brain was yelling at me to run like my ass was on fire, but the other part, the part that feels told me there was no need to run, that this girl was not going to hurt me. The look on her pale face was expectant, and the feeling part of my brain wanted to know what she expected of me.

There was a crashing and cursing behind me, and the grinning sergeant who met me in the morning appeared, leading another, vaguely dry, uniformed cop.

"Your relief is here," the sergeant said happily as he walked into the clearing and clapped me on the shoulder. Now that the body was gone, his discomfort was gone as well, and I had a distinct urge to punch him in the tender spot below his nose.

I looked back to where the girl was standing, but she was gone, leaving nothing to indicate she was ever there; nothing except for the burned spot on the ground and the broken fingernails.

"You don't need to worry about the rats anymore," I said to

the already shivering cop who was replacing me, and walked up the trail and back to my patrol car.

An hour later I was showered and in dry clothes, walking out of the precinct office and heading for my car. I was beginning to think the pale girl in the tank top was nothing more than a hallucination brought on by near hypothermia and exhaustion. I dropped my sodden uniform in the trunk of my car with a wet plop, then slipped into the driver's seat and leaned forward to put the key in the ignition, and promptly started screaming.

In the passenger seat of my car sat the pale girl. I got just the barest whiff of charred meat as she turned and looked at me, her eyes focused on my chest, and as she moved she flickered again, transformed into the burning figure. The change was over in a heartbeat, and the pale girl once again sat in my car, watching me with sad grey eyes.

"What the fuck do you want from me?" I yelled, panic making my voice rise in both pitch and volume.

The girl didn't speak, but turned her head and looked at the driveway leading out of the office parking lot. She looked back at me, her eyes still on my chest, with that awful flicker once again, then turned her eyes back to the driveway.

"You want me to go that way?" I asked.

There was no response, but she kept staring at the driveway.

I tapped my fingers on the gear shift of my car, as the feeling part of my brain tapped on the backs of my eyes, trying to get my attention and force me to make a decision. I studied the back of the pale girl's head, and the uneven part of her hair, as several tumblers in my brain clicked into place. The important thing, right then, was to see what my passenger wanted me to do.

I started my car and pulled from the parking lot, following the direction of her gaze. As I pulled onto the public street she turned her head and looked left, and I turned the car to match her eyes. She never spoke, or pointed, or gave me any indication where we might be going, she just kept staring where she needed me to go and I obliged her.

We travelled from the city center, where the police station sat, and headed north, back to where her body had been. We passed through residential neighborhoods, both good and bad, guided by the turning of her head. As we neared the place where she'd lain and I had watched over her body, she flickered into the burning figure, and stayed that way for several heartbeats. The smell of burning flesh and an intense, awful heat filled my car and it took every ounce of will I could muster not to dive from my vehicle and flee while I let it drift into a ditch. Once we'd passed the place of her death her image stilled, returning to the placid, sad looking girl. But the sight of her burning corpse, the flesh sloughing away in sheets as it blackened and seared, would not fade from my vision and my stomach lurched in rebellion.

The further we went, the more ramshackle the houses became. The yards grew narrower and the houses began to sag, as the property values dropped and the crime rate climbed. I'd been in this neighborhood many times while I was working, but never on my own time, and I was strangely uncomfortable; my morose companion notwithstanding.

The girl looked down a narrow street, flickered once, and disappeared from my car. Her vanishing was as startling as her appearance, and I looked around in alarm for a moment, wondering where she'd gone I saw her a moment later, a slight, washed-out, ghostly pale figure standing against the stained stucco of an old, single-storey house. I drove past the house and parked my car on the side of the road, then got out and carefully walked back towards the old dwelling. The girl was still standing where I'd seen her, looking at the front door of the house, but when I started walking up the driveway, she turned and watched me, her eyes on my feet.

There was a beat up old Chevy pickup in the carport beside the house, the dented cargo box filled with articles of trash. As I got closer, the sad eyes left me and shifted to the box and heaps of garbage. I stopped and followed her eyes which were focused on a small, black purse. I reached down and picked up the shiny vinyl object and looked inside. There was a wallet containing a cracked driver's license, and I held the plastic card up to the light and looked from the small picture to the girl in front of me; it was her.

"Your name was Vanessa," I said, lowering the driver's license.

It felt odd to be talking about her in the past tense when she was right in front of me, but the sad creature was a faded reflection of the pretty girl on the driver's license.

She was still staring at the bed of the truck, and I turned again. I had to look longer this time, but eventually found what she wanted me to see: a small red jerry can, the lid discarded. "Holy fuck," I muttered, looking at the jerry can, and gripping the driver's license.

A shout from inside the house startled me, and I crouched, my heart slapping up against the inside of my rib cage while I put my hand on the butt of the pistol I had concealed under my coat. I took several quick steps and pressed myself against the corner of the house, near a broken front window that was held together with duct tape and plastic sheeting.

"Quit your fucking crying," a rough, tobacco cured voice said from inside the house. "I got no time for it."

"But, what if we get caught, man? I told you we shouldn't have done it." A second voice, higher than the first, had a note of panic in it.

"You weren't fucking complaining yesterday when you had her bent over in that field with your cock in her ass."

I glanced over at the girl, who was still standing in the drive-way, near the back end of the pickup. She was looking at the house mildly, her lank hair framing her sad face. She said nothing, made no movement, but every time the rough voice burst through the thin window her visage flickered. The shift kept up, quick as a strobe light, until I felt ill looking at her.

"I didn't know any better," the second voice wailed. "I was drunk. I didn't want to kill her!"

"No," the first voice said, in reasonable agreement. "You didn't want to. You wanted me to do it. When she started screaming, telling you to stop, saying she was gonna call the cops, you told me to shut her up." There was a pause, and I heard the flick of a lighter and an exaggerated inhaling. "You wanted me to shut her up and I did. So stop your fucking crying."

"It wasn't even my idea! You were the one who grabbed her and shoved her in the truck. That was all you!"

"You'd been fucking complaining, all night, how bad you needed to get laid. So, I got you laid."

"You know that's not what I meant."

"Once again," the first voice said, the rough tones nearly a purr, "you weren't complaining when your dick was getting wet."

The second voice tried to speak, several times, but each time his words were cut off with a heavy sob. "But you burned her, man," the voice finally gagged out. "She was still alive! I can still hear her screaming!"

"Look, shut the fuck up, you fucking pussy! You wanna go to jail? I've been and I ain't going back. You ever heard of DNA? Well it was all over that bitch, yours and mine. I had to sort that shit out. You had problems, I fixed them. Don't whine about it now that the job's done. We ain't gonna get caught, so you ain't gotta worry. Now have a beer and shut up. You're giving me a headache."

The greasy weight of the words crawled through my ears and settled in my gut, making it flip over while my knees turned watery. I watched the girl while the voices inside spoke; with every word and every burning flicker her color faded a little more, and her shoulders slumped further forward, as though each syllable was a memory of her last few, tortured minutes, and they dragged the last vestiges of life from her.

I did not know the girl in front of me, but I could see that she'd been failed. She'd been failed by whatever family she had, who let her wander the dark streets of the worst part of a bad city at night. She'd been failed by a society who allowed bogeymen, like the ones inside, to walk free and snatch children off the street. And she would likely be failed by a system that would not hold to account monsters who raped her and then set her on fire to hide their crime.

But she would not be failed by me; not on this day, anyway.

I drew my pistol from its holster, and couched as I crept under the window towards the front door. I knew the body of the girl was burnt badly enough, right down to the bone, that it would be almost impossible for the forensic guys to get any evidence. If I didn't lay hands on these two assholes, after finding the drivers license and knowing what I did, they'd never be caught. Explaining to a judge that I was led to the plethora of evidence by a ghost, that sometimes looked like it was burning, was going to be problematic, and I would have to do the best I could with what I had.

I stood square in front of the door and held my pistol up at eye level. I glanced behind me at the girl. For the first time since I'd seen her she was looking into my eyes, and her image was steady, her face clear. She nodded once, her chin moving up and down, then she was still.

I turned back to the door, took a deep breath, and kicked it in.

A file folder plopped on the desk in front of me, and I turned from my computer screen to look up at my boss, who stood beside my desk with a coffee cup in his hand.

"Did you see the briefing notes?" he asked.

I looked down, then back up at him. "Well, I have now."

"That scene with the burned up body from a couple weeks ago, the homicide guys figure they know who did it."

"Oh yeah?" I asked, sitting back in my seat, and folding my hands behind my head. "Do they need Uniform to go and bring the guys in?"

My boss shook his head. "Nope. Looks like the guys are dead. Uniform guys in the northern district got a call of a strange smell coming from a house and went in to check. Found two rotting bodies, looks like they were beat to death, but they also found ID from the girl who got burned up, plus a pair of underwear with her DNA on it, in the glove box of the pickup in the driveway."

"Oh, wow," I said.

"Neighbors from across the street said the two guys were assholes, and didn't seem torn up that they were dead. But they also said they saw a guy in the driveway, day after the body was located, who kicked in the door and went inside with a gun in his hand. They say the guy looked like he knew what he was doing, and didn't call it in cause they thought it was probably a cop who was there to bust the two guys on something."

"Oh," I said. "Did they give a description?"

"Yup," my boss said, looking me up and down. "You have any idea what the guy might look like?"

"You haven't given me the description yet, so, no."

"They said he was about six-foot-two, big guy, driving a blue sports car."

"It's a big city, Boss. That doesn't really narrow it down."

"What color is your car?" he asked.

"Blue," I said.

"Uh-huh. Is there anything you wanna tell me?"

"Not a thing," I said, meeting his gaze evenly.

"Okay, then. That's what I thought." He picked up the file folder from my desk and started walking across the big room to his office. He stopped and turned back to me, then took a slurp of coffee. "I told the homicide guys that I didn't know anyone who matched their description, but you'll let me know if you think of anything, though. Won't you?"

"I think the important thing here, Boss," I said as I turned back to my computer. "Is to know those two mother-fuckers won't be setting anymore teenagers on fire." I began typing, not looking up, letting my boss's eyes linger on the top of my head. He took another slurp of coffee and turned away. I often wonder if he knew, or was only guessing; either way he never mentioned it again.

I have seen the girl only once since the day she guided me to her murderers. I attended her funeral, with the other cops who worked on her homicide, and saw her walking among the grave markers, her image steady, the tortured figure gone, and I caught the faint scent of vanilla soap instead of charred flesh.

I do not feel guilty for what I've done, and tell myself the important thing is that sometimes vengeance brings peace; for some of us, anyway.

WHERE'S TOM?

By Kollene McKeown

Kollene began writing many years ago in Direct Marketing and as editor for two newsletters in the Wheelchair sport community. It wasn't until recently that she decided to try her hand at writing fiction. She is in the final stages of her first romantic suspense novel.

An avid reader, particularly of murder and suspense. Some of her favorites include Ian Rankin, Elizabeth George, Lee Child, Dan Brown and Patricia Cornwell.

Kollene lives in near Toronto, Ontario with her husband and two dogs Jack and Sally.

Visit her at: kollenemckeown.com

"I don't know. He's just gone." Anna Johnston shrugged, one hand, palm up and the other dabbing her nose with a tissue. "Gone."

For fifteen minutes, Officer Joshua Samuels had been sitting across the dining room table from her. He ran his hand through his short cropped hair and placed his notebook on his knee. This line of questioning was getting him nowhere. The call had come, just minutes before the end of his shift. His main thought was that his buddies were no doubt gathered around the big screen TV at Shoeless Joe's watching the Leafs game.

"Mrs. Johnston?" Samuels tried to keep the irritation out of his voice. "When you say gone, do you mean he just stepped out, maybe for a drink somewhere, or out with friends?" It would be just his luck that the old guy was at some bar watching the game. "What exactly do you mean by gone?"

Anna Johnston just sat and stared at the china cabinet along the side wall.

"Mrs. Johnston." This time more forcefully, "I can't help you if you don't talk to me. Where did he go?"

This time Anna Johnston turned to him, eyes still moist, again she repeated, "I don't know, he's just gone, he left." She glanced down at her lap and twisted a tissue in her hands, then looked back up and said, "Can you find him?"

Samuels drew in a deep breath and exhaled. What the hell was he supposed to do with that information. Gone? Really? He glanced out the dining room window, only to have his and Anna Johnston's reflection staring back. "I'll do my best ma'am, but you need to give me more information. Does Mr. Johnston work? Maybe he's just working late or away on business." Samuels looked hopefully at her for any kind of response, but there was none.

When he'd received the call earlier, dispatch reported it as a missing person. Samuels picked up his notebook and looked at it. November 15th, Mrs. Anna Johnston, 45 Chester Blvd., Ajax, Ontario. Mr. Thomas (Tom) Johnston – missing, since? Shit he thought, why me?

"Do you mind if I have a look around?"

Mrs. Johnston stopped shredding the tissue and jerked her head up, "where are my manners, officer? Let me get you some tea."

"No, no thank you, that's not necessary." Too late, she was already on her feet heading into the kitchen. "Ma'am, please, I don't really want anything." His request fell on deaf ears.

Dressed in a shapeless pair of pants and an equally shapeless oversize sweater, Anna Johnston was at the sink filling the kettle. Stifling a groan, Samuels sat back in the chair and tucked his notebook back into his breast pocket. From this vantage point, looking out the living room window he could see his cruiser blocking the driveway. The street light cast a filtered glow on the area through the full leafed tree on the boulevard. No doubt the neighbors were peering out through their curtains wondering why the cop car was there.

Pushing himself to his feet, he too entered the kitchen. The kettle forgotten, rested in the stainless steel sink. A box of tea and two cups with the tea bag tags hanging over the rims sat abandoned on the counter.

She was leaning against the countertop staring out the window. A buzzing sound came from the window. Following her gaze, he was only met with their reflections in the glass, too dark outside to see anything, but down on the window sill, the buzzing continued, a fly, trapped between the panes of glass alongside the carcasses of three others. Must be the last of the season, she didn't seem to notice. "Mrs. Johnston, is there any one I can call for you? Family? friends?" Still no response.

It was difficult to determine her age. Initially Samuels had thought her to be in her mid-70s, but now in the light of the kitchen he wasn't so sure. In spite of her unattractive shapeless clothing, short cropped mousy colored hair and oversized glasses, her skin was relatively unlined and there was an inner strength about her he hadn't seen initially. If the job had taught him anything, it was to quickly assess a situation and the people in it. He now determined her to be mid-50s at most.

"Ma'am," he touched her shoulder, "is there someone I can call for you?"

Startled out of her reverie, she turned. "Oh there you are officer, I wondered where you'd gone." She picked the kettle out of the sink and placed it on its base and turned it on. "Now where are those biscuits?"

Dementia? Or just crazy. He wondered.

"Here they are," she turned and smiled, looking at him, but there was something in the eyes. He didn't know what it was, they were looking at him, but didn't appear to see him, they were looking through him. Creepy.

"Mrs. Johnston, I'm just going to take a look around while the kettle boils, would that be okay?"

Turning back to the kettle, she absently waved her hand in response, "of course." Still feeling uneasy about the look, Samuels headed toward the hallway.

Technically, without a warrant, he had no right to search the place, but she seemed oblivious to his actions. The short hallway leading to the front of the house had three doors, most likely a powder room, laundry room and the stairs to the basement. Before heading upstairs, he glanced back into the living room. A large recliner that appeared newer than the balance of the furniture and more masculine was angled to face the large, flat screen television that sat in the corner, against a short stretch of wall separating the living and dining rooms. On the end table, next to this chair were a lamp, a pair of glasses and an ashtray. Was Mr. Johnston a smoker? Yet there was no smell of smoke in the house. With the exception of the recliner the room seemed to be trapped in the Seventies. Conspicuously absent, however, were any personal pictures. No happy couple on their wedding day, no toddlers, no family picnics or graduation pictures. Nothing of a personal nature. Odd.

At the top of the stairs, he could see there were four rooms off the central hallway. Flipping the light on in the first revealed a small bedroom with the same hard-packed beige carpeting that was throughout the house, probably, builder installed. Nothing much in the room other than a few boxes stacked against one wall and a closet with a few empty wire coat hangers. The second room had an assortment of second hand office furniture.

The last room at the front of the house was the master bedroom. Opposite the window were two doors, on the left a closet with a rod running along the side and another across the back. The back rod housed Tom's clothing, no gaps or empty hangers, Mrs. Johnston's clothes were on the side. The other door was the en-suite bathroom. The vanity and a small shelf over the toilet contained an assortment of men's and women's toiletries. If Tom had left, it didn't appear that he took anything. Everything was very neat and orderly.

Anna Johnston was still in the kitchen. Hot water had been poured into the two cups on the counter beside a tray containing cookies, milk and sugar.

"Bag in?"

"What?"

"Tea bag officer, do you want it in the cup or out?"

"Oh, the tea bag, uh, out please."

"Mrs. Johnston, what else can you tell me about Mr. Johnston? Did he work from home?" Samuels asked once they were seated back at the dining table.

Mrs. Johnston absently stirred her tea and munched on a cookie.

"Mrs. Johnston," Samuels prompted again, "your husband, did he work from home? There's an office upstairs." Why do I always seem to get the wackos, he thought. The guys will be well into the game by now and several pints as well, and here I am having tea and cookies ... what's wrong with this picture?

Mrs. Johnston looked up from her tea, looking through him again making the hair on the back of his neck bristle.

"Upstairs," he continued, "the bedroom, is that Mr. Johnston's office?" Again, a blank stare. This was pointless, he thought. Ten more minutes and he would have been off duty and this would have been Hamilton's problem. "Mrs. Johnston," he stated more emphatically, purposely tapping his pen on his notebook.

"Office? Oh yes of course, the office." She picked up the mug and took a sip, her hand trembled. "Well, he attempted to start a business, but failed," she shrugged, "didn't work out. Biscuit?" She pushed the plate toward him.

Still tapping his note book, he looked again at what he'd written, which amounted to just about nothing. "Mrs. Johnston, I'm just going to have a quick look downstairs if that's okay with you," he said, trying to hide his irritation. She'd zoned out again. He headed through the kitchen to the basement door. As he passed the counter beside the fridge, he noticed a pack of cigarettes with a lighter propped on top, sitting alongside some canisters. Strange, he thought, any smokers he knew didn't go anywhere without them. He turned back to the dining room, "Ma'am, do you smoke?" this seemed to startle her.

"What? No, no, I don't smoke."

"It's just that there's a pack of cigarettes on the counter here. Does Mr. Johnston smoke?" She was now on her feet, placing the cups and cookies back on the tray.

"Tom? Uh yes he did."

"Isn't it odd that he'd leave without them? Smokers I know, don't go anywhere without them."

"Oh well, he was trying to cut down. He must have left them behind." She continued clearing the table, never looking up.

Shaking his head, Samuels rounded the corner to the basement door.

Some rooms were partially finished and filled with boxes and an assortment of discarded furniture. Across the back of the house was a large work room, with work benches along the walls and filled with all manner of tools. They all appeared to be well looked after and neatly assembled. Everything was very clean, almost clinical. Strange for a workshop.

Overhead fluorescent lights were positioned above the workbenches leaving the ends of the room in shadow. Clicking on his flashlight, he focused the beam toward the far end. Tucked in an alcove, was the furnace and water heater. The room still had the builders' framing. An assortment of spray and paint cans sat on the cross bars. Shining the light around revealed more of the same. Venturing closer to the furnace, he felt the surface of the floor change. Backing up, he shone the light on the area. It was standard concrete, but this patch looked and felt different, not smooth like the balance of the floor, but rough and darker in color and covering a fairly large area about five or six feet in length and maybe three feet wide.

Samuels stepped to the side, puzzling over the patch. Something brushed his hair, jerking his head up he saw that there was a string dangling from the ceiling attached to another fluorescent. Pulling the string, the light flickered to life, flooding the area in white light.

Turning off his flashlight and clipping it back onto his belt, he stepped back to get a better look at the floor. Bending down he touched the area with his hand. Rough and cold.

It had been done recently, not long enough to cure. His eyes followed the path to a drain by the water heater. Propped against the wall were two large rusty pipes. He stood, sidestepped the area and picked one of them up. A large crack ran the length and it was caked with concrete. It was obvious they had been replaced. Putting the pipe back, he knelt by the drain. Why would they go to all the trouble of changing the pipes and not the rusty drain cover? Shrugging, he stood and pulled the string, returning the area to shadow.

Anna Johnston was back in the dining room, staring at the cabinet again.

"Ma'am?" his notebook was in his hand, "do you think you could answer a few more questions for me?" Samuels made a show of walking around the table to her side, pulling another chair out and sitting down. "Just a few more questions."

"You didn't finish your tea, maybe you'd like coffee instead," she stood up.

"No, really, I don't want anything, thank you. Please have a seat."

Anna Johnston let out a sigh and sat back down. She picked a napkin off the table and began twisting it in her hands.

"Mrs. Johnston." Samuels said again, resisting the urge to sigh himself. At this rate I'll be here all night, he thought. "Why don't you tell me what you remember. When did you see him last?"

Anna Johnston looked up, eyes glistening, she dabbed at them with the twisted napkin. "Yesterday."

"Yesterday?" You last saw your husband yesterday? Was it morning? Did he go to work?" Samuels scribbled in his notebook. Trying to smile consolingly he continued. "I know this is difficult ma'am, but when yesterday?"

"Morning, I think ... maybe it was the day before, but I think it was morning. I'm sorry I'm not more help. Sometimes I forget things." She kept the watery eyes on him and attempted a smile.

"Meoooowwww." The sound made Samuels jump. It echoed through the kitchen. "Meoooowwww." He could see a cat sitting in the middle of the floor, staring up at the counter. Shivers ran down his spine, the sound was like a child wailing.

The sound caught Anna Johnston's attention too. "There you

are kitty, where have you been? I looked everywhere for you, you naughty boy."

Continuing to meow, the cat had made its way into the dining room and rubbed itself on the leg of the chair. Tail held high in the air it wandered into the living room, then turned and looked up at Samuels. Bizarre looking cat, he thought. Ginger and white markings on its back and face and the tail raccoon striped. Long skinny, primarily white legs with odd colored paws, almost a rusty brown color. It lowered itself down on its backside and began grooming.

Anna jumped out of her chair and scooped up the cat. It was not too impressed with this new plan and attempted to leap back to the ground. She clutched it closer and hurried to the patio door. "Off you go," she slid the door aside with one hand and all but threw the cat out then slammed the door.

"Was that more tea then officer?" she asked. Wiping her hands on her pants, she stepped to the counter, grabbing the kettle off its base.

"No, no tea thanks, I'd like to finish up here. Please have a seat."

Giving him a pathetic smile, she put the kettle down and returned to her chair.

"When his business failed, did he find another job? Does he work? Does he drive?" His frustration was mounting. He was asking too many questions without waiting for answers. Not that she had been that forthcoming with answers. If he was ever going to finish here, he had to keep throwing out questions, hoping she'd respond to one of them. "There's a car in the driveway, do you have another vehicle Mrs. Johnston?"

She shook her head, "no," and continued to shred the napkin.

No? What the hell kind of answer was that? His fault he thought, too many questions. "No, he didn't go to work, or no he didn't drive – help me out here Mrs. Johnston."

"No, he didn't go back to work, he'd been looking, but hadn't had much luck. He would take the bus, said it was more economical."

Interesting use of the past tense, he thought.

"Where was he going yesterday?"

"I don't know, he would just go out. He didn't tell me." She looked at him as she said this. Did he see something in her eyes? A hardness? She looked away before he could get a reading.

"All right then." Samuels flipped his notebook closed and put it in his breast pocket along with the pen and did the button up.

I doubt I'll get any more out of her, the old bugger probably just took off, couldn't blame him, he thought. "I'll file a missing person report. Technically, he needs to be missing for 48 hours, so if you haven't heard from him in a day or so, I'll come back and talk to some of the neighbors, maybe someone saw him."

"Oh, I've done that. We don't mingle with the neighbors, they are mostly young with children. We keep to ourselves." She went back to shredding the napkin in her lap.

"Are you sure there isn't anyone I can call for you? Maybe someone you could go and stay with?"

"Oh, no, there's no one. I'll be fine."

Samuels got up from the table and walked into the kitchen. The patio door was closed, but he could see the cat outside, looking in, meowing and pawing at the glass. Down at the level of the cat, the glass looked smudged and dirty, a direct contrast to the cleanliness of the rest of the house. Upon closer inspection, there were more flies trapped between the glass pane and the screen door. Pretty late in the season for so many flies.

Donning his hat, that he'd left at the front door, he repeated, "Mrs. Johnston, are you sure you'll be okay? I could still call someone for you."

Anna was on her feet, leaning against the back of a chair. She shook her head. "No thanks, I'm fine."

Samuels turned to the door, then turned back: "One other thing?" Anna Johnston had been picking at imaginary lint on the back of the chair, but looked up, removed her glasses and perched them on top of her head. "That patch of concrete in the basement? What happened there?"

Habit had him reaching for his notebook, but he hesitated, waiting for her response.

She didn't answer right away. Taking in a long shuddering

breath, she looked at him. "Patch of concrete?"

"Yes ma'am, by the furnace, looks like work done recently," his hand still resting on his breast pocket.

She puzzled over this for a moment, then said, "oh that. There was a problem with the drain pipes, they were leaking. Tom had someone in to replace them." Shrugging her shoulders and attempting a smile, she responded. "I forgot. I don't go down there much." She went back to picking lint off the chair.

Samuels stood for a moment longer watching her, then shrugged himself. "I'll be on my way then. Let us know if he shows up. I'm just going to have a quick look around outside." Without waiting for a response, he pulled the brim of his hat down and opened the door. "G'nite ma'am."

Samuels rounded the corner of the garage and headed for the back gate, his flashlight beam leading the way. A coiled up garden hose was lying on the grass. Stepping over it he opened the latch, the other end of the hose was attached to a tap inside the gate. Why would a hose be around the side, he wondered, there wasn't a garden there, in fact there was only about five feet of patchy grass between the houses.

Stepping around to the back he saw that the cat was still on the concrete step. Spotting Samuels, the cat sauntered over and rubbed itself against the bottom of his pants. He leaned over to scratch the cats head and noticed a rust colored smudge on his trousers where it had rubbed against him. Absently, he brushed at it. Standing up, he shone his flashlight around the back yard. Not much to see, just your basic suburban yard. A tree and unkempt gardens along the sides and back.

Following the hose back around to the side, his light picked up on the well of the basement window. Leaning down to look closer, he could see that it wasn't latched. He hadn't noticed the window when he was in the basement, but then it was dark between the houses, so no light would filter in at night. In fact, there were no other windows on either house.

Dropping to one knee, he pointed the beam back into the well. He nudged the window inward and focused the light into the basement. He could see that this was the section with the repaired drain. The hose was probably used by the contractor for the cement, he thought. Letting the window drop back into place, he leaned back, flicked off the light and used it to nudge the brim of his hat back. Things just didn't add up. Anna Johnston was clearly dealing with some memory loss issues among other things. The house appeared to be spotless, yet there were flies trapped between the window panes. And that cat, it's just creepy. What was on its paws? If a contractor had done the job in the basement, why wasn't the floor finished properly, or why wasn't the drain replaced and the old pipes removed?

Rising to his feet, he brushed the grass off the knee of his trousers. As he straightened up he glimpsed a shadow coming through the gate. Reaching instinctively for his holstered gun, he felt the blow to the side of his head and heard the hollow ring of a metal pipe. Then nothing.

"Bastard," hissed Anna. "You men are all the same, nosey sons of bitches, everyone of you. Lying, cheating bastards."

She continued to rain blows into the empty space that had been occupied by the police officer only seconds before.

"Why couldn't you just come in and file a missing persons report?" she said to herself. "It would have been so simple, but no, you had to go nosing around, didn't you? Well never mind my dear, I've plenty more cement where that came from."

Scooter

by Patricia Kennedy

Patricia enjoys a diverse range of interests enhanced through a passion for reading and writing. She has written non-fiction articles on a variety of topics and her fiction writing includes romance, mystery, paranormal and crime.

Patricia lives in Toronto but loves New York City where she visits family and friends often.

She is a member of Sisters in Crime Toronto, Romance Writers of America and Toronto Romance Writers.

Visit her website: www.patriciaakennedy.com or Facebook: http://www.facebook.com/Patricia.Kennedy.7587

Indy, the notorious criminal, had struck again. Known for his brazen daytime and secretive night-time crimes, he had been escalating his activity from pick-pocketing, convenience store robberies, and break-ins to daring kidnappings, earning him the status of infamous. Nobody had been physically harmed, but that could change as his crime spree continued. This latest incident seemed to be the most outrageous one yet.

During morning activities in the schoolyard, Indy kidnapped a popular pupil and star of the sixth grade soccer team. The victim was nicknamed "Scooter" because of his ability to run fast down the field, scooting around his opponents to score the goal.

A sea of soccer uniforms depicted the school colors, light brown jerseys with cream and black stripes, and dark brown shorts and socks. The students were filing into the school after their early morning soccer practice when Scooter was snatched. The abduction occurred before most of the team realized what was happening. However a fast-acting tech savvy kid known as "The Wiz" caught the horrifying incident on his cell. Terrified shrills were heard as Scooter was stuffed into a waiting car that sped away.

The Wiz called 911, and was told police were on their way.

Detective Parker Knight was in his kitchen reviewing a case and enjoying his morning java when his phone buzzed. "Knight."

"We have another crime in progress."

"Let me guess, it's the elusive Indy."

His superior gave him the name and address of the school. "We're in the process of contacting his parents, so tread lightly when speaking with the other kids."

At the school Knight gathered information from the soccer team, and The Wiz showed him the video of the kidnapping.

Knight answered his phone and told his partner Indy had been spotted entering an abandoned warehouse about a mile from the school. He and his partner headed to the alleged hideout.

Knight was well aware of the volatile situation. Although Indy had a history of committing brazen crimes, he had never hurt anyone. Parker hoped this would be the case today. If they were going to bring this situation to a successful conclusion they would need a plan. The element of surprise would definitely be an advantage.

Detective Knight entered the building, adjusting his eyes to the dimly lit area while his partner guarded the door. He heard someone running and caught a glimpse of the victim scooting behind a pile of boxes. He sympathized with the victim's reluctance to show himself, especially during his ordeal.

Suddenly Knight heard yelling outside the warehouse. "Free Scooter. Free Scooter. Free Scooter." He realized Scooter's friends were chanting non-stop for his release. They must have followed the police car instead of going inside the school. Probably not the best strategy, but he couldn't do anything about them at the moment. Knight slowly walked around the boxes and grabbed the victim while he was distracted by his friends. "It's okay. Let's get you out of here." They both ran to the door. The bright sunlight was a welcomed sight. Scooter's teammates cheered and surrounded him.

Now that the victim was safe, the next task was to capture Indy. The detective had been close to arresting him many times, but Indy had always outsmarted him. Frustration and a bruised ego made him even more determined this time.

Knight walked cautiously through the building. The silence was deafening. He stopped and looked around when he heard a faint rustling from behind some boxes. Parker looked around the corner. He couldn't believe it. Indy was sitting on a wooden box chewing a mouthful of food, as if nothing was out of the ordinary. He wore his signature black jeans and white T-shirt with a dark brown faux fur vest. His hair was dishevelled as if it hadn't been washed in days.

"Don't move," Detective Knight commanded, pointing his gun at Indy.

Indy looked up and offered a taunting Cheshire cat smile, then took a drink of water. "You finally caught me, Detective PK."

Knight, furious at hearing his nickname, was tempted to shoot but held himself back. "Don't be coy, Indy."

"Quite honestly, I don't know why you're interrupting my breakfast." Indy looked down at his cereal and took a mouthful. "What's the problem?" He continued to munch.

"You've committed crimes and terrorized innocent people." Knight didn't know whether he was more annoyed at Indy for being smug or at himself for answering Indy's ridiculous question.

"So, what's next in your world, detective?" Indy asked as he took another sip of water.

Without taking his eyes off Indy, he radioed his partner. Knight was confident he could capture Indy without assistance, but this criminal was a master escape artist, so he wasn't going to fail this time around.

Suddenly Indy looked above Knight's head and yelled, "Look

out!"

"You must think I'm an idiot."

"As a matter of fact..."

Indy made a throaty growling sound as a number of boxes fell on Knight, knocking him to the floor. He recovered almost immediately.

"Damn!" Indy was gone. "Damn!" He'd failed again.

Knight exited the warehouse with his partner to see a jubilant soccer team. They gathered around Knight to thank him for rescuing Scooter. Even though Indy had escaped, the detective felt relieved the boy was safe. The team all shouted in unison, "hip, hip hooray," three times in their high-pitched chipmunk voices.

Thoughts of the escapee troubled Knight. He glanced back at the warehouse then looked to the ground, shaking his head. His partner gave Parker a reassuring jab to the shoulder.

"You'll catch Indy next time."

STRANGERS IN AN ELEVATOR

by Ray Livingston

Ray has loved fantasy and adventure stories for as long as he can re-member. To this day, one of his favorite childhood movies is Goonies, and it was at that moment, that he caught the writing bug. He began by writing stories about superheroes and some of his favorite cartoon characters, incorporating his friends into the stories, before coming up with his own original ideas.

After high school and joining the work force, he went on to study Digital Video Post Production at Trebas College in Toronto. He left that dream behind to focus on writing, working various jobs while working on his first full length novel.

When he is able to leave the imaginary world behind, Ray enjoys playing in basketball leagues or spending time with one of eleven nieces and nephews.

He lives near Toronto. Visit him at: xraylivingston.com

"I know who you are," said a voice over my shoulder.

I turned and saw a creepy guy in a long coat standing at the back of a crowded elevator staring at me. He was aged; less like fine wine, more like life had beaten him down. His alluring hazel eyes drew you in. Some might have thought he was ruggedly handsome, but not me. He wasn't my type, and I'd never seen him before in my life.

"I doubt it," I said, looking forward, waiting for the elevator to reach the lobby.

The elevator opened on the third floor. Several people got off and two men got on, a blond and a brunette. Their finely tailored suits clung to their chiselled bodies, screaming ivy leaguers.

The stench of nicotine was all over the brunette. He pulled out a pack of menthols and was eager to light one up the minute he got outside.

I couldn't stand it.

The blond chewed peppermint gum, and was visibly bothered by the other's habit. I smiled at him, and he smiled back.

I was hungry again.

"I'm pretty sure I've seen you before," the creepy guy said, his voice was hoarse and sinister.

I rolled my eyes. "Maybe I have that type of face," I said, my eyes never leaving the blond.

He was visibly intrigued, and why not, I was gorgeous; young and vibrant skin, hair the colour of a golden sunset, and eyes as blue as the sea. He was shy and looked away as I held his stare. I wouldn't to give up so easily, not when the hunger takes a hold.

I took a couple of steps towards him.

"Maybe we were here to see the same person," the creep said.

I'm not sure what my reaction was, but it was enough that peppermint decided to come to my rescue.

"Hey, pal. The lady says she doesn't know you. Maybe you should leave it alone," he said.

He was brave enough to defend a woman's honor, but not quite as brave when it came to the ladies. I knew the type. He'd take a bullet sooner than tell a woman how he feels about her.

"Hi, my name is Serena. I don't feel comfortable walking out of here alone. Do you mind walking me out?"

"Ah, sure," peppermint said eagerly. "My name is, Richard."

Peppermint shot a gloating stare at the creep at the back of the elevator then moved beside me.

I wrapped my arm in his. "It's so nice to count on a good man."

The elevator opened on the lobby floor to a commotion. Sirens blared outside and the police questioned people inside.

The elevator emptied except for peppermint and the creep.

Peppermint stepped off the elevator, unaware that I hadn't moved until he felt the tug on his arm. "Are you not getting off?"

Hell no.

"Gary Shields, he's a lawyer in this building, right? Didn't I see you coming from his office?" The creep asked.

I turned and looked at him, making no attempt to hide my contempt.

"I had an appointment with him this morning too," the creep said. "He must have been called away after you left."

Called away, or my first meal of the day. Who was this guy? Was I careless? Did I leave a witness behind?

"Serena," peppermint called me, still waiting outside the elevator.

"Do you have a car?" I asked.

"A car? Um, yeah."

"I thought maybe we could get a cup of coffee or something," I said.

Peppermint stepped back onto the elevator with a smile and pressed the button for the first level parking. "I know a great place nearby," he said.

The elevator closed on the panicked lobby and lowered to the first level parking. The doors opened and I quickly stepped out, keeling over gasping for air, as if being in the elevator a second longer would rob me of my ability to breathe.

Peppermint followed. "Are you okay?" he asked.

The creep began to walk out of the elevator. "He's scaring me," I cried. "Don't let him follow us."

Like a puppy, peppermint did as I beckoned. He valiantly stood between me and the creep. "Hold on a second there, pal. Maybe you should get off on another floor," he said and gently, but forcefully pushed the creep back onto the elevator.

The creep didn't put up a fight, and the elevator door closed on him.

"See, there's no need to worry," peppermint said. He turned around to look at me and jumped.

My face, no longer youthful and vibrant, was now withered

and pale. My hair, no longer the color of a golden sunset, was now thin and white, and my eyes turned from the sea to the fires of hell.

I stifled his scream as my hand clenched around his mouth, and hoisted him off the ground, his feet left dangling. I opened my mouth, ready to drain him of life.

Someone cleared their throat behind me.

"My apologies," said that same hoarse and sinister voice. "When I said 'I know who you are', I meant to say, I know what you are."

I dropped peppermint, and turned on the creep faster than any human could move, but it was still too slow.

"How is that possible?" I pathetically asked, as I looked down at the dagger protruding from my heart.

The creep violently pulled it out and I collapsed to the floor. He stood over me until peppermint began to stir.

"When you asked me to get off on another floor, I assumed you were capable of handling one little lady," the creep said.

"She's no woman, Agastino," peppermint said. "She's a wight."

"Always expect the unexpected."

Peppermint moved to stand over me. "I think she's still alive."

The creep handed the still bloody dagger to peppermint. The last thing I saw was the dagger lowering into my skull.

Hit and Miss

by Cindy Carroll

Cindy Carroll is a member of Sisters in Crime and a graduate of Hal Croasmun's screenwriting ProSeries.

Her interviews with writers of CSI and Flashpoint appeared in The Rewrite, *the Scriptscene newsletter, the screenwriting Chapter of RWA.*

She writes screenplays, thrillers, and paranormals, occasionally exploring an erotic twist. A background in banking and IT doesn't allow much in the way of excitement so she turns to writing stories that are a little dark and usually have a dead body.

When she's not writing you can usually find her on Twitter.

Ward noted every exit as he walked into the crowded coffee shop. It bustled with activity at 6 a.m. as regulars bought their lattes, macchiatos, and large coffees. A quiet public place meant it was easy to be overheard. A noisy place meant that would be less likely. His client had chosen well.

He got his coffee and picked a table at the back exit that had a view of the entire shop and the front window. He positioned his sunglasses on the edge of the table positioned just so. Across the street a film crew prepped a shot for a cop show. Live 3D television with the remote stuck alternately on rewind and play.

The moment his client walked in he knew it was her even though this was a blind date of sorts. Dull blonde hair pulled into a pony tail teased her shoulders as she walked. The baggy grey jogging suit drowned her petite form. At her side she clutched a muddy brown purse and a large yellow envelope.

She hastened past the university students, swerved around a toddler running amok, and dodged a waiter carrying a tub of dirty dishes. Her gaze fell on his sunglasses as she neared his table. But instead of sitting, she continued to the back and disappeared into the ladies' washroom.

A few minutes later she emerged and with a glare took a seat across from him.

She grabbed the metal napkin holder and placed it with the metal sides facing the front and back of the shop. He scrutinized her for any tell-tale signs of nervousness. This wasn't an everyday situation and people usually came to their senses in time. Her jaw was set. Her movements steady; thin, pursed lips, bright, intelligent eyes. Not even a tremor when she reached into the envelope and withdrew a picture.

He nodded towards the front window. "You watch the show they're filming out there?"

"I don't watch cop shows. They never get it right."

"How so?" He cocked his head to the right.

"They always catch the bad guy." She pushed the picture across the slippery table top. "Make it look like a robbery gone wrong."

He leaned back in his chair, snatched the picture from the table and studied the man in the photo. Kind eyes, too many teeth exposed by a huge smile, salt and pepper hair. The guy didn't look like a threat but if he'd learned anything doing his job it was that looks could be more than deceiving. They could be deadly.

"He use you for sparring practice?" He picked up the sugar and poured a generous amount into his drink.

Her brows scrunched together. She arranged the condiments on the table in order of size, largest to smallest. She reached into the big envelope again, pulling out another smaller envelope this time. A thick envelope. She took a deep breath, and then handed it over.

"You get the other half when I have proof he's dead," she said.

"He cheats on you?" He picked up the sugar again and added more to his cup, stirring his coffee this time then taking a sip. He set the sugar in front of the saltshaker.

She glared but said nothing. Not that it was any of his business. No names, no details, no getting attached. But to want someone dead badly enough to hire a killer, there was always a motive. He checked the envelope and did a quick count of the cash. She had the means. Now he was her opportunity.

She arranged the condiments again, putting the sugar into its proper place. Her task complete she folded her hands in front of herself on the table. When he reached for the sugar a third time, the glare became a scowl. He'd let her have this one. He sipped his coffee again, wondering what would push Miss Suburbia into hiring a hit man.

"Do we have a deal?"

The question came through clenched teeth and he sensed she didn't like relinquishing control of anything to someone else. He didn't either. When he could do it himself, probably better than anyone else, why risk the job to a stranger? Why didn't she do it herself? The fear of getting caught? Hiring a professional to kill someone brought the same charge to the professional as it did to the person doing the hiring.

Her gaze darted to the napkin holder then back at him. He looked at the side facing him and saw his distorted reflection looking back at him. Was she afraid someone she knew would walk in and see them? The sooner they concluded their business the better.

He nodded. "We have a deal."

Tense shoulders relaxed and he heard her sigh. She shoved a piece of paper at him. "That's his usual routine."

He scanned the list. Perfect, neat script with bullet points for each activity with an approximate time. An address at the top caught his eye. He knew the neighbourhood. Mentally he walked through the streets. If the apartment adjacent to the target's home weren't free, he would have to find another vantage point to view the results of his job.

With precise movements he folded the list and put it in his shirt pocket. From his jeans he pulled out a disposable, pre-paid cell phone. "I'll be in touch," he said as he handed it to her.

With a curt nod she stood, grabbed the phone then fled the coffee shop, glancing around as she went. When she turned right down the main street, he drained the last of his coffee then left through the back door.

Back in town after years of absence, he wasn't convinced he wouldn't be recognized, but he despised wearing a disguise, opting instead for a blue non-descript baseball cap and sunglasses.

He pulled out the list to see where the target, from now on referred to as John, would be in the next hour. His mind raced with possibilities for the hit. Something that looked like a robbery gone bad would have to occur in John's place. Away from prying eyes should ensure no witnesses. Next, he needed to decide on a weapon. A gun made too much noise drew too much interest.

No, he needed something more personal, quiet. A knife would do the job well, be harder to trace. He glanced at his watch. Over an hour before John would be leaving for errands and ultimately work. Ward headed to a little shop he knew on Main Street to get just the right knife.

An hour later he stood on the sidewalk in front of his target's apartment building waiting for him to emerge. He needed to follow John to work, then double back and check out the building, see what his options were for surveying the aftermath. His client had also been kind enough to include John's car make, model and licence plate number. When a late model black sedan pulled out of the underground parking, Ward raced across the street to his car.

Early morning traffic was unusually light. Ward weaved through the streets, John's car never more than one car ahead of him. These kinds of stakeouts turned every minute into a lifetime but they were a necessary part of his job. John made a stop at a dry cleaner, leaving with a couple of hangers of clothes draped with protective plastic.

Ward put his SUV in gear and followed his target. But this time as John drove to work a knot formed in the pit of Ward's stomach. The woman had to be crazy.

John pulled into the parking lot at 23 Division. A cop. Ward threw the car in gear and raced out of there, tires squealing. He didn't stop until he arrived at John's building. Before going through with the rest of the plan, he cursed his client and yanked out his cellphone.

Ward punched in the number of the disposable cell he'd given her.

He answered with a breathless, "What?"

"He's a cop!"

"So? That doesn't change the job that needs to be done."

"I'll need more money."

"Why? It's the same job."

"More risk means more money." Maybe she would come to her senses and call off the contract.

"More risk means more reward. Won't it give you a thrill to off a cop?"

"Offing a cop will bring the entire police force down on me. It will start a manhunt like no other. A first degree murder charge if I'm caught is not more rewarding than making it look like an accident."

"So don't get caught."

"Right. Find someone else who will kill a cop for what you're paying. Go ahead. I'll wait."

Silence greeted him for several seconds. "What if I throw in a bonus?"

"That's what I'm asking for."

"Not money. Me."

He managed to muffle his chuckle with a cough. Still not the best reaction when a woman offers herself to you but she couldn't be serious. It was obvious she wasn't in the habit of hiring a hit man to kill anyone.

"Sorry, lady. No getting involved. That includes as payment. Cold hard cash or no deal."

"Fine. I'll get you more money."

He'd been in enough relationships to know that when a woman said fine the situation was anything but. "Good. You'll know when it's done." He hit the end button and shoved the phone back in his jeans.

Ward sat in the car for an hour watching the people in John's neighborhood. A few smiled at him. Most kept their heads down as they rushed along the sidewalk going who knows where. How many of them would notice someone in the neighborhood who didn't belong?

He shoved the car door open and went to the trunk. From inside he pulled out a black jacket with a zipper and a clipboard. People rarely questioned a person with a clipboard. Act like you belong and just keep walking. He took a deep breath and crossed the street to the building.

A small courtyard with plenty of benches and lush, green shrubs looked inviting. At the entrance to the building a security camera, mounted above the door, promised protection but the wires connected to nothing. Instead of buzzing randomly, he waited for a tenant to arrive then tailgated them. Inside the building another camera gave the illusion of security. The lobby boasted a circular sofa to the right with a brown living room table. Plants, indoor trees, in full bloom evoked a spa like atmosphere complete with fountain in the centre of the lobby. Mailboxes to the left indicated there were fifty apartments. How many of those had tenants?

Seeing everything he needed to see, Ward made his way to the stairwell. He climbed the stairs to John's floor and scoped out the target's place. He couldn't risk setting up shop in one of the apartments. The cops would be checking the building. He found the emergency exit at the end of the hall. A survey of the corridor turned up a garbage can. He opened the lid, searching for anything he could use to keep the door from locking. Hidden under soft drink cans and fast food paper bags he spied a piece of cardboard that usually did the trick. He ripped off enough to cover the door latch then slid, and jumped down the stairs three at a time. At the bottom he used another piece of cardboard on the door latch of the heavy metal door leading outside. He couldn't risk going in the front of the building twice in one day, especially not today.

He looked around the alleyway he found himself in. It was only a few steps to the street and an ice cream parlour. A bell tinkled when he opened the door. The scent of Belgium waffles wafted on the air, teased his nose, and made his stomach grumble. With all the surveillance he'd forgotten to eat. He ordered a double scoop in a cup and sat at one of the metal tables to eat the creamy concoction.

Four hours later, slouched in his car he almost missed the target's exit from the police station. He waited until his mark was almost a block away before pulling into traffic and following him. Not that he needed to. If the list was correct the target was on his way to the mall, then the gym, then home.

Ward debated going inside the mall to follow the target. But with no backup he risked losing sight of John, so he waited in his own SUV listening to rock music.

The thud of bass and heat of June made Ward drowsy. He shook the feeling off and grabbed a forgotten bottle of water from the passenger seat. He splashed the water, warmed by the sun, in his face. Stakeouts had never been his strong suit.

When the torture of waiting reached an unbearable level John came out. Ward followed him to the gym.

Curious about the woman's motives for wanting the guy dead, Ward followed the target into the gym. He hung back, waiting until John picked a treadmill near the window. Ward chose a machine four down and one across. After a few minutes the guy was in a full run on the treadmill and still not breaking a sweat. Ward kept his pace at a steady jog. How long would he be here? Not that he objected to a workout, he worked out every day, he needed to keep in shape for the job. But he'd already done his usual hour of cardio and weights before meeting his client. Insomnia did that to a person. Up at 4 a.m. with nothing to do but watch infomercials or exercise. The only time he liked two workouts in one day was if the second was with a sassy brunette or fiery redhead.

He slowed to a walk prepared to settle in for a long workout when John increased his pace. Just his luck he'd followed his target on the guy's cardio day. If John came here regularly it was hard to tell. No one came over to say hello. No one greeted him when he came in. No one paid him any attention at all. Not even the women. By most accounts John was a good looking guy with a friendly face. But his posture and expression as he pounded the moving belt of the treadmill screamed that he was all business.

After an hour of walking Ward needed a shower but the risk of losing his mark was too great. John finished his run, grabbed a towel and headed to the locker room. Ward left the gym, jumped into his car and started the engine.

Thankfully, John went right home. Ward parked around the corner from the building once John disappeared into the lobby. According to the list his client provided John should be inside for the night. Should he give her one more chance to stop the madness?

Against his better judgment he dug his phone out of his pocket and dialled his client.

"Is it done?" she asked.

"Not yet."

"You're not going to try to shake me down for even more money are you? I had to cash in RRSPs for your last demand."

She didn't have a lot of money to throw around which brought up the question again as to why she was hiring a hit man. How did anyone hate someone so much that you would pay someone to kill them?

"Did he arrest you?" Ward asked.

"What? No."

"Arrest a friend? A family member?"

"Why does it matter why I want him dead? I want him dead and I'm paying you a lot of money to do the job. Whatever happened to the customer is always right?"

The customer was always right, unless they were wrong. Dead wrong. Since he didn't have a full name for the guy doing a background check was out of the question. But everything he'd seen so far gave him the impression of a nice guy.

"He a dirty cop?" he asked.

"Just do your job and don't contact me again until he's dead."

He shoved the phone in his pocket and walked around to the

back of the building. In the fading light he saw the door propped open the way he'd left it. He heaved the door open and climbed the stairs to the third floor. The knife tucked into his belt felt awkward, foreign, not at all like the weight of his Glock.

Outside John's door, Ward rocked his head from side to side to get out the kinks, took a deep breath and reached for the door knob. Surprise filled him when the door offered no resistance. Either this was a good neighborhood or John thought no one would touch a cop. Ward inched the door open, stuck his head inside and looked around. In the immediate vicinity nothing stood out. A small kitchen to the right of the entryway smelled faintly of food. Beyond the entryway the living room boasted a 60" TV that took up half the room. The other half hosted a brown sofa. Sports memorabilia donned the one wall not encumbered by a floor to ceiling bookcase. The apartment had a quiet, empty feel to it. He slipped inside and locked the door.

A carton of left over Chinese food sat on the counter, dirty dishes littered the sink. The TV hissed on, John still pointing a remote control at the device as he walked into the room from a hallway on the left. Ward willed the man to sit, not to turn around. A surprise attack would be best, less mess. When Ward took a step forward a creak filled the room. John spun around, spotted the knife in Ward's hand and frowned.

"She really did it," John said, slumping onto the plush sofa.

"'Fraid so."

Ward walked farther into the room, drew the curtains closed and faced his target. The man looked defeated, all smiles gone, the light from his eyes dimmed. Ward kept his gaze on John, prepared for any sudden movement. There was no telling where a weapon might be hidden in the apartment. For all he knew John might have a gun tucked under the sofa cushions and Ward was in no mood for the man to put on a show of a struggle.

"How is it supposed to go down?"

"Robbery gone bad."

John leaned back in the sofa. "Not an accident? Not what I expected."

"Do you know why she wants you dead?"

The man smiled. He knew why but like his client he wasn't telling.

"Knife, huh? Good choice, no noise. It's hard to muffle a bullet here. The walls are like crepe paper," John said.

"I thought it was a nice touch. Where do you keep your valuables?"

John looked at Ward quizzically then smiled. "Right, robbery. I don't have many valuables. There's a lock box in the bedroom under the bed."

Ward nodded, the awkwardness of the situation almost comical, if a woman hadn't hired him to kill someone that is. Still baffled at her reasons, Ward flicked his gaze around the room in search of a weapon, every few seconds focusing on John again. The guy was amiable enough. He didn't know how well he did his job or if he was a dirty cop. Maybe a lover's spat. In the end it didn't matter why. He'd given her more than one chance to back out but she'd insisted. Now he had a job to do and he had to do it.

John stood. Ward debated where to stab the man. In the stomach? Knife across the throat? A knife wasn't his weapon of choice. Not for the first time since the job started he went for the gun that was not on his hip. Couldn't risk having the Glock with him for this job. Ward let instinct take over and lunged. The knife got John in the stomach. John fell back onto the sofa, eyes closed, a patch of red bloomed on his shirt.

Ward pulled out his phone and took a picture, then another one for good measure. He sent the photo to his client. While he waited for a response he proceeded to toss the apartment to make it look like a robbery. He grabbed the lock box from under the bed and left the apartment.

He had to walk a block before finding a phone booth with a working phone. He called 911 and reported a robbery at John's location. It would take a few minutes for law enforcement to arrive so he walked back to the ice cream parlor, sat and waited for the show.

First responders, two street cops, arrived less than five minutes after he called. They had less trouble getting into the building than he had initially. Minutes after the first responders more cop cars showed up, including an unmarked black sedan with flashing light on top. His client leaped out of the car and rushed into the building.

A few minutes later she emerged from the building, crumpled and broken, tears streaming down her face, looking to the world like she'd lost a best friend. She'd traded her frumpy jogging suit for a crisp pant suit with a white blouse. One of the detectives on scene helped her sit on one of the benches. He would love to hear what she was saying. The distraught bit was a nice touch, making him more curious who the guy was to her.

Officers would be canvassing the neighbourhood, looking for witnesses, interviewing neighbours relentlessly until they found their man. Ward stood, walked through the parlour to the back doors, slipped outside and took the scenic route to his car a block away. He ditched the baseball cap in a garbage can.

Thirty minutes later he arrived back at the coffee shop. He had to come to it from the left this time, the street blocked again for a TV shoot. Despite the chaos outside the shop was busy. He waited in line to get his coffee then made his way to the back, sitting at the same table he had when they first met. Though the sunglasses had served their purpose at their first meeting he still put them on the corner of the table. Ward waited.

He spotted her as soon as she opened the door. It was like opening night compared to the rehearsal of their first meeting, his client's appearance exuded confidence. Before she didn't want to stand out but today they were just two people having coffee with a little money exchange. Her gaze fell on the table and she walked with purpose to it.

This time she sat right away, giving him a glare for taking the seat with the best vantage point. She grabbed a metallic napkin holder and positioned it on the table just to her left with the metal sides facing the front and back of the shop. Out on the street police cars screeched to a halt. A man came running up and spoke to the people in the cars. The cars backed up, out of eye sight, to do it all again.

He nodded to the scene outside the shop. "I thought about it and you're right. They always catch the bad guy."

"I'm always right. Can we get down to business? I'm on the clock." She crossed her arms.

"If you insist. That was some acting." Ward picked up his coffee and took a tentative sip. Still too hot for him, he put it back on the table.

"You were there? You could have been caught!"

"I'm touched. I wasn't though, was I? So what's the deal? You gonna tell me who the guy was to you now?"

She smirked and leaned back in her chair. "Not that it's any of your business but he was my ex-husband."

"You hate him that much? That's pretty cold. Looked like a nice enough guy to me."

Angry red splotches dotted her face. She drew in a deep breath. "He grew a backbone."

Ward smiled. Control freak couldn't control her man anymore and that made her angry. He suspected the divorce was the ex-husband's idea.

"Whatever. I did my job. Where's the rest of my money?"

She reached into her blazer and pulled out a thick yellow envelope. "That's all I have. I can't give you anymore so don't try to shake me down later."

He nodded. On the street police cars screeched to a stop. This time officers jumped out of the cars, shouting ensued as directions were given. Four officers stormed the front of the coffee shop. The bang of the back door bring flung open startled him enough he almost spilled his coffee. He turned to see four more officers storming through the back door.

The initial four officers at the front weaved their way through the shop and more police entered the establishment. All of them converged on his table. With guns drawn, one officer stepped forward from the rest. It was the detective who had helped his client in front of the building.

"Detective Lucy Phillips, you are under arrest for conspiracy to commit murder. Do you understand?"

The detective hauled her to a standing position and put cuffs on her. Ward gave into the song playing in his head when the detective started cautioning her as a suspect and rhyming off her right to counsel.

"What do you think you're doing? Hank, it's me. You're crazy," she protested.

Her puzzled look turned to rage when John walked to the back of the shop. "Not so crazy, Lucy," he said.

The fake blood still stained John's shirt where Ward had "stabbed" him. Ward pulled the knife he'd used out of its sheath, pressed it into the table. "Blood" dripped out as the tip contracted into the handle; then he placed the knife on the table.

"It was faked?" Lucy shrieked.

Ward pulled out a small recorder and placed that beside the knife. Beside the knife and recorder he placed both envelopes of money and the picture of John. He stood and shook John's hand.

"Nice to officially meet you."

"Barry," he said. ``Likewise. Good show at the apartment. But did you have to toss the place and take the lock box?"

"Sorry, man. No way to be sure she wasn't watching. We needed her to believe the job was done. Your lock box is in my car."

To keep it as authentic as possible Ward had insisted on not meeting any of the players beforehand. That and they couldn't risk Lucy seeing him talking to cops, especially her ex-husband Barry. He loved a mystery so he'd also insisted on not knowing the reason for the hit to see if he could get it out of her.

Lucy lurched for Barry, Hank holding her back. She fought against Hank's hold, her face red, nostrils flared, and lips flat. After a minute of struggling she calmed down, her shoulders droope, defeat filled her faced.

"When Barry came to us with his suspicions we were sceptical but we had to act," Hank said. He turned to Ward. "Detective Cooke thank you so much for your help."

"You're a cop?" Lucy lurched for Ward but Hank held her back again."We'll need you at the station for your full statement, Detective Cooke."

Ward nodded. "I do like that show." He jerked his head towards the front of the coffee shop. "They get some of it right. We don't always catch the bad guys, but a lot of times we do."

THE CHRISTMAS PRESENT

by Rick Gustafson

Rick Gustafson is the author of Discipline, Minor Crimes, and the Christmas Present. A former US Army helicopter pilot, Gustafson flew as a commercial helicopter pilot in Alaska during the Exxon Valdez oil spill and later in Croatia and Macedonia in support of the United Nations Peacekeeping Mission in Yugoslavia (UNPROFOR). He later became an airline captain.

In the summer of 2005, he accepted a temporary assignment with the United Nations' peacekeeping mission in the Democratic Republic of Congo (MONUC). During the six-month rotation as an Aviation Officer, he coordinated United Nations' aviation assets in Lubumbashi for the distribution of electoral registration kits to remote villages in the Katanga Province.

His short story, Discipline, *was awarded first place in the Denver Women's Press Club Unknown Writers Competition. In addition to his short stories, he is currently writing a book inspired by his experiences in Africa.*

Rick lives in Denver, Colorado and holds a Masters of Liberal Studies in Global Affairs from the University of Denver along with a Certificate of Advance Studies in Creative Writing. He graduated from the University of North Dakota with bachelor's degrees in Aeronautical Studies, Aviation Administration, and Accounting.

Jenny's flight was scheduled to arrive at 7:30, which gave me three hours to fill the car with gas, kill Sanborne, and still get to the airport in time to pick up my wife. It would be dark soon, and I had just finished lining the trunk of my vintage burgundy 1978 Monte Carlo with plastic. The duct tape didn't stick well in the cold, but I figured it was better than nothing.

My cell phone rang. Sanborne. On his way over with tire chains.

When he arrived, I carried the chains into the garage, and set them near the trunk. Sanborne followed.

"You got the keys?" he asked.

"In the ignition."

"How long do you think you will need em?" Sanborne slipped the keys from the ignition and returned to the trunk, opening it with a metallic click.

"Not long." I turned toward the workbench, my fingers closing around the worn wood handle of an ice pick.

"I might need them back if it snows hard next weekend, heading up to the Aspen for the long..."

The trunk swung open. Inside the trunk lay three photos, evenly spaced on the plastic, the grainy intertwined bodies telling their own story of another weekend in the mountains. Before Sanborne could protest, I slipped up behind him, grabbing his forehead with my left hand, ramming the ice pick through the nape of his neck with my right, the ice pick's newly sharpened tip finding its way through the grisly muscle and cartilage before gliding through the soft tissue where Sanborne kept his some of his hopes, a few of his memories, and most of his autonomic functions.

He stiffened and jerked, and then he relaxed, his brain unplugged from his spinal cord. He fell, face first into the open trunk, his legs collapsing beneath him, kneeling on the cold cement floor as though in a church pew, his torso prostrate in the plastic-lined trunk, a tiny trickle of blood on his neck.

It was much easier than I imagined it would be.

I slid a garbage bag over Sanborne's head, careful not to disturb the ice pick. He was still alive, technically. His heart might beat for a few more minutes, maybe for as much as an hour, not that it mattered. After tying the open end of the bag tightly around his neck, I shoved his legs into the car. He lay cradled in the plastic. I wondered if he slept that way on the sheets Jenny would later wash, the same as my mother had for my father.

"Nice and clean for you," my mother would say as she tucked my father in following one of his twenty-four hour shifts at the hospital.

I closed the trunk.

If I were a smoker, I would have lit a cigarette as I drove to the gas station, my window open, the winter air washing over me. At the station, I pumped the gas with my coat open and watched the numbers roll up on the pump. Three dollars and ninety-two cents a gallon, criminals. I paid cash for the gas and dropped into the car for a leisurely forty-five minute drive to the airport.

Christmas music piped through speakers created a festive atmosphere in the brightly lighted main terminal. I stood waiting among the families, lovers, and limousine drivers.

Seven forty-two, the escalator from the train station one level below bore my wife to the terminal's main level. Smiling, she dropped her small bag and draped her arms over each of my shoulders, her wrists crossing behind my neck.

I returned the embrace, and we kissed long and hard.

"Merry Christmas, Doctor Marshal."

Merry Christmas, Missus Marshal."

"Do you have a special present for me this year?" She leaned back, holding our clinch smiling in a girlish way, her head tilting to one side.

"Yes, I do."

"Really?"

"Yes, really, it's in the trunk."

Love Fades

by Karen Blake-Hall

Karen's sharp-bladed fiction cuts to the heart of the emotions driving her characters in desperate situations.

In her chilling short story, The Hunter *a woman runs from a relentless pursuer determined to bring her down.* The Hunter *was recently featured in the Toronto Sisters in Crime Anthology,* The Whole She-Bang.

She is a member of Sisters in Crime International; Sisters in Crime Toronto; Sisters in Crime Toronto Executive; Romance Writers of America, Toronto Romance Writers; Kiss of Death Chapter; Fantasy, Futuristic and Paranormal Chapter, and Savvy Authors.

When she's not at her day job, she's crafting more tales of love and crime or spending time with her family.

She lives outside of Toronto with her husband and a Jack Russell Terrier who rules, not only the street, but the universe.

Visit her at her website: karenblake-hall.com
or her Facebook page: Karen Blake-Hall

Waking up to the sound of people in my house, I scramble out of bed and throw on some clothes. Damn, I hate it when Sonya invites people over when I'm sleeping. She has always hated my working nights and lately has started her entertaining earlier and earlier. I walk down the steps and rub the sleep from my eyes then comb my fingers through my receding hair.

"Sonya?"

She doesn't answer me. *Nothing new there.* Lately she's been distant, withdrawn and I can't figure out what the hell I've done wrong.

Walking into the living room, I see her holding court, her favorite past-time. Seeing her best tea set out on the coffee table, I know she has special guests today.

"Sonya."

She deliberately ignores me in front of her guests. She doesn't care that I hate the silent treatment. The quieter she gets the deeper shit I'm in.

Sitting down on the couch beside her, I notice she's still in her housecoat. With the closet full of clothes, I can't believe she's still in her housecoat. This makes no sense but lately nothing she does make sense to me.

"Sonya, can we talk?"

She hands a cup of tea to the cop sitting in the chair across from her. *A cop?* What the hell is a cop doing in the house?

"Sonya?"

The cop takes the cup and sets it back down on the table, then he pulls out a notepad and a pen.

I haven't got a clue what's going on and I know she won't tell me.

Not looking up, the cop says, "Has your husband been acting differently?"

"He has always been distant. You know he suffers from depression."

"Hey, don't tell him that." I point at the cop.

He keeps writing in his note pad. "Has he been depressed lately?"

"No. I haven't," I say. "I'm taking my meds and I'm feeling fine."

Nodding Sonya said, "Yes. He's been getting worse."

"No. I haven't." Turning to her I plead, "Sonya, don't do this. I'm fine and you know it." She ignores me so I face the cop but he never makes eye contact with me. "I'm fine. I take my meds and I'm fine." I realize how desperate I sound but hope he doesn't notice.

The cop scribbles his notes. "How?"

"He stays in bed all day. Doesn't seem to have the energy or the will to get up and do anything anymore."

"I work nights." Ramming my fingers through my hair I force myself to calm down. "Look officer, I have to sleep sometime. She doesn't realize that while she's sleeping I'm working. I'm not depressed." I look at her. "Sonya, stop this. Whatever I've done to make you mad, I'm sorry. Turning to the officer I say, "She doesn't mean it. This is just a misunderstanding that's all. Why don't you leave and we'll talk it out?"

The cop doesn't even look at me. He just keeps writing in that damn note pad. She shouldn't have involved them.

"Sonya, let's talk."

She grabs tissues from the box, holds them up to her nose and starts to cry. My heart breaks. I never know what to do when she acts this way. I'm a strong man but when her tears start to flow, I turn into jelly.

"Mrs. Brown, I know this is hard, but I have to ask these questions. Were you happily married?"

"Happy as anyone else. We had our ups and downs but yes, I'd say we were happy."

"She's right there, we're happy." The cop doesn't react to what I've just said. Guess they've been trained to play it cool with husbands.

Sonya starts to sob into her tissues. "It's been hard to watch him fall into depression. I really have tried my best."

"I'm not depressed. I'm not. Sonya, stop this."

"The doctor said it wasn't my fault." She starts to rub her wrist and I see the cop notice it.

"Arthritis."

"What? You don't have arthritis." I look at the cop. "She doesn't have arthritis."

She blows her nose and looks away from me. If she only knew how much it kills me when she's upset. After all these years together she should realize how much I love her.

I follow the cop out into the foyer. Maybe I can convince him this is just a misunderstanding, nothing serious. I see the cops huddling together.

"Seems straight forward," one says. "The empty pill bottle on the dresser says it all."

"I don't keep my pills on the dresser," I say in desperation. "I keep them in the kitchen in a pillbox. You know the kind that has the days of the week on it. That way I take them in the morning and night. I reload it every Sunday morning."

"Doc said there were no signs of trauma."

"Yeah, that would fit with what the wife said."

I look down and notice I'm fading. What the hell? I feel light-headed and dizzy. I touch my head. I feel strange, not warm, not cold, just strange. "What is going on?"

Sonya is standing at the door as the cops leave and closes it after them.

"What the hell are you doing to me? Why did you call the cops? I ask.

She smiles and walks back into the living room. Her robe loosens and I can see a red bra with matching panties under it.

A light is shining so brightly that everything in the room pales. There is a figure with out-stretched hands standing in front of the light. I've never seen him before but he is beckoning me to follow.

Looking back at Sonya I see her running her fingers across her stomach. She picks up the phone and punches in numbers. "Hey lover. Yeah, they bought it hook line and sinker. You want to come over and console the lonely widow?"

Witness Protection

by Stephanie Bedwell-Grime

Stephanie Bedwell-Grime is the author of more than twenty novels and novellas and over fifty short stories.

She has been nominated for the Aurora Award five times and has also been an EPIC eBook Award finalist.

Visit her at: feralmartain.com

"We've got a live one."

Lyra wasn't even halfway through the door, the seal on her stim still unbroken. She clenched the cup in her hand. She wasn't putting it down until she got at least a sip. She nodded to the desk sergeant in passing and then looked back at her fellow detective, Roland. "And a good evening to you, too."

"No, seriously, you've got to see this one."

She broke the seal on the biodegradable cup and took a long swallow of the hot brown watery liquid. It burned all the way down her throat, but its warmth radiated out through her body, kind of the way coffee had, before it got too expensive. She took another sip for good measure because the way Roland was talking she wouldn't be getting any more for a while. "What's so special about this one?"

Roland grinned, showing even, white teeth, all composites of course, but still, it was a nice smile. "You'll see. He's in interrogation."

"Why is he in interrogation? Is the holding cell full?" She sincerely hoped it wasn't because that would make for a very long night.

Roland's grin faded. "No, he tried to eat the other inmates in detention."

Lyra took a long pull on her stim, heedless of the hot temperature. "Tell me you're joking."

Roland shook his head. He started walking toward the back of the precinct. Lyra followed.

It was Saturday night and since the Fall, more people had fled to the city, making every night a challenge for law enforcement. The hallway was crowded with detainees waiting to be processed. Armored police officers stood over them, vainly trying to keep the corridor in some kind of order. The holding cell would be full by night's end. Then again, it usually was. Still, it was rare for inmates to try eating each other.

She called ahead to Roland trying to be heard above the general din. "What's he got? Metal teeth?" Steel dental work had been all the rage for a while once dentists had gotten scarce.

Roland glanced back at her and shook his head. "Just a case of the crazies."

"So, why are we holding a crazy in interrogation?"

Her colleague reached the door to the observation room and opened it. "You'll see."

Lyra looked through the one-way mirror. A man slumped in a chair, his head resting on his chest. At their arrival, his head snapped up. She took an involuntary step backward.

The man didn't have metal teeth, but his were broken and stained with old blood. His left eye was swollen shut. He stared straight at her with his right eye. She was surprised he could see anything at all through that red-rimmed, cloudy orb. His clothes hung in tatters in spite of the unseasonably cold weather. She didn't even want to speculate on what stained his jeans. His bare feet were black with dirt. She thought he had mud caked between his toes, but judging from the rest of him, it could be anything.

95

It wasn't his state of disarray that had startled her, though. Since the Fall, she'd seen every kind of human misery a post-apocalyptic world could offer. It was the slack-jawed, hungry look he gave her even though he couldn't possibly see her through the interrogation room glass. So how had he known she was there?

In a flash he was out of the chair, lurching toward her with blinding speed. He crossed the floor in an instant, not even slowing when he hit the glass. The entire room vibrated with the impact. Stunned, her assailant fell to the floor. His hands left grimy prints. Something yellow and nasty looking smeared the glass where his face had hit. Lyra sucked in a calming breath. Good, she'd held her ground this time. She hadn't embarrassed herself in front of Roland by taking another step backward.

But she almost did when her attacker rose and threw himself at the glass again.

His mouth worked, broken teeth snapping together. He clawed at the observation mirror with filthy hands.

Her eyes darted to where Roland stood, calmly taking it all in. He'd already seen this once tonight. Anger surged through her. She could have been warned.

She drew another breath and tried to muster some of Roland's feigned disinterest. "I'd say he's a little more than a crazy. How'd the guys even get him in here without getting bit?"

The glass shuddered again under another impact.

"Oh, the guys didn't bring him in. He walked in himself. Said he wanted to report a crime. He's a witness."

Lyra glanced back at the man throwing himself against the mirror. "A witness to what?"

"Don't know. Before we could question him he went like that."

"Great." She suddenly remembered the stim in her hand and downed the rest of it.

"C'mon," Roland said, motioning for them to leave the observation room. "No sense in having to replace the glass. Too hard to come by these days."

"Yeah." She followed him out of the room. "So are a lot of things."

96

She cast one backward glance as the door shut. Their attacker was peering one-eyed into the glass, trying to catch a glimpse of where they'd gone.

Lyra hurried to catch up to Roland. "What are we going to do with him?"

"Dunno. Can't toss him back out on the streets like that."

Lyra struggled to calm her racing heart. "Well, the interrogation room is secure. It's not like he's getting out."

"No," Roland agreed. "But here's the funny thing. When we're not in there, he just sits in that chair. Like he's got all the time in the world."

She ducked back into the observation room and cast a quick glance through the observation mirror. Sure enough, the witness had reclaimed his chair. He slouched in it like a rag doll, his head once again resting on his heist. No sooner had she caught a glimpse of him, he somehow sensed her presence. His head jerked up and that one eye centred on her as if he was staring at her through regular glass. Lyra beat a hasty exit.

Roland cocked an eyebrow. "Let me guess, back in the chair?"

"Back in the chair. It's weird, it's like he knows we're there." She suppressed a shudder. On her desk waited a million other tasks. But sooner or later they were going to have to free up the interrogation room. And that meant finding a solution to their biting-mad witness. "Okay, here's an idea. Has anyone tried to feed him? Maybe if we could distract him, we could get some cuffs and a muzzle on him."

Roland barked a laugh, catching the attention of some detainees in the hallway. He lowered his voice. "What do you suggest we do? Hack a leg off one of these guys and toss it in there to him?"

One of the people in the hallway heard him and shied back against the wall.

"Actually, I was thinking a pseudo-steak. That might hold his interest long enough."

A couple of uniformed officers squeezed by them in the corridor wearing heavy armor. "Heard we're holding a zombie in interrogation," one said as they passed. "Can we have a look?"

"You heard wrong," Lyra replied. "Just a crazy." The last thing they needed was a rumor like that spreading through the precinct.

They reached the cramped room that housed their desks. Roland sat down, stretched his long legs out and took up most of the space on Lyra's side of the room.

He still hadn't answered her question. "So what do you think?"

"If I had a pseudo-steak, I'd eat it myself."

"Well, that was my idea," she said, as a hint of annoyance crept through her. She'd learned to deal with Roland long ago, or they wouldn't have survived their first five minutes together as partners. And that meant not taking the verbal bait. Lyra sat at her desk and tossed her empty stim cup in the recycling bin. "What do you suggest?"

"We could always just shoot him in the head. It's not like we wouldn't have cause. All we need is for him to take a run at us."

"He says he's a witness!"

"Not saying much now." He pulled his legs in and sat up in his chair facing her. "Last I checked there wasn't anything in the rule book about being nice to zombies."

She let the barb slide. For one thing, there was no rule book. "You don't really think he's a zombie, do you?"

"Looks like. Guy's biting mad. He tried to get through the glass at us."

She desperately needed another cup of stim. Shouldn't have come in tonight, she thought. Should have called in sick. Like anyone in the precinct cared if you were ill. If you weren't dead, you showed up for duty.

After the Fall, the city functioned pretty much on its own, but rumors from the countryside were rife. People flooded into the city, looking for safety behind its walls, where some semblance of law was maintained. Those responsible for upholding it knew just how tenuous their hold on the law was. But according to the testimony of those fresh from the country, it was worse where they came from.

Lately they'd heard rumors of a strange disease that, like rabies, was spread by biting. People were calling the victims zombies, but a new strain of rabies made more sense. Vaccine was in short supply. In order to put food on the table, people unaccustomed to hunting were now encountering wildlife more than ever. It could be rabies, chances were it was something else. And now they had a living carrier in their interrogation room.

Roland was right. They should shoot him.

"We've got to get back in there." She stood up. "We've got to find a way to communicate with him."

"Knock yourself out," Roland said and began digging through his paperwork. He looked up as she reached the doorway. "Let me know if you want me to shoot him for you."

"Thanks a bunch," she muttered as she made her way down the corridor toward the main desk. She'd start with the desk sergeant. That's where the mystery began.

The hallway was even more crowded. A flash of her badge parted the sea of bodies. No one wanted to add extra charges to their rap sheet. Justice in the city was swift and brutal.

"Guy was waiting in line over there," the desk sergeant told her, pointing to the queue that stretched into the hallway.

"Was he acting odd in any way?"

The sergeant looked at the line clogging the hallway and raised his eyebrows. "Define odd."

"Stranger than usual."

He seemed on the verge of saying something else sarcastic, but instead thought better of it. "Now that you mention it, he was kind of shifting from foot to foot, like he was real impatient. Thought it was drugs."

"So he was agitated?"

"Not agitated so much as in a hurry."

"And what did he say?"

The sergeant glanced down at his notes. "Said he needed to talk to a detective right away. That he wanted to report a crime."

"Did he say what kind of crime?"

He consulted his notes again. "A murder."

"Whose murder?"

"Didn't say. I was in the process of rustling up Roland when he went completely ape-shit on us. The guys tossed him in detention, but as soon as we tried to put another detainee in there, he tried to bite him. So we threw him in interrogation."

Foul pretty much described the stim from the vending machine. Lyra took a sip and grimaced. Still, it gave her something to do as she sidled back down the hallway and mulled over the zombie's fate. She pressed her ear to the door, but couldn't hear any sound coming from inside.

Thunk!

The impact sent her reeling across the narrow corridor. Her hand squeezed the cup of stim sloshing brown liquid after her. A couple of uniform officers passing through the hallway gave her curious glances. They probably hadn't heard the zombie rumor yet.

"You okay there, Detective?"

"Fine," she said, regaining her composure. She took a step back toward the door, but another ominous thud from inside stopped her from going any closer. How did he know she was there? She wouldn't be getting inside even with a pseudo-steak. And it was only a matter of time before the Captain demanded to know what was going on. Once the zombie rumors reached him, he would order Roland to shoot the guy.

Lyra squared her shoulders, ignoring the stim staining the floor, and headed for the observation room.

Their witness was still over by the door when she entered. She could have sworn he was sniffing the door jam, trying to sense what was on the other side. Lyra shook her head. She was starting to think of him as a zombie now herself. She closed the door behind her as softly as she could. But as soon as she moved to stand in front of the one-way mirror, the subject whirled toward her. He launched himself across the room faster than she'd ever seen anyone move.

She steadied herself for the impact, but it still shocked her when it came. He hurled himself against the glass with no concern for pain or bodily damage. Who did that? Even the most hardened criminals, even the worst cases from out in the countryside had some remnants of self-preservation left.

His jaw moved as if he intended to chew through the glass. He clawed at the observation mirror with the stumps of blood-streaked fingers. Rabies, they'd tried to tell her. It didn't look like any case of rabies she'd ever seen, not that she'd seen many. But more diseases than ever were cropping up in the over-crowded city. In some cases diseases that hadn't been seen in hundreds of years. It could be something they'd have to get out the history books to diagnose. Or it could be something new. Was there a disease in the countryside that turned people into zombies? Could it be a biological weapon meant to thin out the crowds and give others a better chance to survive? Was that the crime he wanted to report?

She was a cop, not an epidemiologist. Finding an epidemiologist would be harder than getting her hands on a history book.

Another smash against the mirror shook her from her musing. Her assailant stared at her through the mirror, his one good eye intent. Somehow he knew exactly where she stood. She took a couple of steps to the side and that cloudy eye swivelled to track her. He'd stopped trying to chew through the glass, but his hands moved on the mirror, leaving grimy smears in their wake.

Was he trying to get her attention?

Lyra began to walk toward the door. He slammed his hands against the glass. Was it her imagination or was there was a pleading look in that eye that hadn't been there before?

He was definitely trying to get her attention, she decided. Perhaps it was just a ploy to get her in the interrogation room with him so she could be his dinner. Still, there was something in his rhythmic movements. They seemed deliberate.

She cocked her head and studied the smears on the glass. A lot of blood and other bodily fluids marred its surface, so it was difficult to tell. The strange thing was, while she studied the marks, the zombie on the other side of the glass fell silent, like he was waiting for her to figure it out.

Problem was, it didn't make any sense. All she could see were bands of blood mixed with a yellowish-green fluid. She didn't even want to speculate what it was. She almost walked away, but then within one of the smears, the scratchings started to make sense. Lyra stuck her head out the door and looked for one of the uniformed officers. "Can you tell Roland I need to see him?"

Roland wasn't happy to be roused from his paperwork. Filing reports put him in a bad mood on the best of days. He had a cup of stim from the vending machine just as she did, the universal sign of a bad night.

"Wishful thinking," he proclaimed after the briefest glances at the mess on the glass. "There's nothing there."

"Look at him." Lyra pointed to the zombie standing a few inches from the mirror, waiting. "He's not throwing himself at us anymore."

"Maybe he got tired."

"Zombies don't get tired." She didn't know that for certain, but it sounded good, so she went with it.

"They don't write love letters, either. I think he just likes you."

"Apparently he likes you, too," she said, keeping the tone light. Roland's dismissal annoyed her, but she needed him on her side. He was the best detective they had. After a moment, she asked, "You don't see it?"

"See what?"

She pointed to the marks on the glass. "Look, he's written it here and then tried to make it more legible by writing it backwards so we can read it from this side."

Roland squinted at the mirror. "Read what?"

He wasn't going to see it. She'd have to spell it out for him. Lyra traced her fingers over the letters. They were smeared almost to the point of illegibility. "It says, Help!"

He stared at the scratchings on the glass. "Say again?"

"It says, Help!" Once again, she ran her finger over the letters, certain they were letters now and not just the random scratchings of a madman.

She looked through the glass to find the zombie watching her intently with that one eye. He shouldn't even be able to tell where she was standing, but as he followed the movement of her fingers, she thought she saw a glimmer of intelligence in that eye that hadn't been there earlier. Perhaps he had lucid moments when the person he'd been remained. Maybe its consciousness came and went as the disease progressed. If it was a disease.

The zombie approached the observation mirror. He didn't throw himself against it this time, but his jaw still moved up and down as if he desperately wanted to be chewing on the two detectives behind the glass, but was trying to control the compulsion.

With an unsteady hand, he smeared more letters onto the mirror. Lyra took a step back to decipher them.

"I'm still not seeing it," Roland remarked.

"Here." She drew her finger over the new letters the zombie had tried to smear into the blood and gore on the glass. "It says, murder."

"I think you're just seeing what you want to see. I still say shoot him and have done with the thing. All we need to do is go in there. He'll charge at us and boom!" Roland mimed shooting the zombie in the head.

"He told the desk sergeant he wanted to report a murder. He's trying to tell us the same thing. We're detectives. We're supposed to listen."

Roland pointed in the direction of the hallway. "I've got a whole lineup of people out there who want me to listen to them."

She had to stay calm. If she took Roland's bait, she'd lose her composure and the murder the zombie wanted to them to investigate would go unreported. "You brought me in here," she reminded him.

"To see the sideshow."

"Well, the main act wants to report a murder, so I'm going to take his statement." She glanced at the gore on the observation mirror. "Even if it's written in blood."

"Fine." Roland headed for the door. "Tell me what he says."

Lyra turned her attention to the scratchings She traced her finger over the word murder. Maybe he could sense that small movement.

For a moment he didn't move, he just stood there while she outlined the word. Then he drew on the observation mirror again.

"I as m red," she read aloud. Roland was right. It didn't make sense. She likely was wasting her time.

She traced the letters again. The zombie uttered a slack-jawed moan. It didn't sound like any word she recognized. It was probably an involuntary sound, or perhaps a groan of protest or frustration. She turned down the volume on the mic in the observation room.

He threw himself against the glass again, leaving a trail of clear, slimy liquid. The captain probably would let Roland shoot him. Whatever lucidity had seized the zombie, it seemed gone. She moved to leave the observation room, to head back through the press of bodies in the hall to tell Roland to go ahead. Movement stopped her. The zombie was drawing shapes in the gore again, adding to what he'd written before.

"I was m red." She ran her finger over the new marks and shook her head. "I have no idea what that means." She should give it up. Roland was right. Cases filled their files faster than they could solve them. Often more crimes in one night than they could solve in a lifetime. They did need to prioritize.

The zombie was busy altering his creation. Adding to it. She turned her head to try and make sense of the crooked writing. "I was mu d red." She ran her finger over the new scratchings he'd made. The zombie eyeballed his creation once more and ran a bloody stub of a finger over the words again.

"I was murdered?" Lyra asked aloud. Then the final letter fell into place in her mind. "I was murdered!"

The zombie didn't want to report a murder. He wanted to report his own."

She stuck her head out of the observation room door and snagged a passing police officer. "Find Detective Roland."

"What is it this time?" Roland's words preceded him into the observation room. His eyes snapped to the zombie on the other side of the glass. "Hey, he's not throwing himself at us this time."

Lyra pointed to the smeared words on the observation mirror. "He says he was murdered. That's what he's been trying to tell us."

Roland studied the gore on the glass. "He's reporting his own murder? He's not dead."

"Well, I guess technically he is...or was."

"A bit of a legal gray area, don't you think? Is it actually illegal to make someone a zombie?"

As if on cue, the topic of their conversation picked that moment to launch himself at the glass again. This time after the impact, he stayed hugged against the mirror, staring at them through it.

Lyra swallowed hard, regretting that second cup of vending machine stim. "Not sure there's anything on the books about it. But I suppose if it caused someone to die, even temporarily it could be considered a crime."

"That's judges' territory." Roland shifted his feet, getting ready to leave. "Like we ever see one of those around here."

Lyra opened her mouth to answer him, but as she did, something caught her eye. Until now, she hadn't been able to study the zombie up close. Not until he'd all but glued himself to the mirror. "Wait a minute..." She pointed to a red stain on the front of the zombie's shirt. "He looks like he's been shot."

Roland moved cautiously closer to the glass. "It appears to be a bullet wound."

She stood beside him and studied the area he pointed to. A hole in the zombie's shirt showed where a bullet had entered his chest. He'd bled from the wound because the tear was crusted with dried blood. "He's been shot in the heart."

"Several times." Roland pointed to another small hole just above it and then a couple more below. They hadn't been apparent at first with all the gore on his shirt, but once she saw them, the pattern became obvious. "Someone really wanted to do him in."

"But he must have been alive when he was shot, or he wouldn't have been bleeding."

"True," he said thoughtfully. Roland had lost his some of usual cockiness. The case had to be intriguing him just a little. He wasn't even complaining about his paperwork or his caseload. "But why shoot a guy and then make him a zombie?"

"Maybe the two things aren't related. Perhaps whomever shot him didn't know he'd been bitten."

He looked back at Lyra. "So you're saying you think someone

shot this guy not knowing he was carrying whatever virus causes..." He pointed at the zombie on the other side of the glass. "This. And then the guy dies, reanimates and comes to our station to report his murder?"

Lyra nodded. It did sound bizarre when Roland said it, but the zombie was staring at them from the other side of the glass, apparently waiting for them to figure it out. "There's no doubt a crime has been committed. The evidence is inside him."

Roland eyed the zombie nervously. "And how are we going to get it out?"

He had a point there. After he'd thrown himself against the mirror repeatedly and tried to chew his way through the glass she didn't fancy going in there and trying to carve a bullet out of his hide. She couldn't imagine anyone volunteering for the job, either. "Do we have to? I mean, what happens to zombies if you just leave them?"

"Reckon they rot... eventually," Roland said. "But we're going to need the interrogation room long before that."

"So what do we do?" Her question lingered in the silence.

Then came a wet, squishy noise from the other side of the glass.

"Eww!" Lyra had to look away in disgust. One of the zombie's stubby fingers had disappeared into the bullet wound above his heart. He seemed to be feeling around in there. Even Roland was affected by the sight because he said, "Ugh!" And turned his head.

Something hit the table with a metallic ping. They looked back at the zombie.

He'd finished digging around in his chest. Black blood seeped sluggishly around the edges of the wound.

A single bullet lay on the table.

"Well, I guess that would be our evidence of the crime," Lyra said. "I'm sure there's a whole bunch just like it inside him."

Roland eyed the gore-stained bullet. "I'll have ballistics run this and see what they come up with." He gave the zombie a wary glance. "If he'll let me take it."

As if on cue, the zombie stepped back from the table, as if to say, all yours.

"Which still leaves us with the problem of what to do with him."

Lyra studied the zombie. Now that he'd given them the evidence they needed to solve his crime, he seemed content to wait patiently. For the moment, at least. "What if we keep him in the evidence locker?" To Roland's incredulous stare, she added, "Well, he is the evidence that a crime has been committed."

"It does have that fenced off part at the back. We could keep him there until we solve the crime."

She looked back at the zombie waiting for their decision. "Works for me. Only one thing…"

"What is it?"

"You're the one who has to explain all this to the Captain."

MERCHANDISE

by Karen Dales

*Karen Dales is the award winning author of **The Chosen Chronicles**. She is also the managing editor for Dark Dragon Publishing, when she is not writing further novels or doing freelance editing jobs.*

The written word is her passion, crochet is her hobby and her family (including two cats) is her joy. She is often found at conventions or at Michaels Arts and Craft stores when she's not teaching Creative Writing for the City of Toronto.

Visit her at: www.karendales.com

Seven women in as many months and still they had no leads, not even a single body. Detective Sarita Taggert pushed her reading glasses back up her straight nose and flipped the sheets of information printed in the growing file. The news media called the rash of abductions The Barbie Doll Disappearances. Detective Taggert called it the case that would make or break her career.

"Anything new?"

Taggert startled and glared at Detective Robertson as she leaned against the wooden back of her chair. Despite his sparkling blue eyes, the mischievous curl to his lips belied any intention to be helpful. Taking the steaming mug of coffee out of his hand, Taggert took a deep sip of the bitter drink, the heat nearly scalding her tongue.

"How long have you been here today?" asked Robertson, concern darkening his eyes as he sat on the edge of her desk. The old beige steel desk slid an inch across the worn wooden floor, the sound scraping everyone's ears.

Taggert glared at him and sighed. Robertson's boyish good looks eradicated any irritation. "I've been here for" –she glanced at the smart phone sitting next to the opened file and placed the mug down–"eleven hours and still the only correlation between the abductees is their looks, ages and that they earned about the same income.

"None knew of the others, not even on social media sites. Combing through their emails revealed nothing. I feel like I'm at a dead end." She raked her fingers through her shoulder length blonde hair. A part of her wanted to pull at the locks in frustration. "It's only a matter of time before the perp strikes again."

Robertson released a sigh and shook his head. "You're not going to get anywhere studying paper and photos, especially after staring at them for so long."

"Don't you think I don't know that?" she snapped. The coffee sloshed dangerously in the mug as she went to take another swig.

His strong male fingers gingerly took the offending cup from her before the white porcelain touched her lips. "How many of these have you had today?"

Taggert glared at him, her arms folded across her ample chest. "None of your business."

Blue eyes never wavered from her glare as Robertson closed the folder. "Grab your jacket. We're going out for dinner."

"If this is an attempt to take me on a date, it's not going to work," she smiled slyly.

"Oh yes, everyone knows you don't date guys from work." Robertson rolled his eyes.

"You're right." Taggert stood up and flashed a beatific smile. "You're a handsome man, I'll give you that, but your bits are in the wrong place."

Robertson's deep laugh caressed her ears. "Too bad. One day you'll make some lucky woman happy." He rose to stand in front of her. "I wasn't asking in that way, rather as colleague to colleague, friend to friend. A change of atmosphere can help."

"Then what are we waiting for?" She shrugged into her jacket.

"Great." Robertson placed the mug down on the desk, pulled his coat from the chair across the aisle and slipped it on. "Chinese?"

Taggert shook her head, freeing the locks from under her coat's collar. "Japanese. I know of this great all-you-can-eat joint."

"Lead on," smiled Robertson, his hand outstretched.

"Oh my God! I think I'm going to explode!" laughed Taggert. She held her stomach with one arm, her other leaning on the black table.

"More saki?" Robertson poured the lukewarm clear liquid into her ceramic bowl.

"Are you trying to get me drunk, Detective?" she laughed.

"Now why would I do that?" Robertson batted his brown lashes.

"I thought we're going to discuss the case," she smirked, ignoring the cooling beverage.

"All right." He sat straighter and leaned on the table, dirty and empty dishes abounded. "Do you have a cursory profile set up yet?"

She shook her head. It would be so easy to come up with a fabrication, but it could be wrong, as were so many assumptions. "No one has reported seeing any of the abductions. The perpetrator is very wily about being seen. There's nothing even on the security cameras as to where the women were taken. It's like whomever is doing this is a ghost."

"So no leads? Nothing."

Taggert shook her head. "The only thing we know is that the perpetrator appears to know their schedules intimately. How is still a mystery.

"I've combed through the interviews of the victims' male partners and there may be something there. I don't know, but I think it's a line worth investigating, one that no one thought to study."

Robertson swigged back his full bowl of saki and place it on the table with a thunk. "So the connection between the women could be through their boyfriends."

"Or husbands," nodded Taggert.

Robertson pouted and cocked his head. "Interesting."

"Tomorrow I'm going to start re-interviewing the partners."

Blue eyes widened in surprise. "You've received permission?"

"Yep." Taggert took a sip from her saki bowl. "Why? You wanna come?"

The playful expression normally on Robertson's face dissolved into a cold frown as he leaned back from the table. "Thank you, but no. I have my own cases to attend to."

"It's me."

"Why are you calling so late?"

"It's necessary. The police have a new tactic to find the girls."

"How is it different from the last one that failed?"

"It could expose us all."

"Ridiculous!"

"The lesbian bitch just left. Questions are being asked, difficult ones, and if co-operation isn't given freely I have no doubt she'll go to the courts for search warrants."

Silence.

"Orders, sir?"

"I'll contact our business partner and see if he can make another shipment, even with only one unit. In the meantime, take care of her."

"Shall I add her to the product line?"

"You say she's lesbian, can she be used? Better yet, is she a virgin?"

"I don't know, but I doubt, with her age and lack of experience with me, she'd fetch a worthy price."

"I hate to dispose of potential wares, but sometimes one must remove damaged goods at the manufacturing level so that it doesn't lower the value of the rest of the merchandise."

"I understand."

"Good. I want this taken care of before I have her on my doorstep. Oh, one last thing. Tell my last associate that payment will be deposited in the off-shore account once the transaction is complete."

*   *   *

Robertson hated coming here, but the necessity of it required sac-rifices. The rewards for doing so ensured his avaricious dreams would come true. He looked out across the abandoned wood lot. Well, not so abandoned. His wife's maternal grandfather had owned this land. When he fell ill, Robertson persuaded him to sell it to a developer. Since that transaction closed Robertson had fol-lowed orders in the thousand acres development.

This morning he had transported the goods from storage to the buyer. By now that single unit floated to the Far East as part of a greater shipment.

Now he returned to store the damaged merchandise in perpe-tuity. That did not sit so well, and he hoped the eventual decom-position would require a new storehouse. The worst was ensuring no one would find the goods he destroyed.

Walking toward the abandoned well, shovel in hand, Robert-son knew the payment was worth it, almost as much for what he had received for his wife.

The freezing stone floor set off a spasm of shivering.

Taggert awoke, not sure of her surroundings, for they were as pitch. Panic set in. She had been walking to her car, the interview with Barbie Doll Number Three's husband written into notes. The grand house in the woods, new to the distraught family, faded be-hind trees as she walked the length of the drive. She could not remember how she had gotten here.

Where was she?

Don't panic, she thought in an effort to quiet her beating heart.

Turning over, she crawled on all fours, her hands burning on the cold as they fluttered to feel what she could not see.

Knees aching, her hands scraped against a wall as firm and steadfast as the floor. She whimpered. She needed to get out; needed to be free; needed to bathe in warm sunlight. Above all was the desire to seek revenge against whoever trapped her here, burned.

Following the curved right-angled path of the wall and floor,

Taggert scrabbled to gain purchase of her surroundings. No sound except from her panicked breath, rasping clothes and tapping fingers, filled her consciousness. She flailed about, searching for a break in the wall, a difference between frozen stone and a possible wooden door, but found none.

Stumped, unknowing how many circuits of the small room she had spun, she grasped the brick wall and pulled herself up. If there were no indication in the blackness of a door near the floor, then maybe there would be one higher up. Again, hands outstretched before her, Taggert walked around the midnight stone room.

Nothing.

No door. No window. No way in. No way out.

How did I get here? WHERE AM I?!

A rasping sound, far above, followed by a chuckle.

Something hard hit her on the head before a wash of dirt cascaded, splashing over her. More laughing, deep, male and recognizable as another tumble of dirt struck her.

Her back sliding down against frozen stone, she crumpled to the chilled floor as more and more earth fell into the room. Hugging herself, tears mingled with dirt to eke down her face. She knew now her fate–she was Barbie Doll Number Eight. Far above, in the darkness, must be the door she must have fallen through into this dungeon-like place. It did not explain why she could not see, why all around her was inky-black.

Numb from the cold, her fingers brushed away a droplet threatening to fall in her eye and halted the motion at the strange feeling before her finger tips. Breath staggering, she brought both hands to her eyes and felt...

Nothing!

No glasses, no firm roundness.

Her eyes were gone!

Only empty sockets remained!

Mouth opening, she screamed into the darkness, to the man whose laugh belonged to Detective Robertson as he shovelled more earth into the pit. She wanted to call out to him, plead with him, but the words could not be formed.

Her tongue was gone.

THE LETTER

by Jeffrey Charles

Jeffrey Charles is a writer from Toronto, Ontario, Canada. He has been writing ever since he learned how and hasn't looked back. While he enjoys just about any genre he prefers writing more dark, twisted and frightening stories.

The biggest influence as far as writing is concerned would be Stephen King and H.P Lovecraft. The terrifying and altogether strange has become a niche for Jeffrey and his writing. When not writing or editing, Jeffrey spends his time with his family, reading, hiking or with friends. He finds a lot of inspiration from his close family and friends.

Visit or contact Jeffrey: on facebook - Jeffrey.Charles.562 or on twitter @JeffreyChaz84

The handwriting had to be perfect. The faint aroma of copper had to linger on the envelope. The taunt within had to be subtle but sharp. The faint smears of blood had to jump out and grab the reader by the throat and give him a little shake. The person carrying this out would have to have not one ounce of remorse.

While the effort proved demanding, at worst it would only take a few hours to complete it all. Only a few hours for something that could scar a rational person for a lifetime. And that was the purpose behind this, wasn't it? Not just to destroy one life but to outright damage the lives of many. It was all I knew how to do, unfortunately.

The most recent note I was preparing contained grisly details about my actions from earlier in the evening. Stuff only I could possibly know. Technically a second party was also privy to such information. Regrettably that party was no longer among the living.

I kept the letter shorter than usual. Just over 100 words barely spanning two paragraphs. It was all they deserved in my opinion. Using special gloves to create it, I left not a trace of usable evidence on my letter. I read it over to myself one more time.

Fifteen months, eleven days and approximately six hours since this started and still you have not caught me. I will continue to fill your morgues until I am in a morgue myself. You people still don't understand the ignorance that resonates within all of you. You cannot stop nature, instinct, evolution or me.

I removed the small intestine as well as the tongue and teeth from victim #26 for a laugh. Her clothes are burned, don't bother searching for them. I didn't take her virginity before taking her life. You couldn't have stopped me even if I did.

I will never be stopped. Open your eyes.

Carefully placing a few strands of my most recent victim's hair inside the envelope with the letter, I was finally satisfied. The worst part was travelling hours away to deliver the letter. One can never be too careful or paranoid. I certainly did not wish to be caught but lately I noticed some boredom setting in with my work. Perhaps it had become too easy and the challenge was faltering.

Do not misinterpret why I do this. It's neither a form of lashing out after an abusive upbringing nor a chemical imbalance. I don't hate my parents, teachers or the planet though I do dislike aspects of society. No, what I truly want to convey is a simple message: We are no different than any other species, so why does everyone believe we deserve to be treated so special?

Why is it okay for us to murder defenseless creatures and obliterate entire eco-systems simply out of need and greed? We can justifiably wipe out a family of raccoons for taking shelter in our attics before turning around and patting ourselves on the back for demolishing a 20-acre forest in order to build a suburb. All because of a false fantasy that makes us believe we are the civilized leader of the food chain.

No, I will not accept that belief and neither should the rest of humanity. Therefore my work must continue, opening the eyes and minds of millions. Yes millions. The majority of North America has now heard about me, an added bonus when you're placed on the FBI's most wanted list. It only took nine murders to crack the list, too.

As I check the time I decide I'm too exhausted and that mailing the letter can wait until tomorrow. Frankly, I'm not even interested in going miles upon miles to send it. Nobody has even come close to catching me, I could mail it from anywhere and still be free as a bird. I drift off to sleep thinking about this.

I wake up to the song of a bird, no doubt free, somewhere outside my window. An odd coincidence I shrug off.

My fading dream slips from memory as I try to figure out why I slept so poorly. I force myself to get ready and decide to mail my letter. No long journey though, this time I will walk to the nearby post office. On the way, I smile and nod to strangers, laughing at them in my head. They have no idea, it is incredible. I take my time mailing the letter and as I finish, I hear someone clear his throat. Turning, I see a police officer behind me.

My blackened heart is in my throat for a moment before I notice the package he is waiting to mail. I produce a wide grin and apologize for making him wait.

"No trouble at all," he replies.

"Good, I never like to cause trouble," I remark before taking my leave.

The officer gives me a strange look before moving on. I smile, certain he will never know how close he was to stopping me. Like everyone else though, he'll never catch me.

And even if by a fluke I am caught, it will in no way stop my work. The message will spread like a disease after I'm dead and gone. My work is and forever will be immortal. If you're reading this, I can only hope your mind has been opened. Good luck.

THE PRE-PAID FUNERAL

by Rosemary McCracken

Born and raised in Montreal, Rosemary McCracken has worked on newspapers across Canada as a reporter, arts reviewer, editorial writer and editor. She is now a Toronto-based fiction writer and free-lance journalist specializing in personal finance and the financial services industry.

Rosemary's short fiction has been published by Room of One's Own, Kaleidoscope Press, Sisters of Crime Canada—and now Nefarious North! *Rosemary's first mystery novel,* Safe Harbor, *was shortlisted for Britain's Crime Writers' Association's Debut Dagger in 2010, and was published by Imajin Books in 2012. Its sequel,* Black Water, *was released in May 2013.*

Visit her at: rosemarymacracken.com

"Have you considered arranging your own funeral, Annie?" Floyd Toole asked as I wrote out a cheque for my Marty's arrangements.

I was so shocked that my pen dropped to the floor. "I just turned 56, Floyd. I won't be needin' a funeral for another thirty years."

"Of course not." A smile creased the funeral director's face into a map of wrinkles. "But think about it. When your time comes, everything will be in order. Just as you wanted. The casket you liked. Your favorite hymns. You can even write your own eulogy. Think of the peace of mind you'll have."

"Hymns?" I'd heard "Abide With Me" at the past five funerals I'd gone to. If that fool song is sung at mine, I swear I'll sit up in the casket and demand the congregation shut up.

"Whatever hymns you like," Floyd said in that honey voice of his. "And you can name the friends or family members you want to do the readings and deliver the eulogy."

"I can?" I'd turn right over in the box if Ann, my son Bobby's wife, had anything to do with my funeral. "Can I say who attends and who don't?"

"If you want a private service here at the funeral home, attendance can be by invitation only. Of course, if you decide on a church service, anyone is welcome to come."

He paused for a moment or two before delivering his final pitch. "And the best thing about pre-arranging is the money you'd save. Say you pay for a $5,000 funeral, and you pass on twenty years from now. Why, that funeral would probably cost $10,000 maybe $15,000 by then. But you'd be locked in at today's prices."

Marty had left me pretty comfortable, but I've always believed a penny saved is a penny gained. This sounded like the deal of a lifetime. I told Floyd I'd be back to see him real soon.

I spent the next few days getting my garden ready for winter. It was lovely to be outdoors again. Those past months, watching Marty inch towards death, had drained me. I was putting mulch around the monkshood and the purple foxglove when Ann's beat-up red Toyota pulled into the drive. Bobby got out as I walked over to the car.

Ann rolled down her window and stuck out her head. Her platinum hair sprang out from her head like a dandelion gone to seed. "I've had it, Mom," she said. "It's been two months since Bob got laid off at HomeWorld and he's not even looking for work. All he does is sit around the house listenin' to music. Hell, he can do that at your place."

I cringed every time Ann called me Mom. I'd told her to call me Annie. She was a good 10 years older than my Bobby, and I was too young to have a daughter of 45. But she said Annie was so much like her own name, and she went on calling me Mom.

She jerked a thumb at some cartons on the back seat, and

Bobby started taking them out of the car. "His country and western tunes," she said. "Hundreds of CDs and tapes in there."

When Bobby had finished unloading, Ann turned on the ignition. "He's all yours, Mom, and welcome to him. You'll be hearin' from my lawyer. I can't go out to work with this faulty ticker of mine, can I?"

With that, she rolled up her window and roared off.

Bobby turned to me, tears in his blue eyes. "She don't want me no more, Mom. What'll I do?"

What will I do, I thought as I watched him carry his boxes into the house. Just when I'd planted Marty in the cemetery and had the house to myself, here was Bobby on my hands again. And it seemed like I'd be supporting his ex for the rest of my days.

The following week, I took a cheque out to Ann's place in the country. I found her still in her bathrobe, even though it was the middle of the afternoon. Without makeup, she looked older than her 45 years.

"I suppose you'll be wantin' a cup of tea," she said when I gave her the cheque.

"Wouldn't mind."

I sat at the table while Raggedy Ann banged around the kitchen. The counter and the tabletop were littered with dirty dishes. A prescription vial sat beside the sugar bowl in front of me. Digoxin, the label read. A fancy way of saying digitalis, I knew, because my Marty had taken it for his heart.

I held up the vial. "You're takin' this stuff, Ann?"

She banged a teapot, a creamer and two mugs down on the table. "Yeah. Looks like I'm on it for good."

"Make sure you take enough. Turned out Marty should've been gettin' more when he was feelin' low."

That got me thinking about how the big drug companies get rich on plants that people like me grow in our gardens. Digitalis comes from my foxglove.

"This cheque you brung, Mom," Ann said, splashing tea into the mugs, "it's only $300 dollars."

"Should tide you over a while."

"It's not enough." She wiped the table with the sleeve of her bathrobe. "I'll be speaking to my lawyer. I got bills to pay."

I poured milk into my tea. "You really want to go through with this divorce? Bobby's been a good husband."

She pounded the table with her fist. Tea sloshed out of our mugs. "I've had it with that asshole–pardon my French, Mom. He's a lazy good-for-nothin'."

The nerve of her. "There are worse men out there. He didn't cheat on you. Never hit you."

"The best thing about bein' married to Bob will be the support I'll get now he's gone."

We stared at each other for a bit, then I pasted a smile on my face. "You might feel better if you cleaned up around here," I said. "I'll give you a hand now, if you like."

I'd always mopped up Bobby's messes. Now I had another one on my hands.

It was the end of October before I made it back to Toole's Funeral Home. And that was the last time I saw Floyd. Our little town's funeral director passed away a week later, and his widow sold to Wilf MacTeague who ran a funeral business in the next township.

Wilf kept the Toole's Funeral Home sign up. When I dropped by to see him, he assured me he would honor all arrangements that had been made with Floyd.

Winter set in early that year. Bobby moped about the house, playing his hurtin' music. He only went out at night to drink beer at the Legion. Those tunes drove me crazy, all that whining about lost love, but I couldn't tell him to shut them off. His heart was broke, poor boy.

So I helped out at Our Lady of Fatima Church. I polished candlesticks until Father Pat told me that, at the rate I was going, they'd have to be re-silvered soon. I laundered and pressed the altar cloths. I typed up the pastor's message for the Sunday bulletin on the rectory computer. When I'd done all I could at the church, I drove out to the country to made Ann a cup of tea.

*   *   *

"Mom!" Bobby stood gaping at me when I got home late one afternoon in January. "You're...you're alive," he finally managed to sputter out.

I shrugged off my coat and unzipped my boots.

"Wilf MacTeague just called," Bobby went on. "He told me you was brought in to Toole's and he was goin' ahead with the arrangements."

"Arrangements?"

"Wilf said he was following the funeral instructions you'd given Floyd."

"Bobby," I said in my sternest voice, "how can I be over at Toole's when I'm standin' right here in my own home?"

But I put my coat and boots back on, and we drove over to the funeral home.

Wilf peered at me through his dark-rimmed glasses. Then he looked at Bobby and back at me again. "If this is your mother, Bob, who do I have back there?" He inclined his head towards the back of the building where the last rites take place.

Bobby shook his head.

Wilf picked up a cream-colored folder from his wooden desk. "Paperwork's all in order." He pulled a sheet from the folder.

"Direct cremation," he read. "No embalming, no visitation, no church service. I was about to send the body off to the crematorium, when I remembered meeting Bob here at the Legion. So I called, thinking this might be a relative."

Wilf pulled another piece of paper from the folder. "I have a medical certificate of death for Ann Dolan."

"That's me." I reached out and slid the paper to my side of the desk. It was signed by Dr. Eric Knowler, who'd put down heart failure as the cause of death. "Doc Knowler works over in Kincaid, don't he?"

Bobby got all red in the face. "Who's back there pretendin' to be my mom?"

"I got a call from Doc Knowler around noon today," Wilf said. "He was at a house out in the country where a woman had passed on. An Ann Dolan."

"We oughta see who this is, Mom."

"I don't think I'm up to it, dear."

Bobby stood up. "I'll take a look."

When I was alone in the office, I pulled the file across the desk and studied it. Everything was written down, just as I'd arranged with Floyd.

When Bobby returned, his face was ashen. "It's Ann, Mom. My wife's back there."

I told Wilf that the confusion must have come about because of Ann and me having the same name. "I was tellin' her that I was thinkin' of arranging my funeral," I said. "I guess she liked the idea."

Bobby picked out a handsome urn, and we arranged for a memorial service at Toole's the following Saturday. Ann was my daughter-in-law, and people would talk if her passing went unmarked.

When we got back to the house, Bobby called Doc Knowler in Kincaid. The doctor told him the woman who did Ann's house-cleaning had found her that morning and called him. When he saw the vial of Digoxin on the bedside table, he realized the deceased had a heart condition, and he confirmed it with Ann's doctor. Doc Knowler told Bobby he was very sorry, but these things sometimes happened.

"The poor woman must have increased her medication and her heart gave out," was how Bobby said he'd put it. "Digoxin does a nice job of regulating the heartbeat. Too much, though, and it slows the heart down. Completely."

Doc Knowler went on to say he'd found a note in Ann's hand-bag, saying she had a funeral all arranged at Toole's. So he called Wilf.

"Funny thing, Mom," Bobby said when he'd got off the phone, "about Ann having someone in to do cleaning. That don't sound like her."

I thought about the drive out to the country I'd no longer have to make, the house I wouldn't have to clean, the tea I wouldn't have to brew. All the cheques I wouldn't have to write.

I smiled at Bobby. "She must've been feelin' poorly, son."

Life Sentence

by Helen Nelson

In her day job Helen Nelson is a project manager and IT consultant. At night and on weekends she morphs into a reader who has a strong commitment to the mystery community. She has spent the past four and a half years as president of the Toronto Chapter of Sisters in Crime.

In 2017 she will be the co-host of Bouchercon, to be held in Toronto.

Helen began her story telling career with ghost stories she made up for younger cousins. Family lore has it that the stories gave the cousins nightmares, and got Helen in a bit of hot water. The story telling continued – but mostly as a background activity to her reading. Some of her many nieces and nephews have been the recipients of stories just for them.

Her first published stories were in the Sisters in Crime Anthology, The Whole She-Bang.

I think I'll kill him. Today. Twenty-six years is long enough to be married to this guy. And really, it's more like forever. When you think about it, it is all our 44 years. He was just always there. Our Moms used to walk us down the street side by side in our strollers. We shared our first smoke when we were about nine. Did I steal those smokes from my Dad or did he? Probably me; he would have stood guard.

I'm pulling the covers over my head now so I can figure this out. How, how do I do this? Because, believe me, I'm not getting caught. Prison isn't for me. I've already served my life sentence – with no parole. And I want out. Thank you very much. How do you spell freedom? G-O-N-E J-O-H-N!

I don't even know anyone who owns a gun anymore. My grandpa did, when he lived on the farm. He used it to shoot rabbits, I think. I don't know where it went when he died. Maybe one of my cousins has it. But who needs a gun in the city? It's not like it's legal to pot pigeons in the park. Pity. Sure would come in handy now though. John is a klutz. Nobody would have a hard time believing he'd offed himself accidentally trying to bag a raccoon. He hates raccoons. Shit, who am I kidding, I hate them too. They are the bane of our existence, scampering over the roof tops, scratching their way into the attic. If I had grandpa's old gun I could just give it to John. He'd be bound to try to shoot a raccoon and almost for sure he'd get himself instead. I wouldn't need to do a thing. That's not even murder, just cosmic justice.

But heck, even if I had to finish him myself, who'd believe I did it? Everyone would believe it was John who did it to himself. And I could put on a good show you know. Lots of tears and sniffling. Red rimmed eyes. The works.

Who'd really miss him anyway? The best part about having three kids before you are 21 is that by the time you are 44, they are long gone. He's a pretty good grandfather. I have to admit that. Our granddaughter is only 2 years old. She's just too young to remember him. The kids all decided that Vancouver was where they wanted to live. They are happy enough to live near each other, even if they don't want to be too near Toronto. They weren't going to suffer the fate of John and I – born in the Junction and likely to die in the Junction. Well John sure will anyway. Today, if all goes well. And me? Well I think I'll take up traveling. But I don't have a gun. And I suppose if I went out and bought one it might look fishy. I'm not even sure I could get one today, just like that. And this has to be today. I'm not waiting.

I've pulled the covers over my head again. I should have started to think about this a couple of days ago. But you know me. I'm kind of impulsive. And the impulse is on me really strong right now.

Take a deep breath. Don't even think about a knife. Oh, John deserves it. For sure. But, who kills themselves by stabbing themselves? I'd have to sedate him or something to slit his wrists. Anyway he's not the sort for suicide. Maybe I could try some variant on Lorena Bobbit. With my luck he'd wake up while I was in the act. Just as I'd grabbed him by the appropriate part. OK, at that point he might think he'd died. Well, never mind. I get kind of queasy at the sight of blood anyway. Some days I don't know how I made it through all the scrapes and bruises of three kids. I took it harder than they did the few times stitches were required. I want John gone, but I don't think I could bear to see him bleed.

I remember the first knife John had. We were twelve. John wanted a jack knife and I wanted a pair of panty hose my mom just wouldn't spring for. Mrs. Johnston from down the street caught us shop-lifting them from Woolworth's, around the corner on Dundas Street. I think she must have been one of the managers there. Woolworth's and Kresge's sat right next to each other, just like in every other city. The two of them are gone now. These days, our old Kresge's store sells antiques. Woolworth's was a Blockbuster for a while. But that's done too. Now its back to the twenty-first century equivalent of the five and dime: it's a dollar store.

I stood guard while John got his knife and he stood guard while I got my panty hose. I kind of thought maybe Mrs. Johnston had seen us, but she didn't say anything while we were in the store. She didn't want to get us in serious trouble, I guess. But later that afternoon she caught us smoking in the park on Vine Avenue. Double trouble. Thieves and smokers. She told us we either had to go back to Woolworth's with her and pay up or she'd tell our parents – and I mean tell all. Mrs. Johnston just always seemed to be around when we were up to no good, so she had lots to tell. If she would have told, I wouldn't be here now worrying about how to kill John – our parents would have killed us both right then. At the time, I'd never have thought such a jolly old gal would have had such a tough streak. Goodness knows though, she sure thinks it funny enough these days. I don't know if she ever sees John or me without giving us a hard time about our misspent youth. But I have to admit, she never does it in front of our parents; she's still keeping her end of the bargain.

But I need to get to the task at hand.

I'm wondering if I could just push him down the stairs. I can't see it working on the stairs from the attic or second floor. There are too many things to grab. He probably wouldn't even break anything. I don't know how many times I've fallen down those stairs from the second floor. I hardly ever got so much as a bruise except for once when I got a very sore butt – bruised my coccyx. Now there's a word I never would have learned if I hadn't fallen on my butt. Cock six, Cock six, Cock su... John had a sore knee at the time so he used his knee to hold the ice pack to my butt. We did that for a week. What a pair.

He'd look fine as a crumpled heap on the basement floor. If I pushed him down the basement stairs, could I bury him right there, in the basement? Not likely – I think that floor down there is pretty thick and I can't quite see me digging it up. Maybe I could stash him in the freezer. But then no one would know he was dead and I couldn't get the insurance. No, I need that insurance money for my travel fund. And I'd lose the food he'd displace in the freezer too. That's a bad deal all the way round. Of course, I could always just say he tripped on the stupid cat. But, what if he just broke his neck or something and I wound up looking after an invalid for the rest of my days? Noooo. Double life sentence? I think not. He'd never tell if I just broke his neck. He'd just sit back and enjoy the pleasure of watching me suffer rather than just divorcing me and sending me to jail. He'd love it. I know it.

The first time we made it, we did it in the basement. Well, not our basement; it was my Mom's basement a few doors down. We used to have these block parties every summer. All the streets around here end at the CPR tracks so it was really easy to just close off our end of the street and have a party. Everyone would serve up food and booze in their front yards. All the adults and kids were back and forth among the houses and the front yards, tasting each other's food and drinking a ton of beer.

My dad always made wine. Everyone on the block had to have

a taste because no one wanted to hurt his feelings. But mostly no one ever really drank it; it was just too awful. Every year us kids would haul about a dozen bottles out to the front yard. And every year we'd haul about 6 or 8 of them back down those stairs.

John and I had slipped away and spread a blanket on an air mattress on the basement floor. No, we didn't get caught – but it was close. We had just finished up and were lying there without a stitch on, contemplating having a smoke, when I heard my dad talking upstairs. He was telling my Mom there was only 2 bottles of wine left and he was going to have to get more. I swear, I got on my clothes in the time it took my Mom to tell him he wouldn't need any more. While Dad was arguing back, I managed to take two more bottles up the stairs to him. Fortunately both he and Mom had had more than enough of his wine. They didn't wonder why I was down the basement. John and I rejoined the party. Not exactly what one would call post-coital bliss. Ah heck, we were thirteen. We were a pair of fumbling know nothings. Not exactly bliss period. And we had to hide out in the park for our smoke.

After that we just had to keep practicing till we got better at it. OK, till I got pregnant. And there we were – we had our first kid at 16. Our parents thought they were keeping us apart after that. But, when I got pregnant again shortly after my 18th birthday our parents relented and we got married. So we had our second kid at 18 and our third at 20. Even with all the practice it was obvious we weren't ever going to get much better at birth control so we got ourselves fixed as a 21st birthday present to each other.

Poison. I suppose it's a bit of a stretch to think that might be seen as an accident, but you never know. There's got to be something in the garden. Do they still kill wasps with cyanide? Didn't I read about that in an Agatha Christie? We have wasps up in the eaves. Now wouldn't that be ironic? Here's John, he's quit smoking, runs all the time, rides a bicycle and has basically gone all health conscious. And what does he do but go and get himself poisoned? I love the irony, but where would I get cyanide? Do you just go into Home Depot and ask for it? Just pick it up alongside a few screws and drill bits. Somehow I can't see that.

And who'd believe he accidentally poisoned himself just

before going up a ladder to poison a bunch of Wasps? He's never made it as high on a ladder as the roof of the shed, never mind the eaves on the roof of the house. No, we'll call the exterminator. Maybe he already has. Or his dad has. One of the benefits of living attached to your in-laws. You can share some of these tasks. We lived with them for the first 5 years we were married while we finished High School and then while John did his apprenticeship. Just before he got his papers this place came up for sale and we bought it, with a little help from both sets of parents. Child care was really handy with both parents living on the same street. Privacy, well that's another issue. God, maybe I should kill all our parents too. Yeah, right. I can't even figure out how to get rid of one man, let alone the whole family. This is getting depressing. I'm going to have to concentrate here.

I got it! I got it! I'm almost leaping with excitement. I saw it in the garden store just the other day. Warfarin. Rat poison for a rat. That's good. But how much would I need? How fast would it be? All these things I don't know. I should look it up on the internet. Don't those rats bleed to death internally? Ugh.

OK, so not Warfarin. But, maybe I could take him to the bar on the corner and slip something in his drink. Our little corner of Toronto used to be dry. A few years back, we were there when the Junction Gardens restaurant served up the first booze in almost 100 years – 1998 I think it was. Some of the folks on the street printed up some T-Shirts. John still wears his. Or maybe he's working his way through mine now. Damn that man is cheap. So anyway, yeah I could slip him something in his drink. But, something like what? I need an odorless, tasteless, traceless poison. Better yet, something that makes it look like he's had a heart attack. You know, from all that running and not smoking and being so damn healthy. Can I just cry now?

So yeah, he deserves to die. There we were two peas in a pod. OK, more like a couple of couch potatoes in a haze of smoke. And he went and got all healthy, went trendy just like the neighbourhood. Shit he even eats broccoli now. I used to have almost as hard a time to get him to eat it as I did the kids. That came out wrong; I never tried to get him to eat the kids. And he wants me to run with him now. As if.

I'm getting pretty desperate for an idea now. Cut the brake cable? On what? His bicycle? Right, maybe he'd trip in a street car track because he couldn't stop in time. Or maybe he'd just see it cut and accuse some of the kids from the park. Yeah, there's always the car. But I use it more than he does these days. My luck I'd forget and use it first. Bye bye Dana.

It would be nice to think of something long and delicious and slow. Just so I could watch him suffer. But no blood. I can imagine the look of horror on his face as he realizes that he is about to meet his end. Hmmm. I like it.

I can hear him coming up the stairs now. He must be back from his run. I can see his shadow now. What's that he has in his hand? Is that a knife? Is he going to kill me? Self Defense! Perfect. I can, I can grab something and brain him. Oh how I'll cry. I didn't realize it was him. I thought it was...

No, it's just a bottle of shampoo. He's just going to shower and come to bed.

Maybe I can hide behind the door and whack him when he comes into the room. I'll stand on the dresser, almost behind the door and hit him over the head. But what with? This bedroom isn't long on blunt instruments, unless you count books. But even the collected works of Shakespeare doesn't quite have the weight to do the job.

The hammer, the hammer is here, on the window sill. No wonder he can never find his tools. That would work. I could pounce on him from the dresser with the hammer and give his head a great whack. Oh, but the blood, and who'd believe I just fell on him with a hammer? Yes sir, it was an accident – I just fell off the dresser as he happened by. Come on Dana, you need something better than that –something devious! Something...

All I've done all day is sleep and pull the covers over my head to sing a rousing chorus, or six, of "Make the World Go Away". OK, I had a couple of good cries. And tried to figure out how to kill John. Fail.

John is crawling into bed. His arms are around me. "I love you, Dana. So, how was day two?" he asks. Funny what a hug will do. I really do love him. I guess I'll let him live, today. Tomorrow? Maybe I'll rob a bank.

I roll over to face him and give him a hug. "I'm OK. I really want to do this. But I want a cigarette so bad, I'd just about kill for one." Little does he know.

THE CRIME OF THE CENTURY

by Graham Freeman

It was well past midnight on a January morning as David picked up another gold bar and cursed the howling Quebec wind.

"*Tabernac*, it's cold", he said as he passed the gold bar to The Other David.

Darkness hid the swirling snow beyond the soft glow of the red taillights of the van.

Clunk. Another bar stacked.

David brushed a light dusting of snow from a bar of gold in the pile before him and heaved it with both hands.

"Merde", he cursed again.

He held it aloft for The Other Dave to take.

"Where's David Two?" asked The Other David from the back of the van.

"Somewhere warmer, I bet." replied David. "I have no idea but he better get here soon". The two of them were alone in the dark, if you discounted the bricks of gold bullion that had fallen from the pallet as the van had rounded a corner too hastily. David had backed up to the pile 30 minutes earlier and the two of them were attempting to recover their lost load. Extremely heavy metals bars don't roll away, or bounce very well, which is why the mound was still together rather than all over the road.

Clunk. Another bar stacked.

David miserably thought about where this all began. Probably at the University. Yes, at the University. Definitely at the University. Or maybe the tea shop. No...absolutely it was the University, he remembered the lab. There were glass beakers, a chalkboard, Bunsen burners and everything. So not the tea shop. Well, probably not the tea shop. There was a tea shop at the University it's true, and it did have a reputation for its unorthodox methods of brewing tea, which sometimes made use of test tubes.

Clunk. Another bar stacked.

So it was positively at the University. And possibly at the tea shop. But when? When was harder than where. It might have been in the past, he thought, but recent events made that sort of thing uncertain. For a subjective version of recent, he added. Things were...complicated. It had all started when he had knocked himself out. To be clearer, it had started when he had punched himself so hard that he knocked himself out.

Clunk. Another bar stacked.

"There he is", shouted The Other David, just a little too loud for someone trying to be criminally quiet.

David turned and saw the headlights before he heard the sound of the car over the swoosh of the wind. Snowflakes passed horizontally from one side of the country road to the other as the car came slowly to a halt in the slush, the yellowish-blue glow of the halogens stabbing into the winter darkness.

There was a brief moment wherein after the car had stopped, nothing happened. When that moment had passed, the driver's door opened just a crack, and then another moment passed. This time something did happen. The "uh-oh" gland deep within David's soul began to stir, and the car door opened further. It swung fully open and a gloved hand appeared, gripping the edge of the door as though ready to do something else, but hadn't quite decided exactly what just yet. Another "uh-oh" length pause and that something deep in David's soul that now rather wanted to be left alone, stirred again. This time it also splashed around a little and called for help.

David didn't like this. In the swooshes of snow, most things tended to happen as fast as possible, you know – to keep warm. But this gloved hand was taking its time and David was sure that attached to it was something menacing that either didn't mind the cold, or had decided that staying in the car was the best thing for everyone all round.

CRACK

It sounded like someone had taken a slap-shot from the blue line. It was followed by a THUMP, like that of a puck hitting leather. The inside of the car must be huge, David thought. Its own private hockey rink.

Before the face-plam of absurdity could hit him squarely on the forehead, the gloved hand disappeared and swiftly reappeared on the slushy ground below the door. On the way down it seemed to have picked up some blood. Things were most definitely going south, David thought, and not in a warm way.

"Errr, David," said David, craning his neck slightly so he could keep his eyes on the car. "I think we should be leaving now."

The Other David had already taken that leap of deducted faith and was currently scrambling over the back of the van's driver's seat. He stabbed the key into the steering column a few times before he found the key slot, and franticly twisted it to start the engine. Miracle of miracles, the van started first time and the Other David slid the lever into gear and gunned the engine. David, now inside the rear of the van, fell backwards onto a large pile of gold bars and bruised his arm in way that would be difficult to explain later, if he were ever called to do so. Perhaps the gold bars in the van didn't think too well of the situation that some of their brethren were being left at the road side. Gold bars can hold a grudge, it seems.

Flat on his back, David painfully twisted himself over so that he could see the car, now just a dwindling point within a white maelstrom of snow. He was sure he could see a figure running after the van, flailing its arms.

New Dave ran after the van, flailing his arms, but it was now just a dwindling point within a white maelstrom of snow. Crap. Not only was he never going to catch up by running, he was now a hundred metres from the warmth of the car.

Oh yes, the car, he thought. The one with the dead body in the driver's seat. The one with the dead body in the driver's seat that you just shot in the back of the head, he reminded himself. Oh go screw yourself, he retorted. It had to be done, he said back to himself. It was still a shitty thing to do, he thought – again, to himself. A third voice in his head piped up and said that standing around arguing with yourself wasn't getting him any closer to the warmth of the car. The first two voices told the third one to sod off.

With a dejected jog, New Dave made his way back to the car. As he approached the vehicle he could see a pool of blood making a ruddy mush beneath the car door. Feeling more than a little sick to the stomach, New Dave stopped to take in the scene. It was not something he wanted to remember, but he had to fathom how to get into the car while getting the body out of the car. He walked around to the other side of the vehicle hoping to get in through a door there and somehow push the body out with his feet.

He grasped the door handle and pulled. Locked. Dammit. The keys were probably in the ignition. Double dammit. He pulled the door again in the off-chance that it had somehow become unlocked through the magic of positive thinking. No such luck. He peered in through the window but the interior was too dark to see anything. He slouched and let out a wail.

Back again at the open door, New Dave stood on tippy-toes trying to see how well the dead body was wedged into the car. The results were inconclusive. There was nothing for it, he'd have to grab the body itself and drag it out of the vehicle.

Normally, this was something that he'd gladly pay someone else to do, but right now there was a distinct lack of anyone else around. He gritted his teeth and closed his eyes.

New Dave opened his eyes after determining that moving a dead body with your eyes closed was asking for trouble. Well, asking for more trouble, to be honest.

He tugged at the body, pulling at the lapels of its dirty coat. The dead weight moved a couple of inches and then seemed to snag on something. New Dave checked the coat – nothing stuck there. He ventured further into the car and noticed a foot was caught in the emergency brake lever, requiring him to climb over the body to release it. He could now smell the blood, which made him gag. Great, he muttered. Let's add vomit to the smell of death. And at that thought he almost vomited. Perhaps I should stop thinking, he thought.

The dead body, now on the ground beside the car, was accumulating a dusting of snow despite the wind. New Dave winced as he caught sight of the all too familiar face, then shuddered into the driver's seat and closed the car door. Reaching to turn the ignition key, he panicked as his hand closed on thin air. A part of him sobbed as he imagined having to search his own dead body for a set of car keys. Before the sobbing could turn to full-on wailing, the toe of his shoe found the bunch of keys wedged under the gas pedal.

Key in. Engine started. Car moving. Wipers wiping. And New Dave was praying as he drove off in the direction the van took. How fast could a van laden with hundreds of gold bars go? In a blizzard? With yourself as a back seat driver? The road jinked to the right, and New Dave almost missed the turn. The car was sticking to the road quite well, he thought. Perhaps things were going better than they seemed. At that overly optimistic assumption the sound of tree branches scraping the passenger side doors shook him back to pessimistic reality. He turned the steering wheel slightly, and the noise stopped. New Dave leaned as far forward as he could, screwing his eyes almost shut as though to filter out the snow flakes, and pressed harder on the gas pedal.

[If you've ever been in a car crash, you probably wished that you were sitting as far back as possible, held safely in the motherly embraces of the seat belt. Pressing your nose against the windshield as a means of gaining more in the way of visibility isn't in the drivers handbook anywhere (I checked), nor is almost closing your eyes in an attempt to see more. In a rare attempt at research I called an optometrist friend of mine from high school and he confirmed exactly that. I had to agree to go fishing with him before he would answer my questions, and he went on and on about how great fishing is and how he and I had not been in touch for years and that I simply had to meet his wife Irene. Did I mention that I hate fishing? I'm going next Thursday. I hope you are happy. Anyway – car crashes. Two rules: don't lean forward, and don't close your eyes. And don't have them. OK, three rules.]

New Dave's eyes opened wide and not because he'd just realized that squinting while driving was A Bad Thing. Out of the sleety turbulence loomed large the van. Which had stopped. Sideways. Blocking the road in front of him.

According to the police report there was "an incident" involving a car and a van on a remote rural road of northern Quebec. Three people were declared dead at the scene, though Constable Gardineau in his report neglected to mention the striking similarity in height, weight, build, facial features and (this was the kicker) fingerprints of all three of the victims. He also neglected to mention anything about gold bars. Constable Gardineau resigned from the police force the next day and was last seen having a heated conversation with a real estate agent in Aruba.

In the heart of the United States Bullion Depository, Fort Knox, Kentucky, Big Dave frowned as he watched another himself appear in front of him. This was the "I can't remember how many'th time" he'd witnessed this, and it still gave him the heebie-jeebies. There was a slight popping sound, and the brand new David apparated, blinked, then fainted.

Well that was new, thought Big Dave.

"Dave", shouted Big Dave. Fourteen Davids looked up from their duties.

I'll never get used to this, thought Big Dave.

"You", he said, pointing at a David with a clipboard. "Wake him up, brief him, and put him to work".

"Sure" said Clipboard Dave. "Whatever I say, boss".

Smartass. Big Dave scanned the vault they were all in. Its dimensions were huge by enormous, and are-you-kidding-me high. The immaculately polished walls reflected the fluorescent lights (all this gold and Uncle Sam couldn't spring for something more chic) and bathed in artificial warmth the approximately seventy-three trillion dollars of auric metal bars. At one end of the vault a forklift was attempting to negotiate a path through the neatly stacked rows of gold while the driver, Dave, called out for guidance. At the other end of the vault three jump-suited figures measured the wall and ran a marker between two points. That these three figures went by the names of David, D-Man and Big D should by now come as no surprise. They continued their geometry sketches as Big Dave checked his watch, grasped at the lanyard-held whistle around his neck, placed it between his lips and blew. The shrill noise cut through the clunking of metal on metal and the yammering of Davids. All faces turned toward him.

"OK people, thirty seconds – let's get it right this time. Places PLEASE!" he shouted. A silence measured in nanoseconds was followed by a shuffling of feet and more clanking of metal on metal. He looked back down the vault at the markings drawn by D-Man and strode toward them with purpose.

Clipboard Dave flashed a disarming smile as Fainting David nodded solemnly.

"So you're up to speed now?" he asked, checking off the final item on a list attached to his clipboard.

"Yes, I was given a pre-flight introduction by me before I left," said Fainting David.

"And what did I just say about self-references?" asked Clipboard Dave.

"That it's best to think of other instances of me as different people. Sorry. I forgot" said Fainting David.

"That's OK", assured Clipboard Dave. "You're new here, I suppose we can excuse it just this once", he added, patting Fainting David on the knee. "Let's get ready for the wall to come down, and you can get yourself going", he said, standing up from the impromptu seat made of gold bars.

Fainting David followed suit and stood up, rubbing his now numb backside.

"Thanks" he said. "See you later", and marched off in the direction of Big Dave and the marker-be-spoiled wall.

He stopped beside Big Dave, just outside an area on the vault floor marked "DONUT STNAD HERE" in large squiggles. Accuracy in lettering need to be worked on, obviously.

"Any second now", said Big Dave loudly, to the line of identical bodies assembling beside him.

A number of other Davids had joined them, including Clipboard Dave, all with toes just outside the squiggly marker line.

There was a rumble.

RUMBLE

There was a high-pitched "eeeeeee".

EEEEEEE

There was a POOMF, and puffs of dust emerged from the lines drawn on the vault wall, which ever so slowly started to fall towards them. Amid "oohs" and "ahhs" the wall continued its descent and finally hit the bags of sand that had been placed at the point where the wall's apex would have met with the floor. A splurge of sand escaped at high speed from a rip in one of the sand bags.

Big Dave blew his whistle again and immediately an orchestrated dance of Davids began to move across the fallen wall. Ropes were pulled, winches were wound and an odd looking contraption about the size of an SUV was dragged from the dusty darkness outside the vault wall.

Once completely inside the vault, the contraption could be seen from all angles thanks to the generosity of Uncle Sam's array of 59¢ fluorescent bulbs.

Although it was indeed roughly the size of an SUV, all similarity ended there. At what was presumably the front, a protruding fishing net-like mesh wobbled as the contraption was Dave-handled into the heart of the vault. Atop the contrivance, someone it seemed had affixed a whole junkyard crane-load of tubing, rods of varying sizes and an entire day's worth of rejects from a golf umbrella factory. The whole thing was painted black, even the dozens of protuberances that lined the sides making it look like a twenty foot pineapple that had been roasted to a crisp, or an enormous sea mine with accompanying Brobdinagian shuttlecock attachment.

Once it had quivered to a halt, Clipboard Dave boldly strode forward and grasped one of the pipes sticking out at head height near the rear of the machine. With nary a missed step he hauled himself upwards and forwards to stand atop the centre of the vehicle.

"Gentlemen, please clear a path in front of this thing so we can get underway," he called out and motioned toward the centre of the hangar-sized room.

A gaggle of Davids heaved upon a rope and the front of the machine turned towards the first pile of gold bars. Clipboard Dave fished in his lab coat pocket and produced a pair of military grade goggles, which he wiggled into place over his eyes and snapped the ties behind his head. He gestured ahead of the machine, and called out his intention to begin.

"Here we go!" he said, pulling on a lever at a panel by his feet.

There was a rumble, a high-pitched "eeeeeee' and a POOMF.

Where there was a pile of gold bars before, there now was nothing except a settling cloud of dust.

There was a slight popping sound, and millions of dollars worth of gold bullion appeared as if from nowhere, upon a tungsten carbide woven mat three centimetres thick.

Of course, the gold hadn't appeared from nowhere. That would be silly. It appeared at exactly the same spot that it had disappeared from, only this time a few thousand years earlier.

It was a warm spring morning in what would become Kentucky in a millennia or three. Two men of uncanny resemblance watched as the pile of gold bars settled into place. Both were sitting on the deflated skirt of an exceedingly large hovercraft. They looked at each other and nodded, then at a leisurely pace one stood and made a move toward the gold while the other pulled a map from his breast pocket. The dog-eared map showed two points marked with a red X and a blue X. A dotted route ran from one to the other in a not so straight line.

The man with the job of securing the gold did exactly that. He checked the chains attached to the mat at eight points, ensuring that each was fastened as per the briefing he'd given himself only yesterday/three-thousand years from now.

The other man replaced the map into his breast pocket, stood, and climbed the ladder into the bridge of the 40 metre long vehicle. Once inside he tapped the compass, flicked some switches into the ON position, and made sure all the fuel gauges were reading at 95% or above. Satisfied that this baby was ready to lift-off, he sounded the horn, donned a pair of sunglasses and waited.

Thirty seconds later, the door to the bridge opened and in stepped the other gent, who had only minutes ago been scrutinising chain links and tungsten carbide integrity.

Again they nodded to each other, and the now bespectacled driver pushed forward with both hands on a set of levers in the bridge console. What had until now been an almost silent whisper grew into a cacophony of engines, fan blades, blasts of air and some creaks and groans thrown in for good measure.

The hovercraft started to rise off the ground, the skirt pushing out to resemble a naked bicycle tyre pumped to the point of almost blowing a puncture. The chains attached to the mat grew taut, and slowly the edges of the bundle began to lift. When the weight of the gold began to be felt, the hovercraft began to tilt backwards.

"Ready", said the driver.

The other man walked to the rear of the bridge, and peered through a port hole looking out onto the stern of the hovercraft. The crane arm could be seen from where it was attached to the hull of the hovercraft just below where he was standing, to all the way out beyond the back half of the vehicle and over the gold. The thick chains were stretched tight. He looked down at the set of controls at his fingertips, and pressed a red button.

The hovercraft tilted further backwards as the crane arm began to rise, lifting the gold completely off the ground. When he could see the bottom of the mat, he pressed another red button. The crane continued to rise but now began to shorten, bringing the gold over the deck of the hovercraft. At the press of yet another button, this time a green one, the gold descended and touched the deck. Before the entire load was completely laid out, the operator turned a key at the controls and the crane arm ceased its movement.

"Make fast the load", yelled the driver, and the operator exited the bridge.

A monitor on the dashboard allowed the operator to watch as his doppelganger strung cables across the load, and locked them down securely to the deck. Everything to his satisfaction, the driver placed a thumb on a large red button and waited for the bridge door to open, and then close. With both men in the bridge room, the thumb was depressed, the button engaged, and the hovercraft began to inch forward.

Accelerating slowly, it took a few minutes for the hovercraft to reach 50 kilometres per hour. A few minutes later it was cruising at 100 kilometres per hour, and the operator turned on the Guidance Control System.

"That's not a GPS", he said knowingly. "That won't be invented for another few hundred generations".

The other man gave him a withering look. "As though I don't know that too", he said.

"At one hundred kay-pee-aitch we'll make Quebec tomorrow morning. River crossings no problemo in this baby", the operator obliviously carried on.

The other man shook his head morosely and made off to slouch in a corner, and perhaps catch some shut eye.

Sally Arnold looked across the café table at her boyfriend. His face was twitching almost in time with the splurts from the latte steamer as he spoke. The words were coming so fast that sometimes they ran into each other. Sally was having trouble keeping up.

"David, slow down", she pleaded as she held up a hand to show defeat.

The café fell silent again as the barista ceased foaming the milk, and scooped the resulting mass into a large paper cup.

David stopped in mid-sentence, his mouth not sure whether his next syllable should fall out or be sucked back in.

"Sorry", he said. "I'm just so excited about this" he added with a huge smile.

"Yes, but please remember I'm not a scientist. I do love you, but sometimes you just make no sense".

David furrowed his brow a little, trying to take that in.

The barista handed the large paper cup – now complete with a lid – to the only other customer in the café. The customer, one of the university's many students, took the cup and exited the café leaving a smallest of small tips on the counter.

"It's not that hard, Sally," said David, "My RNA zipper needed a neutral bio-meme, something that doesn't occur naturally, but I've managed to coalesce a substitution agent using living tissue AT ROOM TEMPERATURE. Do you know what that means?" he half screamed.

"You lost me soon after 'Sally'", she said.

An old lady entered the café and made a bee-line for the register.

Again, David's brow wrinkled.

"All other attempts at merging one strand with free-floating proteins have..."

Sally cut him off by placing a hand gently on his lips.

"David", she said slowly, "talk to me as though I know nothing about this".

The old lady at the register was obviously asking the barista a tough question, if his shrugs were anything to go by.

"Right", said David, cautiously. "Biology ... ?" he started, with a questioning intonation.

"Yes", said Sally, "that's a good place to start. Now take a LITTLE step further?" she continued, mirroring his tone of voice.

The old lady was now waving a ten dollar bill in the barista's face. His eyes followed the fluttering of the purple bill.

"I know how to clone people" said David, quietly.

Sally said nothing.

"You see", blurted David, taking Sally's stony face as licence to jump headlong back into rambling mode, "I can get the entire sequence duplicated without ANY possibility of error by adding a specific substrate so that the enzymes..."

"STOP", cried Sally. "I don't know what's worse; that you're mad enough to experiment in all this, or that I'm mad enough to listen. Please try to find an answer to THAT while I go to the little girls' room", she said, extricating herself from the booth.

As she made her way to the washrooms, the little old lady, now ten dollars poorer, shuffled over to where David was sitting alone, totally perplexed.

"And you must be David?" she asked.

"Er, yes?" he asked back, not so sure whether to believe himself or not.

The old lady sat down and pinned David's complete attention with an eagle-eyed stare.

"I am Sally." She said, "and I am here to give you a righteous bollocking".

The hovercraft passed over Northern Quebec's rocky terrain as though it were out for a Sunday drive in Saskatchewan. It crested a small hill with ease, and coasted to a noisy halt at the bottom of a shallow valley approximately 400 metres wide.

The sun was shining, the sky was an almost azure light blue, and an ever so slight breeze was blowing away the merest hint of a mist. It was a beautiful spring morning three thousand years before mankind would pave over this idyllic scene with a succession of industrial attempts to screw money out of anyone with more of it than sense.

After almost a day's travel, the hovercraft had come to rest next to a spiky, black vehicle about the size of an SUV. Sitting on top of this monstrosity was a triplet to the hovercraft's twins. He looked at his watch and checked off an item in a list attached to his clipboard.

Big Dave watched as the last of the piles of gold bullion disappeared in a mixture of EEEEEEs and POOMFs. He waited until the dust had settled before blowing his whistle. A small cheer erupted from the throngs of simulacra.

This was it. They had done it. In all the attempts they had never got this far before. Something had always gone wrong and they'd had to be zapped by that black vehicle (they should have thought of a name for it, he mused) and sent to wherever and whenever it was they used as a base of operations. Now it was all over, he realised that he had no idea what to do next. It was the last realisation he had before a bullet entered the back of his skull, said "excuse me, coming through" to the grey squishy parts of his brain, and exited taking half his face with it.

Big Dave fell forward and never blew his whistle again.

David looked at the old lady who claimed to be Sally, then at the door to the washrooms, and back to the old lady again. His mouth wanted to say something, but his brain was running round in circles with its pants down screaming "WOOHOO, WOOHOO!"

"That's me, David" said the old lady, pointing at the washroom door. "I just walked in there, and now sixty years later I am here. If I remember rightly you were trying to tell me something that I had trouble grasping. Nice to have turned the tables on you" she continued.

David's brain had ceased its Daffy Duck impressions and was now drooling out of his ears. Metaphorically, of course.

"Buh, buh, buh ..." he tried to make sense. Something of the scientist kicked in, because he followed that with "But you're OLD".

"Long story", said Sally. "You'll have to come with me if we're to stop all this unravelling again" and with that started the laborious process of getting her aged frame into a standing position.

'Wait", said David. "I was explaining to her, I mean you, I mean ... anyway, I was explaining that I'd just worked out how to easily clone humans. Are ... are you a clone?" he asked.

"No, David, not in a million years would I ever let you clone me. There's only one of me, thank heaven."

David looked towards the washroom doors.

"Just the one?" he ventured.

"Yes – that's the same me. Come on, help me up, I'm not as young as I am now, if you catch my drift" she said. She held out a hand waiting for David to take it and assist her.

A few seconds after they had left, the washroom door opened and Sally returned. With her hands on her hips she considered the empty booth and shot an annoyed, questioning stare at the barista.

144

The barista shrugged and did his best to project at Sally the psychic image of a ten dollar bribe. It didn't work.

"Why are we in a broom cupboard?" asked David in the darkness.

"No-one would think to look in here" said the older version of Sally. "I have some important things to explain to you and I don't want you interrupting. The dark will calm you down a bit and right now I need you to be quiet".

"OK", said David. "I'm all ears"

"You were right when you said you had worked out how to clone people, and if it had been anyone else that would be the end of it. But you, my love, are so very impatient".

"I can't help it. It's something that makes me push for answers. So tell me more, I'm dying to know!"

"Well, your impatience made you think of a way round the problem of a clone starting life as a baby." She said.

"Accelerated hormonal pre-growth steroids? I KNEW it!" exclaimed David.

"Shush", said Sally, batting him on the top of his head. "Nothing so biological. You invented a time machine".

"Cool!" said David. "Wait, what?"

"Yes, in order to have a clone be adult age now, you had to take the infant back in time" she said.

"Wow, I am awesome. So I built a clone machine AND a time machine?"

"Yes", said Sally, sadly. "Yes you did."

"But wouldn't that be...", said David.

"Very expensive? Yes. I see you're piecing it together" said Sally.

"How expensive, exactly?"

"More than it costs to make a nuclear power station. But you found a way," answered Sally, quietly.

"Ha, next you'll be telling me I stole all the gold in Fort Knox or something" said David.

The silence expanded to envelop the darkness.

"No way!! I am SO awesome!!!" squealed David.

"No David. It was a big mistake. Think it through now, before you start down the path I know you've already taken" said Sally.

Once again David furrowed his brow, this time unseen in the darkness.

"How did I rob Fort Knox? I'm a scientist, not a criminal" said David.

"The two are not mutually exclusive, my love. But with a cloning machine and all the time in the world thanks to a time machine, you had all you needed to take the gold" said Sally.

"So I took the gold to pay for the machines, and I built the machines using the proceeds from the stolen gold?" asked David.

"Yes. The paradox is not lost on me, and I thought long and hard about how to stop you" said Sally.

"Why would you stop me?" asked David.

"Think about it", said Sally, flatly.

"Whoa. There'd be tonnes of gold for sure, but I'd need an army of helpers to take it, helpers I could rely on," he mused. "Hmm, but with a cloning machine I could make more than one of me" he continued. "Dozens of me I know I could trust".

"Hundreds of you, yes." The pain in Sally's voice was obvious now.

"So where are all the versions of me? What did I do with them?" asked David.

"I killed them, and towards the end, you did too." cried Sally. "I had no choice", she sobbed.

"I don't understand" said David, shocked.

"I shot them all, David. I trained to be an expert shot with a high powered rifle and I shot them all, David, with your help. I killed you so many times. The universe can take an extra one or two paradoxical inconsistencies, but you took the piss, David, you really did. You didn't stop to think of the consequences, you only focussed on the goal, of getting into Fort Knox and stealing the gold" said Sally.

David's brow was still furrowed.

"So what do we do now?" asked David.

"Well, if you promise to never clone yourself, and follow through on that promise, there may be a chance that things will sort themselves out. You'll have to promise never to pursue designing a time machine or that infernal cloning machine." said Sally sternly.

"I promise" said David, crossing his fingers in the dark.

"OK, I believe you my love. Let's get out of here, we need to destroy some of your paperwork" said Sally.

David opened the door of the broom cupboard, and stepped into the light. Standing right in front of him was someone who looked like he could be his twin brother.

"You bastard!" screamed the non-brother. "You crossed your fucking fingers!" and with that, he punched David squarely on the nose and knocked him out cold.

Murder Trumps Madness

by Heather Mac Archer

Bunny Fisher closed the big drawers of her wardrobe and leaned her forehead against the cool smooth wood. Twelve pairs of shoes were lined up neatly along the bottom with no greater space than five inches exactly between each shoe. She knew that because she'd counted those shoes five times this morning and now she'd be late for her interview with the museum curator. She sighed, both hands on the knobs of the doors willing herself to back away and leave the bedroom.

She'd checked the bathroom taps four times, the stove (she only used one burner to boil an egg) and had made sure six times the latches were securely caught on the French doors that opened onto her small balcony. These she checked once more, hurrying through the living room and rattling the handles. She paused to look out the doors' windows, highly polished and without a speck of dust on them, and gazed at the small park that served the residents of this small square in Notting Hill.

Her ground floor neighbor was strolling casually along the paths, heedless of the beautifully structured flowerbeds the neighborhood's older ladies had cultivated so tirelessly. Hands behind his back, head down, Raulf Renshaw was unaware of the blaze of reds and pinks that lay at his feet, the sweep of the willow trees, the noise of the tight green leaves on the shrubs that rattled gently in the soft wind.

Perhaps he was taking a break from practice. She'd heard him earlier, the rich vibrating and mellifluous tones of his cello sending sad notes out across the small lawn that divided the house from the park. Something in the music he played struck a chord deep inside her and she longed to tell him how much she loved to hear him play. But he spoke to no one in the house, not a hello, goodbye or a nod. He was odd, this principal of the symphony, and teacher of pimply youths who streamed through the front door to be taught how to play sad music.

The basement flat was let to two young women, not the kind Bunny wanted to befriend, although she could use a good friend or two, and the occupant of the first floor was new and unknown. Bunny sometimes heard a radio playing, the clunk of the pipes as the shower started up in the morning but little else. She was glad her nearest tenant was not only quiet, but not around much

Bunny checked the doors once more, grabbed her handbag and fled her flat. She ran past the door of her first floor neighbor, skipped quickly to the ground floor and ran to the gate before the compulsion to check anything else overcame her. She was on the pavement now and felt safe. Next door, a young man she only knew by the name of Molloy was staring at her, a half smile on his face, a rag in his hand. He was fixing his bicycle – again – and he raised a hand in greeting.

Bunny smiled at him and turned her back and walked quickly to the nearest bus stop. If she hurried, she'd be just a few minutes late. If she caught the bus and made the tube quickly, she might even be on time.

She'd be fine in a few days. Dr. Braslow had promised her. And she believed him. It took a while for the meds to kick in, he said, and she was ten days into her new prescription. Soon, he'd reassured her yesterday. Soon the compulsions and obsessive activities would stop. Soon she could get on with her life. Coupled with behavior modification sessions, she'd be fine in no time.

Bunny was highly suspicious of all her neighbors. No one actually said hello, no one stopped to chat. They were an odd collection of people. And she suspected one or more of them were getting into her flat. Did someone else have a key?

A few times, after she'd been out for a walk, or to go shopping – she could now afford some of the nicer fashions she saw in Selfridge's or John Lewis – she came home to find a few things out of place. The dish soap would be on the other side of the sink, a book taken from the coffee table and placed on the arm of the sofa. Another time, she swore someone had made toast, for she could smell it, as though it had just been eaten.

This frightened her, but she felt so vulnerable these days, she couldn't be sure she wasn't imagining things. She tried to put it all to the back of her mind, but she was careful to look over the flat for details whenever she came back, even if she'd just gone out for a pint of milk.

The basement tenants got off the bus as Bunny waited and giggled at her. The two women were supposed to be models, well-paid and famous, but Bunny couldn't remember seeing them in any of the publications she used to peruse while waiting for the train to take her home to Norfolk. But Bunny didn't pay much attention to fashion.

For the life of her, she couldn't see why these women were thought to be so beautiful. They were tall, stick-like figures with an appalling sense of style. Most of the time they wore torn jeans and stretched T-shirts and shapeless sweaters. One of them often wore a tight leather jacket over tiny tops that exposed her midriff. It wasn't Bunny's idea of glamour.

She said hello to their giggles and got no response, climbed aboard the bus and held her Oyster card to the sensor. She missed the bemused look of the bus driver. Bunny's zealous work with the duster this morning, all surfaces, picture frames and knick-knacks, had left her with a long brown feather caught in the top of her pale, fine hair.

Bunny was a nickname her father had given her due the shortness of her nose. She much preferred Adeline, her real name, but Bunny had stuck. The fact she was albino had only reinforced it and so here she was; a compulsive obsessive with pale angel hair, large eyes and thick glasses. The only thing that kept her from being completely odd was, as her mother never ceased to tell her, the fact that Bunny was 'extraordinarily beautiful under those unsightly glasses,' which was cruel, for Bunny really struggled to see well. She squinted to see up close and read. And she peered into people's faces when she talked to them. Most found this unnerving but no one told Bunny this.

She was really hoping this morning she'd get the job at the little museum of medical oddities because she was tired of counting shoes, arranging the cutlery drawer and spending two hours at night making sure the flat was safe and secure. She hated it, but felt powerless to stop the need to do these things. Even now, she plunged into her purse and counted the bills in her wallet. She hadn't done that since last night. Yes, there were five 20-pound notes, five pound coins and other assorted pence. She planned to get a few things at Sainsbury's after the interview and she wanted enough money.

Bunny didn't trust debit or credit cards. That would present her with a whole other set of problems and she wasn't sure she could bear the compulsion to check her bank accounts several times a day. No, it was better to go to the bank, take out the money, count it, and have a little book that told you exactly how much was left.

Bunny hadn't always been like this. Well, she was odd-looking, to be sure, but the obsessive behavior really started three years ago when her beloved father – a country doctor whose kindness to patients had been legion – began his slow and painful descent to the grave. Cancer. The word that sent chills down the stoutest spines and rocked the hearts of the bravest and fiercest. Her father had been both; he never raised his voice to his whining, belligerent and frequently drunk wife. Nor did he ever swear or hit his son, Earl, Bunny's errant and erratic older brother, who wrecked his father's cars, was caught drinking underage, was kicked out of private schools and got an underage teen pregnant.

No. He spoke quietly, evenly, with enough force to make himself heard, and enough conviction so you knew he meant business. You didn't mess with him. If you did, he'd cut you off, entirely and completely. And that is exactly what he had done to his wife and son.

Bunny was horrified when he finally died – in a hospice because her mother didn't want that mess in her home – to find he'd left everything to her; the house, his savings, his investments, his cars, his belongings. To his son, not a penny; to his wife, not even a roof over her head.

Bunny remembered the day the will was read two years ago. She'd not really been interested. She had just graduated from university – a real challenge for her – and she was high on the possibility of the future.

She'd come to accept the fact her father wouldn't be around and although she loved him dearly, she hated his suffering, his silence, the sunken eyes, the smells, the dry, thin hands on her wrists when she visited. She was embarrassed by the hoarse voice that tried to communicate with her at the end, the strings of spittle, and the drawn-back lips that once so easily stretched into a huge smile.

He couldn't laugh or sing anymore. There were no jokes, no cynicism, and no barbs about the political scandals du jour, no quips, no practicing his atrocious French. There was just the shell of a lovely man that Bunny didn't recognize. But still she visited every day, cycling the familiar route from their home on the outskirts of King's Lynn to the tall, narrow little hospice in the city's center.

She'd been the only one with him at the end. A nurse hovered close by, administering pain killers through a "butterfly" IV in his arm every few hours. As his shallow breathing wound down, she'd held his hand, stroked his arm, and talked about good times, family outings spent on Norfolk beaches, picnics in the country. She left out the fact these days usually ended in tears; Melda, Bunny's mother would over-imbibe and Earl would either steal from someone nearby or pick a fight. Still, Bunny would be forever grateful for her father's encouragement to live her life as normally as possible.

It was only through these final hours that Bunny realized how completely she depended on her father. He knew her condition, explained it to her, had monitored her vision, and watched for signs of her skin being damaged by sun. Her devastation and grief grew as his life dimmed.

Only afterward, when they'd pulled the sheet up over his face, when she'd called her mother – who sounded slightly drunk – and was retrieving her bicycle from the rack at the front of the hospital, did Bunny feel compelled to reach inside the bag and count her money. She stopped twice on the way home to count again and when she finally made her way past her drunk and argumentative mother and her bombastic and idiotic brother, ("What right had you to be with him at the end?" "Well where the hell were you, anyway?" she'd retorted. "Surely you knew the end was imminent!"), she fell to her knees and went through all her drawers, counting scarves, underwear and shoes. It comforted her and she was able to tune out the ruckus that was unfolding downstairs as her mother and brother fought over the funeral, the money, the house, and the cars.

Bunny had been home five times since her father died to try and mend fences, talk about sharing the estate, even things up. But that wouldn't do. Her mother and brother wanted it all: She'd never been normal, they said; she'd done a deal with her father, coerced him on his deathbed (she hadn't, the lawyer assured them all, the will had been made ten years earlier); she'd gone behind their backs, etc. They never missed an opportunity to rant and rave.

The upshot was she wasn't welcome at home anymore, which was even odder since the home was actually hers now. She was within her legal rights to kick them out, but she couldn't.

In retaliation, her mother and brother had hired lawyers to contest the will to get their fair share of Dr. Fisher's estate and Bunny had fled as far away as she could. Her father's lawyer, a seasoned legal brain called Owen Thropp, who knew the family situation and was confident no amount of legal wrangling could change things in favor of Melda and Earl, had suggested the flat in Notting Hill. She could more than afford it. Indeed, he'd found it for her as he knew the owner of the house and had gone to law school with the woman. Mr. Thropp suggested Bunny take a good six months to recover from her ordeal and then he'd even helped her try to find a job that would suit her. He'd set up the interview today with the museum and Bunny desperately didn't want to let him down.

She knew the problem with counting and checking – OCD, they called it – was out of hand and when she explained to Mr. Thropp what was happening, he'd sent her to one of the best psychiatrists in London, arranging to have the bills paid out of her father's estate, which was still being probated. He'd assured Dr. Braslow that Dr. Fisher had been of sound mind and in good health when he'd written the will. He'd explained it was a sort of vengeance from beyond the grave and the psychiatrist was to do all he could to aid Bunny.

Bunny was relieved. But she was still wondering when the meds would kick in. Would it be something she felt immediately? Would her bizarre behavior end quickly?

In the meanwhile, she was doing everything she could to move on and forget the past two years. She wanted a new life, one that wasn't fraught with confrontation and legal wrangling. She had tried, God knows she had, but her mother and brother were so incensed, they were determined to strip her of everything.

Bunny stood at the bottom of the steps that led to the museum. She really wanted the job – it housed exhibits of various medical devices and instruments used over the centuries – and she combed her hair and removed her glasses to check her lipstick in a small mirror before she went in.

She had a good degree in history and felt reasonably qualified for the position, but she was shaky and took several deep breaths before opening the door. Mr. Thropp had given her the name of the curator on the telephone but Bunny, who'd just cleaned the entire kitchen, was exhausted and she wasn't sure whether he'd said the person was a Mr. or Mrs. Beringer.

An elderly woman sat at an old desk just inside the door. She was surrounded by pamphlets and had what looked like, to Bunny at least, knitting needles stuck in the back of her head. Bunny tried not to stare, knowing her stare through her magnified glasses sometimes frightened people.

The woman laughed. "Yes, dear, they are knitting needles.

154

Believe it or not they actually keep my hair up. So do pencils, but I just finished these mitts," she waved a pair of knobby purple wool objects, "and the needles were handy." She laughed at herself, a great guffawing sound and asked Bunny if she wanted admission to the museum.

"Er...no I have an interview with someone named Beringer. It's for a job."

"Oh, you're here to see Nick. Come with me," she said rising, all twenty stone of her rustling and rolling in a mauve and pink caftan, her large hips making her lumber as she led Bunny to the back of the building, past frightening displays, to an office that had a sign Curator on the door.

"I'm Betty Chu, by the way," she said, sticking out a fat hand.

"Adeline Fisher."

"Good luck, Bunny Fisher, we could sure use your help around here," Betty whispered, winking.

She knocked on the door and said loudly. "Nick? Miss Fisher is here. Oops, you are a miss?"

Bunny nodded.

From within the office came the sound of a heavy chair being wheeled back along a bare floor. "Come, come,'" said a gruff voice.

"There you go!" Betty flung open the door.

Bunny gaped. Nick Beringer must have weighed a quarter of a ton and was wedged in an enormous chair between a wall and a long desk covered with paper, old books and vials filled with liquid. Balled bits of cotton lay strewn the length of the desk. Crumbs lay across his massive chest and his lovely blue shirt seemed to be stained and marked by something that had eaten into the fabric.

"How do you do?" she offered.

"Sit, sit. I hear you've a got a pretty new degree in history? A first?"

"I have. I studied at Cambridge."

"Well, bless me. That is good news. Are you interested in museums? Old stuff? Medicine in particular?"

Well, duh, thought Bunny, my dad was a doctor. "Yes. I'm

very interested, sir."

"Good. How about tomorrow?"

"Pardon?"

"Can you start tomorrow?"

"That's it?" Bunny sputtered.

"Look, Thropp told me your history. You come highly recommended. He tells me you're bright, conscientious and affable. You're what we need. Betty?"

The door popped open almost immediately and Betty's face appeared. "Can you show Miss Fisher around? I tell you Miss Fisher ... may I call you Bunny? Or would you prefer your proper name?"

"Adeline is better for me," Bunny said. "I prefer it."

"Adeline it is – although we're apt to call you Addie, you know. Anyway ... where was I? Oh yes. I tell you, you'll end up cleaning up a lot of these old bits and pieces of medical equipment for display – among other things. Look at this." He held up an old scalpel and handed it to her.

"Blood still on it!" He grinned, showing perfect teeth in what Bunny realized was an extremely handsome face.

"I look forward to it," she said, surprising herself with the enthusiastic tone.

She was still holding the thin scalpel and had popped it into her pocket without thinking.

Later, when Bunny got off at her stop in Notting Hill, she was amazed at how easy it had been. And at how much she liked Nick and Betty. It was a strange little place to be sure, but she somehow felt entirely at home in the macabre and gloomy museum. She'd peered into glass cases, examined gadgets for holding open insides during operations, hoses for God knows what and other horrible looking devices. But she'd enjoyed it. And best of all? Not once on her way home had she counted her money or checked her bag. Had her meds begun to work since this morning's painful exit from her flat? In fact, she was so excited she hadn't even stopped at Sainsbury's for fresh fruit or milk. Halfway home she'd reached into her overcoat for a tissue and felt the dull prick of the scalpel. She'd gasped and her first thought was Beringer would accuse her of stealing. Well, she'd go online and see if she could discover how to clean it up. It would be a surprise for her new boss. She took out the tissue, but instead of using it wrapped it around the tiny knife. The long narrow shape felt good in Bunny's hand. She tucked it inside the deep pocket of her coat, excited now to please Beringer, to see that handsome face light up and have him flash those perfect teeth in approval.

Bunny fairly bounced along the street and almost bumped into Raulf Renshaw as he exited his flat into the small lobby. Presumably he was leaving to perform at this evening's symphony, wherever that was, and he was struggling with his instrument. Bunny graciously stood back and held the door open for him, smiling and watching.

"Thanks," he said, winking, the corners of his mouth lifting slightly in a leer. Bunny found this alarming. She'd never suspected he might be that sort. But you never knew.

"Pleasure," Bunny said, bounding once more up to the next flight. She paused. She would like to see who lived in the flat below hers, but she'd never been able to catch sight of him. A few times she'd heard a male voice murmuring into a telephone. She had yet to hear the door open or close, a window slide or a TV blare, even briefly. She stood now, listening, but heard nothing.

She moved lightly upstairs to the second floor and turned the key in the door. She threw it carelessly into a small bowl that sat on a table beside the door. Then she froze. Something was dreadfully wrong. She could feel it. She peered into the living room and noticed the curtains had been drawn over the French doors. She'd left them open to get the best of the afternoon sunlight. It helped warm the room. She moved into the kitchen and noticed a wet ring, from a cup or glass, on the counter. She had scrubbed it clean that morning and there hadn't been a mark on it. There was no cup in the sink and her kettle was cold.

Bunny ran into her bedroom and stood there. Nothing seemed to have been touched, the bedspread didn't have a wrinkle on it and it fell to one inch off the floor on all sides. The curtains hadn't been touched. The pillows were piled against the headboard, just as she'd arranged them. Her laptop computer sat on the small desk in front of the window, the pens and pencils still arranged with precision.

She moved cautiously to the wardrobe. Had someone gone through her clothes? No. They hung perfectly, shirts, skirts, dresses and jackets, all arranged neatly, just as she'd arranged them.

Then she looked down, gasped, and fell to her knees. Her shoes. Her shoes had been placed in a huge pile at the bottom of the wardrobe. Bunny's hands flew to her mouth and she began rocking back and forth, back and forth, a strange keening noise coming from between those clenched fingers. Her heart hammered in her chest and tiny lights flickered before her eyes. She felt as though she couldn't breathe.

What should she do? Run downstairs to the stick figures in the basement flat? They'd laugh, say she was imagining things. Should she call the landlady?

No. She'd call Dr. Braslow. She crawled to her dresser and fumbled in the top drawer for the small card he'd given her if she needed to talk to him after hours. Her hands shook as she lifted the handset from the receiver and punched in the number. It took two attempts to connect she was shaking so hard.

"Hello?" It was his voice.

"Dr. Braslow?"

"Yes," he said impatiently, "who is this?"

"It's Ad—it's Bunny Fisher. I have a problem."

"Is it the medication? Are you having a reaction of some kind?"

"Ah. No, sir. I've just found a job today."

"Well that's good, isn't it?"

"Yes. Yes it is. But there's a problem. While I was out at the interview, someone has been in my flat. Things are out of place, moved about." She realized her voice was rising to an almost hysterical level. "And it has happened before. I did mention it to you."

"Well why in God's name are you calling me? I can't do anything. Are you taking the meds? Eh? Sure you're not imagining things? Really, you mustn't call me unless it has to do with your medication. Alright?"

"Sorry, sir. But your name came to mind. You said if I was in trouble…"

"Miss Fisher. I don't do break-ins."

"Of course. I'm sorry I bothered you." Bunny hung up abruptly, her face flaming. Her hand reached for the comfortable cotton-wrapped scalpel, still in her pocket.

What had she been thinking? Dr. Braslow had seemed like a kind man – at least in the paneled surroundings of his office, dark leather furniture lining the walls, warm red shades on the lamps, his desk a bulwark against madness. His low voice was comforting and controlled. But she realized now, as she leaned against her bed, feet stuck out in front of her, that warmth never reached his eyes and his body language was constrained, his torso tucked into his chair as far away from her as he could get. If she leaned forward to make a point, he wheeled backward. Did he do that with all his patients? He'd even refused to shake her hand. He was a cold fish. She wouldn't go back to him. She'd find someone else. Another doctor could provide her with the meds. And were they even working? She thought so, but couldn't be entirely sure.

Bunny was not about to call the police. She would, however, ask the young women in the garden flat if they'd seen anyone about today who didn't live in the house. They'd laugh at her, but she didn't really care.

She locked her door and made her way downstairs. The thinner, blonder of the two women opened the door and gave her a perky "Hiya. What's up?"

"I was wondering if either you or your roommate saw anyone around the house today? I seem to have been broken into. Nothing taken, but still scary."

"Gosh. Just a minute. Helena, get out here. The top flat lady has been broken into."

The other model appeared from the bathroom, towel around her head, bare feet and fingernails tipped in black nail polish. "Did you say break-in? Was anything taken?"

"No, but things were moved around, left a mess. I just wondered if you'd seen anyone," Bunny managed to say smoothly and without embarrassment.

"Shit, Mug, I bet it was that creep in the first floor flat, the one that's just moved in. I don't know his name but the young guy next door, Molloy, says he regularly helps himself to his bicycle and he's never even met him. Molloy's had to put double locks on the door because the guy got the first lock off easily. Weirdo."

Mug stood thoughtfully and looked at the floor. "Or could it be Molloy? He's pretty weird himself. I've seen him sneaking about the gardens at night, smoking weed. And God knows where he gets his money. No one seems to know."

The three women stood silently for a moment.

"Wait," said Mug, "There were break-ins two doors up last spring, remember?"

"They caught that burglar, though," Helena said. "He's doing his time by now, I bet. He took computers and cameras."

Mug looked at Bunny as though seeing her for the first time. "I'm Marguerite Wytham, by the way. Mug just seems easier. This is Helena Grosman," she said.

"Adeline Fisher. But I'm known as Bunny."

"Where do you work Bunny? Sorry, but you do suit that name," Helena said, her face lit with a smile. "I don't mean that in a bad way, either."

"A museum. Just starting."

"Oh good for you. Well, good luck with that." Mug paused. "Look, I'm going to try and keep a lookout for you, see if I can find out more about the new tenant. I'll ask around. I'll bloody well ask Molloy if I see him, too. We haven't had any problems, except someone has been using our garden furniture and leaving cigarette butts all over."

"Could it be Raulf?" Bunny asked.

"God no," said Helena. "He's a complete dear. He'd ask first if he wanted to use our stuff. No," the two women exchanged glances, "we've suspected the new tenant. But we haven't caught him."

"Have you seen him?" Bunny asked. "What does he look like?"

"Just from the back, going out the front door. Slight, tall, light brown hair. Pretty ordinary."

Bunny shrugged. "Well, let me know if you find out anything. And thanks."

"Would you like a drink? We've got a bottle of red open."

All Bunny's awkwardness and suspicions had fallen away. "Thank you. I really must eat, but another time?"

"Anytime," Mug said. "Just holler. We keep an erratic schedule, with shoots and stuff, but if you see us, just knock on the door."

"Very kind. I appreciate it."

Bunny hadn't expected the models to be so friendly, polite or welcoming. And they too had noticed a few things out of place.

She climbed the stairs, past Raulf's ground-floor flat to the first floor. She paused. Just who was this new neighbor? Without pausing – or thinking – she knocked rapidly and loudly on the door. Flooded with anger, she wanted to confront the unknown tenant and demand if he'd been in her flat and why.

But her knocks were answered only by a deep silence that went on and on, until Bunny heard a slight "chink" – the sound of a piece of cutlery tapping against a plate.

"We all know you're in there. We all know you're a thief and a creep and we're watching your every movement," she shrieked at the door. "You won't get away with sneaking around and upsetting the neighbors because the police have been called and we've all told them we think you're our culprit."

Bunny was shaking with shock – at her own reaction and outburst – and her braveness. She'd brought the scalpel out of her pocket and found she was waving it about. The Bunny of just yesterday would never have done such a thing.

"Did you hear me? You got all that? We know about you."

And then she kicked the door twice for good measure before storming up the stairs to her own flat. She was shaking so badly she could hardly get the key in the door or get it turned. She now wished she could run back to the garden flat and take up the offer of wine.

Tea would have to do. She filled the kettle, got out a cup, plopped in a teabag and rummaged in the little fridge for some yogurt. She poured it into a bowl and threw some muesli and put a sliced banana on top. Bunny devoured this makeshift meal before her little television, swearing under her breath at the idiocy of people who think they've got talent and can sing and the assholes who think up such ridiculous shows.

She flung her dish and cup in the sink and went to run a bath. She was still furious but the shaking had stopped and her anger had ebbed. In its place was a curious new feeling, a kind of steely assertiveness. Bunny spent an hour in the bath, topping up the hot water again and again and scrubbing her skin until it was shiny and wrinkled. It was as though she couldn't get clean enough. In that hour, Bunny tried to rub out all the hurt and pain she'd felt over the past two years, the endless compulsions, the strange obsessions, that spiraling feeling of losing control.

Getting out of the tub, she heard a curious thumping noise coming from downstairs. Had she angered her neighbor? She wrapped herself in a robe, her head light from the hot water, her legs wobbly, that curious object wrapped in the tissue in her robe pocket. Barefoot, she stood in her living room. The thumping was getting louder and faster, a rat-a-tat that sounded like gunfire. It banged on and on, and Bunny stood, bemused at first then annoyed at the man's audacity.

Still in her bathrobe and bare-footed, Bunny slowly descended the stairs and stood at the neighbor's door. She rapped, first lightly and slowly, then hard and rapid-fire, pummeling the door with her left hand.

A click made her stop. He'd slid a lock. Then nothing. She began tapping again, fingernails beating and scratching like an enraged feline. The knob turned and the door opened a fraction of an inch. Bunny's hand had unwrapped the rusty scalpel and she clutched it now, her fingers slippery along the handle.

She knew that face, recognized the slight, tall form with light brown hair.

"I should have known," she said simply as she looked at her brother Earl. "I should have known you'd do everything you could. I think part of me knew it must be you." She laughed, the sound ragged in her throat. She was surprised, but not afraid.

162

The door was flung open wide and a hand reached out and violently grabbed the front of Bunny's robe, jerking her into the room. She was thrown on the floor.

"Of course I'd never give up, you bitch." He had a broken broom handle in his hand. His face, never attractive, was positively hideous and Bunny realized she'd never noticed the deep blue veins that ran along his forehead, the lower lip that dipped in a scowl.

She lay on living room floor and gazed up at him.

"Now what?" she asked.

"Well, that would seem fairly obvious," he said, turning to a small table. He scooped up the small gun, but wasn't as quick as Bunny. She bounced up on her feet just as he turned to aim the gun at her chest. Lightning fast, she plunged the rusty scalpel as far into his heart as it would go.

He gasped and the gun dropped to the floor. A look of complete astonishment swept across his face. He tried to talk, but his voice had become a gurgle, his words a dribble of blood.

Bunny was neither horrified nor frightened by what she'd done. She pulled the scalpel from his chest and wiped it neatly along the knife-edge of his khaki trousers. She felt exhilarated and free and couldn't help smile as she looked down at her "neighbor."

She knew exactly where she would put him. It was dark now and it would be easy. The square's garden ladies had spent the better part of last week digging a new bed just outside their gate. He wasn't that heavy and Bunny felt especially strong now. And the house was deadly silent. Bunny could be ever so quiet when she wanted to be. She'd make light work of the job.

Now that Earl was gone, Melda would buckle. She'd do exactly what Bunny wanted. And Bunny wanted to sell that big house in Norfolk, perhaps buy herself a little property in London. Something she could call her own. A place where she didn't have to count shoes and check doors and taps .....

The next morning, when Bunny arrived for work, she headed for Nick Beringer's office and knocked.

"Come in," he called.

"Good morning," she said brightly, reaching into her pocket

for the square of cotton. "Sorry, but such was my intense interest, I found last night I'd pocketed this by mistake. But guess what, I also figured out how to get it clean!"

She unwrapped the scalpel and placed it gently on the desk. "Just don't ask how I did it" she said, laughing lightly, her hands raised.

"Good God. I'm astonished," said Beringer. "It's like brand new!"

Night Work

by Steve Shrott

"Robert, is that you?"

"Yes, Miss McNally," I said, entering the basement of the two-storey brownstone, where I live. "Just me. Sorry to wake you."

"You didn't wake me, honey, you know I'm a night owl. I love watching all those late-night news shows. Why don't you come up for a nice cup of tea? I've got the kettle on and..."

"I'm a little tired."

"C'mon. Help a bored old lady get a bit of excitement in her life."

I sighed. "Okay, I'll be up in a sec."

I limped down the stairs to my tiny room, cursing myself, as always, for being in that car accident on my sixteenth birthday.

The room had all the amenities–fridge, hotplate, even an old TV. The paint on the sky-blue walls had peeled in sections showing yellow underneath, but it didn't bother me. I'm kind of a loner and seldom have guests.

I yawned. I could have fallen asleep on the spot. Still I had to admit I enjoyed these Friday night chats with my landlady. We often talked for hours. She had travelled extensively and always had a tale to tell. Of course, I had to be tight-lipped about what I really did at night.

As I opened the door to the upper level, I could smell the distinct minty aroma of Jasmine Tea. Miss McNally shut off the TV that had been playing some special news report, and directed me to the two clay cups sitting on her Ecuadorian coffee table. She had explained many times how they had been hand-crafted by artisans from the Azande tribe in New Guinea.

She took her usual spot in the rocking chair and leaned back. I made myself comfortable, next to her, in the rattan chair she had purchased from an outdoor vendor in Mozambique for a handful of centavos.

She smiled at me, her eyes still bright at 72. She used to travel around the world. I assumed she couldn't do that anymore because of her heart condition. I truly felt sorry for her being stuck in a small town like Westport.

She took a sip of her tea. I took a sip of mine.

"So how's work going, Robert?"

"Good, good."

She leaned in close and whispered. "Everything went off okay tonight?"

"Uh, yes, absolutely."

"You robbed the bank?"

My body froze.

She chortled. "It's an old Welsh saying, Robert. It just means you got paid."

"Oh," I said, relieved. "Yes, as a matter of fact I did."

"It's always nice to get an honest day's pay for an honest day's work. Honesty, that's the key, isn't it?"

I crinkled my eyebrows. "Uh, yes, of course."

"You know, I don't often have boarders in your line of work. I guess you got interested because you like to steal from people."

A shiver flew up my spine, then down and across my back. What was going on here? "I don't know what you're referring..."

She patted me on the shoulder. "I'm sorry, Robert. I'm in a bit of a mood today. It's just that most of the lawyers I've dealt with seem to charge an arm and a leg. Of course, I'm sure you're not like that."

I gave her a toothy smile. "No, no."

"But you know," she said, giving me a suspicious glance, "isn't it a little odd for a small town lawyer to work till the wee hours of the morning?"

I started breathing heavily and my mind went into overdrive trying to figure out what to tell her. "Well, uh, the truth is, I have so many clients I can't get to them all during the day. So, I have to see them late at night. You know, some, uh, dentists and chiropractors are doing that now too."

She seemed to believe that explanation. Thank goodness. To be honest, I did feel bad making up that wonky story.

"You know your boss should be throttled for making you work so much. I hear the door banging shut at two or three sometimes."

"I'm sorry."

"I'm thinking of you. You're probably not getting enough sleep. Would you like some cream for those lines under your eyes?"

I grinned. "No, no thank you. Yes, it is a bit of a grind, but I don't mind."

"I suppose that kind of work can be rewarding."

I sipped some tea, hoping that talk about "my work" had ended.

She picked up a copy of the Westport Chronicle that lay on the table and turned the pages. "Lots of bad news in the papers these days."

"You're so right."

"Oh my goodness, there was a bank robbery the other night."

My bad leg started to twitch. "You know I really don't like hearing about things like that...makes me worry that my money's not safe, and everything."

"Apparently, the First National got robbed by a man who limped. You have a limp don't you, Robert?"

"Yes. I, uh, guess a lot of people have limps."

"You're certainly right about that. My Uncle Ted had a bad leg himself. Couldn't get around without a cane."

I looked her in the eye. "How is your sister doing–the hip replacement operation?"

"Apparently, they've made some strides in the case. They

found a glove that belonged to the thief and—"

"Oh?" I tried again to divert her. "Did you play cards this week, Miss McNally?"

"—they were able to get prints off the glove and find out who it belonged to. They're currently searching for him. The name of the man is—this is hard to read. It's all smeared—Rober...St—let me get my glasses."

As she reached for the glasses case, I grabbed the paper from her. "Miss McNally, as I said, it makes me nervous hearing about this. Could we change the subject and talk—"

The next thing I knew, she had a gun in her hand.

"What are you doing?"

"The article says the prints belong to a Robert Stanton. You. You're the bank robber."

"What? That's wrong."

"They knew the prints were yours because of the record you got when you were 16, stealing girlie magazines from variety stores." She shook her head. "Such a dirty boy. I guess your crimes escalated after that."

"No, they didn't escalate. My dad grounded me for three months and I vowed never to steal again." I looked into her warm brown eyes. "Please believe me. I didn't do this, Miss McNally."

She frowned for a moment, and then a maternal smile broke through. "I believe you, honey."

My breath slowed down; my heart calmed. "Thank you."

"I did it."

"What?"

"I robbed the bank."

I stared at her, stunned. "Did you take too much of your medication?" I asked, pointing to the numerous pill bottles on her shelf. Sometimes that can give you weird hallucinations. I've..."

"Those aren't my pills. They were my mothers. She had congestive heart failure, passed away a year ago. Just haven't gotten around to tossing them yet. My heart's as strong as a newborn's." She slapped her chest. "You gotta be in good shape to be a thief."

I couldn't believe this.

A moment later, however, I noticed her running shoes. Actually, my running shoes on her feet.

"On Tuesday, when you left for your doctor appointment, I went into your room."

"You can't do..."

"Afraid I can. It's in the contract you signed. The thing is, I noticed some odd items lying around–a gun, a pair of gloves, a ski mask. You told me you were a lawyer, but I began to think otherwise. Actually, I started to get a tiny bit of respect for you." She moved the gun closer to my chest. "Now, I see you're just a lying little weasel."

"I can explain."

"You don't have to. I also found the program from the Glenview Theatrical Production of "Stick 'Em Up!" You're listed as playing the bank robber, Lefty Goldstein. Those items were just props, the gun was a fake!" Her voice started to rise. "You're no lawyer, no bank robber. You're a damn actor!"

"I'm sorry. I had to lie. I heard about your husband leaving you for that young actress and how bitter you were about it. People said you wouldn't rent a room to anyone in the theatre."

"That vixen screwed up my life. She took away my George, and now I don't have a penny to do one iota of travelling." She kicked the Ecuadorian coffee table, our cups spilling and smashing to the ground.

She moved toward me, raising and lowering the gun, as if deciding where to shoot me for the most pain. My whole body began to quiver.

"That's why I dressed up in your clothes and ski mask and robbed the bank. I limped like you, then I dropped a glove with your juicy fingerprints all over it onto the floor of the First National."

She pulled me out of the chair. "Okay, let's stage this properly. I guess you know a thing or two about staging, right?" She glared at me. "Go lie on the ground with your hands behind your head."

I did as she asked; after all she had the gun–a real one. I looked up at her. "You'll never get away with this. I'll tell them everything."

"Good luck with that, sweetie. I'm sure they're going to believe a 72-year-old woman with a heart condition, got dressed as her male tenant, to rob a bank." She snickered. "They'll think you're a loon." She took off the running shoes, put them on my feet, and hid my shoes under the couch. Then she picked up the phone.

"Hello police? I have the thief who robbed the First National Bank trapped here. Please come soon, I'm just a helpless old woman."

THE WARNING

by Linda Cahill

"I thought we would be somewhere else."

The man in front of me just smiled: "Don't you like it here?"

Well of course I did. We were in my office, my favourite room, not counting the church and the Glen Edward Club, but I guess he knew that.

One wall of my sanctum is glass and looks out on the downhill runs of Mount Templeton, the highest peak in this part of Ontario. In the summer it's a green paradise of fern and fir trees with blue wild flowers growing at the edges of the runs. The Club is in the valley below, exquisite fairways hacked from the virgin forest.

"Yes I love it," I told the stranger.

Today, sunshine was glancing off the hard packed snow outside and filling my cozy retreat with that beautiful winter light we get here in the mountains.

The stranger moved between me and the view.

"Won't you sit down?"

He shook his head.

"You don't mind if I do?" I took my seat in the oak captain's chair on my side of the desk and tried to take a deep breath.

"So is this where you ask me questions?"

"I thought you might have some for me."

I did actually. "Alright then, is there anything you have, ah, against me?"

The stranger paused as if listening for something. Outside my window, people were enjoying the New Year holiday in the bright sun and bracing temperatures. Skiers whizzed by just beyond the fence, I could see the red, blue and green of their jackets and the light flashing off their poles. Closer in, the sun glittered off the oversize satellite dish crouching like a big black bird in my garden.

Inside, the same sun illuminated the single malt whisky on the polished table before the fireplace, and some junky pamphlets requesting money for a leper colony. It also warmed the ochre leather arm chairs drawn up on either side of the fieldstone hearth.

"Why would I have anything against you?"

Was it my imagination or was the temperature dropping?

"Umm, if we're going to chat you may as well take a chair," I tried again. To please me, he took one of the leather ones, the one at the left of the fireplace and closest to where I sat at my desk. He was still backlit and I couldn't see his face very well except his eyes, a very bright blue.

"My friends," I began.

"Rich and thoughtless lifestyle?"

"Yes."

"It's not about them," the stranger said firmly. "Except, did you give them a good example?"

"What do you mean?"

"You know what I mean."

I turned away from his piercing look with an effort and sneaked a peek at the ornate clock on my desk, an antique that pealed the hours.

As if on cue, the bells sounded five o'clock. Drink time. But somehow I didn't crave the smooth whisky in its crystal decanter.

"I'm thinking about all the different people you turned yourself into a pretzel for; being all things to all men so to speak."

I couldn't lie. Not now. "I gave up the club. Well, except for the occasional round of golf or dinner with the members of my old investment firm. I don't attend meetings for instance." I felt on safe ground here.

"But you didn't give up the money."

"And I've been celibate for years."

He nodded.

Then a thought came to me.

"You think I don't spend enough time with the flock."

"You're saying it, William."

"I'm always on deck," I protested. "Three masses on the week-end, baptisms, funerals, weddings...I visit the sick when someone calls me..."

"And your parishioners don't like Opera" the stranger said with the ghost of a smile.

"They play guitar and hunt ducks. My Bay Street friends and the Club members are the only people I could be myself with."

The stranger sighed and cast his eyes around my study. "No vows of poverty here. What about works of charity?"

"You mean feed the hungry, clothe the naked...? I'm still learning. You know I'm a convert," I said.

The stranger looked grave.

"You should have made a clean break."

"You mean?"

"Your Club members feel cheated because you're half in and half out, the parishioners are suspicious for the same reason. And none of your congregation could afford that golf club of yours – even if you let them in."

"But everyone likes me."

"Apparently not."

"I'm still affiliated with my club," I went on. "As for the pa-rishioners, just last week one of the council members came to in-stall that satellite dish for me, for free." I gestured to the outdated receiver outside my window.

"Does it only get religious channels?"

"I should insult him and ask him to take it away?"

The stranger said nothing. It was definitely getting cold in here. I pushed myself up from my desk and brushed by him to get a log for the fire. The sun was still glistening on the mahogany desk top and the cheap flyers the parishioners flooded me with about preparing for the end times or giving money to the missions. I always keep dried birch logs in the shining copper at the right of the fireplace. The leaflets make good fire starters. But the smooth white bark slipped through my fingers.

"Your hands are too cold," he said.

It was true, they were as white as the logs, very cold and they weren't obeying me like they should.

"We don't have a lot of time left," he said. "They will be coming for you soon."

"What are you talking about?" I said, or at least I thought I said. The words seemed stuck in my mouth and my knees were bending, I reached out for the armchair holding on to keep from falling but I was going down, in slow motion, so slow I felt and saw every millisecond of the descent. The stranger somehow broke my fall holding me by the shoulders as I crumpled on the rug. I loved that rug, Turkish, a country style with lots of red and beige and blue. I had purchased it on a European vacation, long before my conversion... No one thought I could stick with it: taking instruction, conversion, and becoming a priest. Not even me. Then here I was, removed from the world of hedge funds and derivatives and posted to a parish near the small town where I grew up. Everyone knew who I was; it was hard to convince them I had changed. But had I really?

From my vantage point on the floor I saw the beige in my carpet was slowly turning red. Blood red. Blood? Yes. Blood was seeping down my forehead, and dripping onto my carpet. Blood? What? How could that be? And then I began to remember.

"Last night," I said it in my mind because I could no longer talk.

The stranger nodded. He had cradled my bleeding head but his shirt or tunic or whatever was still clean, white, whiter than the snow and sun outside. Gently, he let my head down to rest on the carpet.

"I told them, I told him," it was coming back to me now; I had been out with friends. Then we went to a party at the Club. Alan came back for a drink...

The stranger's clothing gleamed brighter as the daylight faded outside and shadows took over the room.

"And last night?" the stranger prompted in a voice far away.

"Last night?" I struggled to remember. My chin was still digging into the Persian carpet. It was no longer welcoming; I could feel the strands harsh against my skin.

"Oh, I got into an argument with one of them. He said I had sworn an oath when I joined the club and I betrayed them by leaving."

The stranger nodded and stretched me out on the floor. I was lying on my side, in front of the cold fireplace.

"And then?"

"He left and someone else came in..." I was struggling now, thoughts were hazy, scattered. I found myself focusing on the threads of the carpet, their perfect intersection red, blue, green woven together.

"Sheila," I paused for breath although it didn't matter since I was now talking only in my mind. Sheila the volunteer parish secretary had burst in on me as I sat before the fire with my single malt scotch. "She accused me..." I struggled even more.

"Of mishandling her money."

"The market tanked, everybody lost!"

"She couldn't afford it William. And you're not supposed to be a banker anymore, the stranger said.

"I was doing her a favour...anyway then she was gone, Sheila was gone and a man came in with a pistol. My pistol, my Ruger 22 calibre for target shooting! Who?" I struggled to see the face of my attacker. But the face dissolved and an acquaintance from the club loomed up instead. My own club how could they? Then that face disappeared too. For a second the face stayed blank, all I could see was light but no features. And then a new face materialized. At first I was comforted to see Alan and then realized to my horror that he was the one raising the pistol...

"He shot me!" I shouted. "Twice. He shot me!" I couldn't believe it. Alan, one of my oldest friends from the club.

The stranger shook his head.

"Who shot me, then? You know!" The stranger gently disengaged from me and rose.

"You've upset lots of people William. It doesn't matter which one of them pulled the trigger.

"I'm sorry" I said, and this time I realized my tongue was thick and my lips didn't move which is why I was talking just with my mind. "I meant well."

"This isn't just about you William; you have warring factions here, you're just one of the prizes."

The stranger was fading away.

"I can't see you," I shrieked but no sound came out.

"Where's the tunnel of light, the bright vistas?"

"You watch too many movies. Maybe you should have prayed more, helped the poor...," I heard the stranger say, but his voice was receding and mingling somehow with the whine of snowmobiles, the distinct shrillness of an OPP siren and the wail of an ambulance.

"Wait! Wait! Don't leave me!"

I felt the stranger's hand, pleasantly warm against my cold forehead.

"You're afraid to die," he said.

"No! I'm afraid of losing you!"

He smiled again and this time it seemed as if the smile was all I could see. But outside my door the sound was deafening, ambulance and police sirens, then fists pounding on wood, axes smashing their way in...

"Then try again."

And suddenly I was in great pain. The room was freezing, someone had turned the heat off and the blood on my face was cold and congealing and my eyes hurt where the blood filled them and they were sticking me with tubes and needles. My body hurt more than I thought was possible.

Two rookie cops, a beautiful blond with freckles, and a thick-set farm boy who didn't look more than twenty-two were talking.

"Look at the gun he was holding and the angle of the bullet in his head," the farm boy said as an EMS paramedic clamped oxygen on my face.

"Suicide?" the blond responded. "But what about the bullet in his shoulder? It's an awkward angle for self-harm."

"I'm not dead yet," I thought and the paramedic, now sticking me with needles agreed.

"Keep a lid on it officers; Father William here is going to make it."

The blond turned from her companion and looked me in the eye, past the mask clamped uncomfortably to my face, and the bandages that now decorated my forehead.

"And you're going to tell us who did it," she said firmly as they hoisted me off the floor onto a stretcher.

Maybe. Maybe not, I thought as they jerked me up and around my desk and out the door.

I would have to pray about it. From the leper colony where I would go as a volunteer. After I sell my house and give the money to the poor. Well, I would keep some for the airfare.

THE LAWFULLY DEAD

by Tyner Gillies

The air was thick with the heavy, sour stench of fear, and it clung to my face as I stepped into the broad corridor. The fluorescent lights in the ceiling hummed as Rudy, stripes of rank glinting dully on his shoulders, led the way.

I was young then, hard in my body and attitude. While Rudy slouched his way beneath the harsh lights, I stood ramrod straight, a bounce in my step and my brow furrowed as I tilted my chin up and glared at nothing.

As we walked, the dark entrances of empty cells yawned open like the mouths of hungry beasts, waiting for us to step too close. Those cells were the punctuation at the end of a story. If you spent the night in one, you were already dead.

Ahead of us a small square of sparse light spilled into the hallway from the lone occupied cell on The Row. The smell got thicker the closer we got to that little patch of light, and I could almost feel it clinging to my skin like the condensation from a heavy mist.

Rudy stopped and turned, and held up his hand for me to do the same. He started to speak, then held a fist in front of his mouth and gave a wet belch. He grimaced and rubbed at the gut that hung over his gun belt. Too many years of watching over the walking dead had given him ulcers.

"Remember what I told you?" Rudy asked, still rubbing his stomach.

I nodded, a typical cocky smirk carefully crafted on my face for the dual purpose of making me look like I knew what I was doing, and giving the impression I was hot shit. The only thing my smirk really affected, I learned later in life, was that I looked exactly like what I was: a cocky little prick.

Rudy, who despite his bad posture and mild foot odour was not an idiot, called me on my foolishness. "Oh yeah, Clint, what did I say then?"

I, in truth, had been far too busy thinking about how awesome I looked in my crisp uniform, and how many phone numbers I was going to receive at the grocery store, to concentrate very hard on what Rudy, also my probationary trainer, had been telling me about my job.

"Uh," I muttered, distracted again by the brass buttons on the sleeve of my black coat, "To make sure I talk to him?"

"No," Rudy said, stepping close and jabbing me in the chest with a thick finger. "We keep them calm. That is what we do. Whether that means you talk to him, bake him a cake, or sing the entire fucking score from Fiddler on the Roof, you keep him calm. You try and even him out so that when his time comes for the long walk he can hold his head up and do it with a little dignity."

The murderer's dignity mattered less to me than a scrap of dog shit on my boot heel, but I nodded obediently and tried to keep my smirk off my face so I could avoid the ass kicking Rudy undoubtedly wanted to give me.

"Dinner comes in about half an hour," Rudy said, removing his finger from my chest, but keeping his glare firmly on my face. "It's all prepared, so you don't have to worry about it. Just slide it under the bars and make sure he's got everything he asked for. If not, you call the kitchen and get it brought up. They give you any shit, you call me and I'll take care of it."

I raised my hands, my smirk coming out again, and started to tell him that I knew all that, but he reinforced his glare, and I shut my mouth with a faint click.

"You got four hours," he looked at his watch, "until me and the Warden come for him. So be professional, be polite, and don't, fuck, this, up." Each of his last four words was punctuated with a tap from his favorite pointing finger. Despite the fact Rudy was at least twenty years my senior, thirty pounds overweight, and shuffled like an old man, I had an inkling he might break me in half if I pushed him too far.

"You got that?" he asked, jabbing me once more.

I nodded.

"Good. Now come meet your best friend for the next few hours."

As soon as Rudy turned from me I, once again, fixed my smirk into place. I wanted the piece of shit in the cell to know that I was not a man to be fucked with.

We stepped up to the mouth of the cell. Rudy put one hand casually on the bars of the door, and the other on the butt of his gun. I stood a little behind him, my back so straight it ached a little, and my thumbs tucked behind the thick leather of my gun belt.

The man inside was not what I'd expected. From the stories in the newspapers during the months of his trial, the same months that I'd spent in basic training for this job, I'd expected someone a little more...aggressive. The papers had portrayed him as a raving lunatic who brutally tortured people to death; a madman who hid in his basement without any company and plotted the kidnapping of his next victim, and a maladjusted freak who got his jollies hurting people. When the other recruits in my class heard I was coming to this prison, and was posted to The Row, they all stared at me in awe and fear, wondering who I'd pissed off to have to guard "The Carver," as the papers had dubbed him. My smirk had only gotten wider as I strutted around thinking I was the hardest man going.

But, the man in front of me didn't look evil. He didn't look like a lunatic, or a madman, or a freak. He only looked sad. Maybe tired. And more than a little broken. He was sitting on the edge of his bunk, elbows on his knees, hands and head dangling towards the floor.

"Mr Connors?" Rudy said.

The man lifted his head. "Evening, Rudy," he said.

Rudy tilted his chin towards me. "This is Clint Davis, the new member of our team. He'll be looking after you for the next few hours, making sure you get what you need." Rudy paused, and glanced at me, then back at Connors. "How you holding up?"

Connors stood from his bunk and gave a small shrug as he stepped quietly towards us. "I'm okay, Rudy. I'm keeping it together better than I thought I would, now that my time is running down."

I wanted very much to step back as Connors approached the cell door and put his hand near Rudy's on the bars. It unnerved me to be close enough to the man to reach out and touch him, but stepping back would have indicated fear, and the most important thing about being a cocky prick is you can't look scared.

I'd pictured Jeffery Connors, the man who kidnapped four men and tortured them to death, to be a scowling, tattooed giant. Instead he was best described as average; the kind of man you wouldn't look at twice on the street. He had a bland face and a bland expression. There was no evil in it. No malice. Like I said before, he just looked sad. And afraid.

He looked at me with his bland eyes for a moment, then stuck his hand out through the bars towards me. "Pleased to meet you, Officer Davis."

This time I did step back, the crawling of my skin giving me momentum. Despite his demeanour, the idea of shaking Connors's hand made my ass pucker and my shoulders twitch. I hated to admit it, even to myself, but I knew what the man was capable of and he scared the shit out of me.

When I stepped back Rudy sighed wearily and shook his head. He looked at Connors. "Don't be offended. He's new, and we're still waiting for his nuts to drop."

That got a chuckle out of Connors and I felt my face burn.

"That's okay, Rudy," Connors said, withdrawing his hand. "You can't expect too much on the kid's first day."

I burned hotter. Hearing a convicted murderer talk about me like a patiently chastising father chapped my ass so much it nearly caught fire beneath my wool pants. I stood a little straighter, if that was even possible, and gave my cocky smirk a little more juice. Neither Rudy nor Connors paid me any attention.

Rudy held out a broad hand, and Connors clasped it. "You take it easy, and I'll see you in a few hours."

One edge of Connors' mouth turned up slightly, a sad imitation of a smile. "I'd like to say that I was looking forward to seeing you again Rudy, but... you know."

"I do," Rudy said and released Connors' hand. He walked past me, stopping to lean close and whisper in my ear. "Remember what I said, Clint. Fuck this up, and I'll have you working kitchen detail, standing elbow to elbow washing dishes with the prisoners."

I struggled to keep my smirk fixed, and Rudy laid one hand on my shoulder in what looked like a friendly gesture, but was really filled with warning. I swallowed thickly as his footsteps receded down the dim hallway.

Connors moved away from the bars, sat back down on his bunk, and resumed his drooping posture. Not really knowing what else to do, I stood by the door, out of arms reach from the bars as we'd been taught in training, hooked my thumbs behind my belt and glared down the hallway.

As I stood there, I fully intended to spend the next four hours staring at nothing, pretending the murderer in the cell, close enough I could smell his fear charged sweat, didn't exist. But, as I did my best impression of an old Roman legionnaire from a Charlton Heston movie, I found my eyes drifting away from the grey wall, to the man sitting on the bunk.

"Its okay if you wanna have a look, kid," he said. "I've been stared at plenty in the last six months, so it won't bother me at all."

I cleared my throat in what I thought was going to be a manly fashion, but it came out like a fluttering squeak, and kept staring at the wall. I was determined to show this man he wasn't able to get under my skin, that I wasn't afraid of him.

"Holy shit, you really are a hard case, aren't you?" Connors stood and walked towards the bars again.

My eyes flicked down, carefully measuring the distance between me and the cell door. Even though I knew he couldn't possibly reach me, I had to fight down the urge to step farther away.

"I ain't gonna try nothing with you, kid. I got nothing left in me, even if I wanted to. My killing's done. I just want the time to run down so I can get this over with and stop this waiting."

I still said nothing, my pulse pounding in my ears so hard I could barely hear his words over the thump of it. My face burned all the more, the heat of it making bright spots in my vision, as the killer looked at me. In my peripheral vision I saw Connors shrug, then sit back down on his bunk.

There was a click from the end of the hall, and it echoed like a gunshot in the stillness of The Row. The steel door opened and a cook in a white smock pushed a cart through and turned down the hallway. I breathed deep, trying not to sigh in relief, and felt like I'd never been so glad to see anyone in my entire life.

The cook was a hound-eyed man who had his heavy lids turned towards the handle of his little cart. I nodded at him, but he didn't even look up at me as he came to a stop in front of the cell. He didn't seem to worry overly about being right near the bars where Connors could grab him if the murderer had been inclined.

The cook pulled the lid off a tray to reveal Connors's last meal: a steak, mashed potatoes with dark gravy, a heavy glop of creamed corned, and a large slice of blueberry pie. Next to the tray was a glass bottle of Coca-Cola, misted with condensation, and one of those little single serving cups of ice cream sitting in a small bowl filled with round cubes of ice.

I looked at the food blankly, waiting for the cook to do something with it. When I didn't move he finally turned his eyes up to me and nodded his head towards the cell.

"Oh, right," I said as I removed my thumbs from my belt and clumsily lurched towards the tray. The civilian staff were not allowed to have any contact with the prisoners, even something so simple as handing them a tray of food. I slid the tray, carefully, through the gap beneath the cell door, and followed it with the Coke and the ice cream.

Connors got up from his bunk and took the two steps required to bring him in front of the food. He looked from the tray and up at the cook. Connors nodded to the droop-faced man, and the cook nodded back, one slow movement of his head, up and down.

The murderer set his food on the little table in his cell, and pulled the lot of it over to the edge of his bed. He picked up his utensils, turned his plate a quarter of the way around, and carefully began cutting the steak. He took small bites, savouring each mouthful, eating like it was his last meal, which in fact it was.

Connors ate in silence. The only sound that reached my ears was the scrape of his knife on the ceramic plate, and the sound of him breathing as he chewed. I found myself staring at him in horrid fascination as he consumed the last bits of food he would ever have. He saved the blueberry pie for last, spooning the ice cream into the middle of it.

"Nothing like warm blueberry pie with a good dollop of ice cream, is there Officer Davis?"

When he was done, he set his utensils down, leaned back against the wall and patted his belly with a small, slightly sad, grin.

"Best prison meal I've had so far," he said, and gave a small belch, followed by, "excuse me."

He turned his head, looked me up and down, and I felt my face colour again while I kept my teeth together and stared at the distant wall, my cocky smirk forgotten.

"So," he said, after looking at the side of my face for a while, "you know any good jokes?"

"Uh, what?" I said and looked down near his feet. I didn't make eye contact with him; I couldn't force my eyes to do it.

"Jokes? You know any? Cause my clock says we still got another three hours to go, and it's gonna be a long night if you don't want to say anything to me at all."

I turned my eyes back up and placed them on the distant wall. "No," I said, trying to build my smirk around the words, "I don't know any jokes."

Connors stood from the bunk, walked to the wall of his cell, farthest from where I was standing and turned to face me. "Okay, kid, I'll bite," he said in his gentle voice as he leaned back against the wall, and crossed his arms. "What exactly is your problem with me?"

The very ridiculousness of his question offended my senses, making all my indignant synapses fire at once, and rendering my brain incapable of forming a response. I could only stare at the distant wall, my smirk frozen. What possible problem might I have with a mass murderer? If Connors was honestly asking me that question, then he was not only psychotic, but a moron as well.

My incredulity overcame my fear of this man, and I turned to look at him, meeting his eyes for the first time. "Are you serious?" I asked, my self-righteousness lending strength to my smirk.

"Yeah," Connors said. "You've never met me before in your life, but you're standing there, hatred painted over every inch of you."

I scoffed, a phlegmy sound in my throat. "I don't need to know you, Connors. I know what you did, and that's enough for me to hate you."

"Oh," Connors said softly. "There it is." He rubbed a weary hand over his face. "Okay, Officer Davis, what is it you think I did?"

"What do I think you did? I don't have to think about it." Righteous fury practically dripped off my words as I spoke. "I know exactly what you did, like everyone else in the country. You kidnapped four college students, one at a time, and tortured them to death in your basement, before burying them in the woods. You murdered four innocent young men." I found myself leaning forward, getting emotional, which I knew I shouldn't be doing, but couldn't help myself. I straightened. "That's what you did, Connors."

"I didn't murder them," he said, looking at the floor, his voice barely above a whisper. "I punished them."

I scoffed again. "You what?"

"THEY DESERVED TO DIE!"

His shout was brutal and harsh in the quiet of The Row, and it made me jump and gasp. My heart pounded and my hand went to my gun as my feet touched the ground again. Connors still had his arms crossed, but he was glaring at me with wide eyed intensity, the veins in his neck and forehead standing out and writhing like worms beneath his skin. I stared back at him, adrenaline spiking with a hot bloom in my chest, my own breath ragged in my ears.

"They deserved to die for what they did," Connors said, his voice reverting to its gentle tone, his body relaxing and his eyes going back to the floor.

During the trial, and the following appeal, Connors never once denied the fact that he killed the four. Neither did he deny he killed them horribly, and they died in pain. His whole argument was based upon the fact they had committed a crime that deserved death in retribution, and he was not guilty of murder.

The apparent crime these men had committed had been glossed over, unimportant, by most of the papers. There was an allegation of a sexual assault against the men, a date rape one story said, but they hadn't been arrested and nothing was ever proven against them.

I marshalled my own emotions, willing my hands to stop shaking and working my tongue in my dry mouth. "Yeah?" I asked, hoping my voice didn't waver. "What is it you think they did that justified their deaths?"

Connors sighed, and looked up at me. "If any of the papers had shown a picture of the child they raped, I'd never have been convicted. They'd have patted me on the back and set me free, and that trash I took out never would have been given a second thought."

"What are you talking about?" My voice was steadier now, speech and disbelief lending it strength.

"I lived next door to the child they ruined. I saw her grow up, learn to ride a bike, knock on my door to sell me cookies. I saw her turn from a toddler into a beautiful girl, filled with life and promise and future. Then, four pieces of shit with a sense of entitlement picked her up from a high school dance and took her to a basement party. They gave her liquor, gave her drugs, and took her body in payment. When she said no and tried to fight, they took turns holding her down and used her so that she couldn't walk right for a week.

"When she finally came home from the hospital, the child I knew was gone. She couldn't smile, couldn't laugh, couldn't hardly close her eyes for the memories she had in the darkness of her own mind. Those boys stole the child I knew, and all they left behind was a ghost."

I found myself shaking my head, denying Connors' words. "That's bullshit," I said. "The papers said her complaint was proven to be false. It was all consensual. She went looking for a party and found one."

"Consensual? You think a 15-year-old girl, who'd probably never been kissed before, would choose to be brutalized by four men for her first sexual experience?" Now it was Connors's turn to shake his head. "No, there was nothing consensual about it. The only consensual sex in the whole ordeal was when the justice system bent over and took it dry."

"The court system works," I said. "There was never any evidence to support a charge." I had to admit my words sounded hollow in my own ears. Even in my short time as a cog in the greater machine of the justice system I could see that it was flawed, mostly to the benefit of the bad guys, but I had to uphold my belief in it or my job meant nothing more than a pay cheque.

"There were charges," Connors said, tilting his head back until it rested against the wall. "The police investigated and laid charges, but the father of one of those boys works somewhere in city hall, and the right ear was whispered in. A key piece of evidence, a warrant or an exhibit or some such, was deemed "inadmissable," and the charges against those evil bastards were dropped. They went on merrily about their lives while that child struggled just to make it through the day. I couldn't let that sit."

The argument Connors was making had been made before, although not quite from the same perspective. A couple of reporters, whose names did not appear in the local papers again once their stories were printed, made allegations of legal misconduct in the rape case. But the story was quickly forgotten, or quashed, and never heard of again. With such little evidence, I could not give validity to the arguments of a mad man.

"Even if you did have a point," I said, "and you don't, you

weren't justified in doing what you did. It wasn't lawful."

"Lawful?" It was Connors turn to scoff. "Son, what's lawful ain't always right."

"With your execution it is."

"I guess that makes me lawfully dead."

As I stood looking at Connors, all the anger and self right-eousness, all the smug cockiness drained out of me. I no longer felt like a guard watching a prisoner. I felt like man, looking at another man who was soon to die.

"Why, then?" I asked. "Why did you think they had to die? If you were so sure they were guilty, why not raise a stink? Go to the media? Tell anyone who would listen?"

"I did tell anyone who would listen, and it was a short fucking list. I was a cabinet maker. A nobody. And when a nobody goes up against a group of affluent people out to protect their own, the nobody doesn't get very far." Connors shook his head. "I tired to go the peaceful route, but it was a dead end. I couldn't let those pricks walk, knowing what they did, so I took a harder route."

"A route that led to the death of four people."

Connors shrugged. "I didn't kill them, Clint."

It gave me a horrible shiver to hear Connors use my first name.

"They killed themselves. They wished for their own death when they broke that poor kid. I just granted the wish."

I opened my mouth to make an argument, but there were no words inside my head. Connors moved back to his bunk and sat down, suddenly looking very old, sad, and tired. As I looked at him, I could not tell him that he was right, but I couldn't tell him he was wrong either.

The rest of my watch over Connors passed in silence; him seem-ingly unwilling to speak, and me not knowing what to say. Even-tually the door at the end of the hallway opened again and Rudy slouched through, followed by the warden, grim and tall in a grey suit. Rudy trudged down the hallway, stopping to give me a hard look, scanning to my face to find any trace of fuckery that might have been there.

His inspection concluded, Rudy turned to face the man in the cell. "Its time, Mr Connors." Connors sighed and stood up as Rudy took an elaborate key from his belt and turned it in the lock.

Connors stepped past me, and with his passing he seemed to blur the carefully constructed notions that I'd carried with me for all my adult life. My self-assured cockiness, my absolute belief in right and wrong – including the ultimate belief that I was always right – even the smirk on my face, were all shifted a little. With that shift came cracks.

When I'd walked up to Connors' cell, I'd seen nothing but a piece of trash on the edge of a society that would be better served by his death. But when he walked out of that cell, I saw a man who maybe didn't deserve the lawful death that awaited him.

As he passed I put a firm hand on his chest. When he stopped I extended that hand to him. Connors looked down at it for a moment, then, very slowly, clasped it. He didn't shake my hand, just held it for a moment, and gave me his sad grin.

The grin I returned to him was equally sad, but I'd like to think it was a little smarter than the ones I'd given before.

"I'd like to say 'take care'," I told him, "but...you know."

He nodded. "I do."

As I stood there and watched Connors take his long walk, Rudy on one side of him and the warden on the other, it was like a shade of me walked with him. The carefully crafted, fine tuned facade of the cocky prick I'd been building and hanging onto all my life had somehow been sent for his own long walk. What was left was just a man, with a lot of unanswered questions.

You Just Weren't Listening

by Kollene McKeown

"Em!" Don't make me call you again. I need you to fix Jack's breakfast. I'm already running late," Kara said.

Teenagers, she shook her head and continued making the school lunches. "Emily, this is the last time," she called over her shoulder.

"I'm right here. Stop shouting," responded Emily, Kara's 15-year-old daughter, cell phone velcroed to her hand, madly texting as she sauntered into the kitchen. "I'm not deaf."

"Sometimes I wonder," Kara replied, putting the last piece of fruit into her daughter's bag.

Emily rolled her eyes, "if I am, it's your fault, you're always yelling at me." Flipping back her dark hair, she pulled a stool out from the breakfast nook with her foot and propped herself against it forearms resting on the counter, never missing a beat.

"Jack come and get your breakfast. Please put that phone down for five minutes and get his breakfast. I'm supposed to be at work by nine."

"Why do I always have to do it?"

"It's not always, and by the way, I still haven't said you can spend the weekend at Zoë's, so come on, move it please. Jack, turn that TV off and come here right now."

Kara's 4-year-old son sat mesmerized by the morning cartoons. Sighing, Kara put her coffee cup in the dishwasher, walked into the family room and turned the set off. "M-o-m" cried Jack, his eyes meeting hers.

One hand on her hip the other pointing to the kitchen Kara said, "now, mister, no arguments."

"But."

"Now."

Throwing his "blankie" to the floor, he jumped off the couch and stomped to the breakfast counter, pulled out the stool and crawled onto it.

"Emily," she shouted this time, "I won't tell you again."

'Okay, okay, I'm nearly done."

"Now, young lady. You won't be very happy if I take that phone away from you, and I will."

Talking a deep breath to keep her temper in check, Kara headed upstairs.

Suitcases lined the wall at the top of the stairs. Kara sighed, she'd have to spend the afternoon, unpacking and doing laundry. Being away for a week was a much needed break however, being back home meant working around the clock, just maintaining the family and fitting in her part time job. Ollie, their terrier, bounded up the stairs on her heels. "Sorry little one, no walkies this morning." The little dog flopped down, chin on paws and soulful black eyes staring up. "Sorry little one."

The last touches of her make-up done, Kara picked up her hairbrush and ran it through her short-cropped curls. Opening the drawer to put it away, she paused, something wasn't right. Jason, her husband of sixteen years, shared the main bathroom with the kids, so she had the ensuite to herself. "I'm imagining things,'" she said, and headed back downstairs.

The breakfast remains were on the counter and the floor and Ollie was happily retrieving the escaped Cheerios. Jack was back on the couch, his blankie clutched to his chest with the TV blaring again. Emily was sprawled in a chair, thumbs flying across the keypad and her ear buds firmly in place.

Grabbing the remnants of everyone's breakfast, Kara loaded

the dishwasher and slid the patio door open for Ollie to go out.

A glance at the clock told her that she'd be late if she didn't move it. At that moment the door bell chimed. "Great," she mumbled, "that's all I need."

"Yes?" she greeted the woman standing on the top step. Dreading a sales pitch of some kind. "Can I help you?"

Lots of hair and large sunglasses perched on her nose, the woman waved a cell phone around. "Sorry to bother you," she smiled, "but I'm lost. I'm looking for Andrews Street." Gesturing with the phone, "my battery's dead," she shrugged.

"Mommy," wailed Jack, racing from the kitchen, "Emily's a meanie."

Reaching out, Kara stopped him then lifting up his chin, she said, "go back and tell Emily to take you upstairs to brush your teeth."

'I can do it myself," he responded, partially hiding behind his mother, but eyeing the stranger at the door.

The woman bent down to his level and pushed the sunglasses to the top of her head. "What a big boy you are. Can you really brush your teeth by yourself?"

Kara reached down and patted his bottom, "off you go honey, show Emily how well you can do it. Turning back to the woman, "Andrews Street is the second stop on your left," pointing in the direction. She began closing the door.

"Of course, I obviously drove right past it, thanks." Bringing the sunglasses down, she paused for a moment, her eyes never leaving Kara's.

A chill ran down her spine as she headed back to the kitchen. Shaking the feeling off, she shouted up the stairs. "Come on kids, time to go."

Jack raced down the stairs, and stood directly in front of the TV, remote in his hand. Emily appeared behind him, and flopped into a chair.

"We're going to be late. Emily please put that phone away and don't even think about rolling your eyes at me. Jack, come on, let's get in the car.

Her purse over her shoulder and the lunch bags and keys in

hand, Kara stuck her head out the patio door. "Jack, let's go, it's paint day today, you like that. Ollie," she shouted out the door, "come on girl, where are you? Stepping out onto the deck, "come Ollie, that's a good girl. Oh, who opened the back gate?" Dropping her purse and the lunch bags on the deck, she shouted "Ollie, where are you, come on, that's a good girl. Racing down the steps Kara dashed through the open gate, "Ollie, come." Rounding the corner to the front Kara spotted Harvey, their neighbor guiding Ollie back with one hand and rolled newspapers in the other.

"Oh, thank God. Thanks Harvey, I don't know who opened the gate."

"No problem, she wandered into the garage. Did you have a good vacation?"

"It was good to get away. Sadly, it's over too soon, back to the grind. Thanks for watching the place and taking the papers." She reached for the dog and papers.

"Always happy to help. I don't think I know the woman you had checking on things."

"What woman?" Kara said shaking her head. There was no one else."

"No?" shrugging his shoulders, "I thought I saw a woman checking the house while you were gone. Must have been someone selling something. Anyway, good to have you back Kara, see you later."

"M-o-m," called Emily from the front door.

"Coming honey," responded Kara, shaking her head wondering whom Harvey saw. He's probably right, someone selling something. "Take Ollie while I lock the gate."

Work finished for the day, Kara entered the day care center.

"Mommy, mommy," bellowed Jack running to meet her at the door. "We drew pictures today." Waving a sheet of paper in her face.

Stooping to his level, she accepted the hug and the picture. "Go get your things, we need to pick Em up."

Tucking the paper into her bag, she took Jack's backpack in

one hand and held his tiny hand in the other.

She had the last of the laundry done and the kid's dinner in the oven, when Jason walked into the kitchen. "What a day." He said brushing past her. Dropping his briefcase on the floor, he picked up the mail and began flipping through it, tossing aside flyers and other junk mail.

Donning oven mitts, Kara pulled the casserole out, removed the lid and stirred the contents. "It was a pretty crazy day for me too." She put the lid back on the dish and returned it to the oven.

"Ollie got out this morning, the back gate was open and Harvey thought he saw some woman checking out the house while we were away."

"Oh yeah? A woman? Hmm," tossing the mail aside, "I'll check the gate."

"Never mind, it's locked now and Ollie just wandered over to Harvey's. Dinners nearly ready, would you call the kids please."

The kids fed and tucked in for the night, Kara poured herself a glass of wine while waiting for Jason to finish showering. They had dinner plans for the evening. 'Date night,' the marriage counselor they had been seeing called it. She had been the one to suggest therapy and the vacation. After sixteen years, she felt things were a little stale.

Sitting on one of the stools to the breakfast bar, she saw Jack's drawing poking out of the top of her bag. Smiling, she pulled it out and smoothed it on the counter top. He loved to draw and considered the fridge his own personal gallery. Today's picture was of a woman with lots of yellow hair and Jack beside her holding an airplane. Kara's brows knitted together. Must be one of the new teachers in play school. Mindlessly she moved to the fridge and placed the crumpled paper on the side, just as Jason appeared.

A last minute check on the kids, Kara opened Emily's door. "M-o-m" Emily screeched, slamming the cover down on her lap top. "Why can't you knock before bursting in here? You never give me any privacy, it's not fair."

"Whoa, don't talk to me like that young lady. What are you doing that's so private?" Kara walked over to the desk, where Emily sat arms on top of the computer. "What are you hiding?"

"Nothing, why can't you just leave me alone? God, I hate it here, you're so controlling." Grabbing the laptop, Emily moved to the bed, placing the unit beside her and crossing her arms defiantly over her chest.

Kara took a deep breath to stop her from lashing out. 'God please let this horrible stage pass soon.' She thought. "Your dad and I are leaving, I just wanted to let you know. The numbers are all on the fridge, and my phone is on, if you need anything…"

"I know." Emily snapped. "Stop treating me like a kid, I know where the numbers are, they're always there." Still with arms crossed and a defiant look.

"Okay. Kara said backing out of the room and closing the door, "we won't be late."

"Whatever." Came Emily's muffled reply.

"I feel like I'm loosing the battle with her." Kara complained to Jason over dinner. "No matter what I say to her, she becomes defensive and snaps at me. What happened to my little girl?"

"She growing up. It's just a phase, all teenagers go through it."

"I hope you're right, she's so secretive about everything. I think we need to put some parental controls on her computer and phone, I'm sure she's hiding something from me. Tonight she closed her laptop when I opened her door. I hope she's not into one of those on-line chat rooms."

Placing his napkin on his plate, Jason, signaled for the bill. "I think you're blowing it out of proportion, she's always been a good kid. She's probably just testing you. She knows how to push your buttons. If it makes you feel better, I'll talk to her."

Smoothing Jack's Thomas the Train comforter over him and Ollie sleeping at his feet, Kara moved an unruly lock of his hair back and kissed his forehead. Leaving his night light on, she pulled the door closed.

Rapping gently on her daughter's door, Kara called softly as she turned the knob. "Em, honey, we're home." No reply. Pushing the door open, "Em?"

Emily's bedside lamp was on and the bed still made. "Emily?"

Kara crossed the hall and knocked on the bathroom door. "Are you in there honey? Jason," she called from the top of the stairs, "is Emily down there?"

"No," he responded, climbing the stairs.

"She's not in her room," Hurrying back down the hall, Kara pushed the door to the master bedroom open, "Emily, are you in here?"

"She's not here." Panic evident in her voice.

"Well she can't have gone far, she wouldn't just disappear."

"Zoë's, that's probably where she is. I'll call." She said, running down to the kitchen.

"She's not there, or at any of her friends houses." Tossing the phone on the counter, Kara buried her face in her hands. Tears that had threatened earlier, now flooded down her cheeks. "No one has seen her. She hates me, thinks I'm too controlling."

"She's a teenager, she hates everyone. That's what they do."

"I don't know, we fight so much lately. It's like she's pushing me away. What if she ran away?"

'She's fifteen, for God sake, where would she go?"

"She's getting more secretive, tonight she hid her laptop from me, wouldn't let me get to it." Wiping at the tears. "I should have just taken it from her. Oh God Jason what if she's met someone online? What if she's with him now?" Dropping her head back into her hands, she began sobbing. "Why didn't I do something earlier?"

I'll go out and look for her," he said, heading for the door.

"I'll come to, let me get Jack."

"No, you stay here in case she comes back or phones."

"I can't just sit here, waiting, what if...?"

"We'll find her, she'll be fine."

Not knowing what to do with herself, Kara paced from room to room. Checking once more on Jack, she headed into Emily's room and stood by the window.

Thinking she heard the patio door open, she ran down the stairs.

"Emily? Honey is that you? Don't think you can sneak back in without my hearing you." The patio door was open. "I know it's you, stop playing games."

She stepped out onto the deck, there was a chill in the air and she wrapped her arms around her waist. "Emily, it's not funny, your dad is out looking for you, so come on, enough!"

Kara wasn't sure if she heard the noise first, or the movement from behind her. Something cold and sharp was pressed against her throat. "Don't make a sound," a woman's voice demanded. She was pushed through the patio door into the kitchen.

A million thoughts ricocheted through Kara's mind. She was shoved down the hall to the garage. It was dark inside; she could just make out her Honda and Jason's Lexus by the little light that came through the windows in the garage door. "Down the steps," hissed the voice." The sharp object, probably a knife, dug further into her throat. Bile rose from her stomach, she resisted the urge to swallow, for fear the knife would cut. She imagined she could feel blood trickling down her neck. Her assailant's other hand on her arm steered her toward the back of the Lexus.

Oh my God, she thought, Jason is back. Where is he? He must have come back when I was upstairs. Surely if he's in the house, he'll come looking for me. Did he find Emily? Where is he?

Kara's mind raced madly. The elbow, that's it, the elbow is a great weapon. Use it, her mind screamed. As her knees came up against the back bumper, she drew in a breath, and with all her strength she slammed her untethered elbow into her assailant's solar plexus.

The knife clattered to the concrete floor, as her attacker, expelling air, doubled up and fell behind her. Kara frantically reached out and scrabbled on the floor in search of it. With it firmly in her hand, she backed away from the moaning creature on the floor. "Jason," Kara yelled. "Help me." Where the hell was he? She was thinking the attacker got to him first. Tucking the knife into the back of her pants, she grabbed a shovel and brought it down on her assailant. Another groan.

"Jason, Emily, where are you?" she yelled, sprinting out of the garage. Taking the stairs two at a time she threw Jack's bedroom door open. Her hand flew to her mouth. "Jack." She screamed. "Oh my God, Jack where are you? "Jack, my baby, where are you?"

She raced across the hall to the bathroom, slamming the light on. "Jack," she continued to yell as she frantically searched the rooms upstairs. Heart pounding madly in her chest, she raced back down the stairs. About to yank the door to the basement open, she spotted movement in a corner of the darkened family room. Fear that her attacker had gained consciousness, she inched her way forward and peered around the corner.

"Jason! Oh thank God, Jason it's you." Holding her chest, she paused for a moment to catch her breath. "Where have you been? Jack, I can't find him, is he with you? Oh God, Jason, someone broke in here, she's in the garage, I hit her with a shovel." She rushed toward him and fell against his chest sobbing. "Emily still hasn't come home," she cried into his shoulder. Pulling herself back, "We have to find the kids Jason, help me look."

He grabbed her by the shoulders, "You're hysterical Kara, get a grip on yourself. Jack's fine, I tucked him back into bed, he's sound asleep."

"But I just looked...he wasn't...he isn't, the woman, she's in the garage," I've gone mad, she thought.

"Shh, we'll take care of it, come on." Turning her around, he led her back to the door.

"No, we can't go in there, no, I hit her, the cops, Jason, call the cops. Jack, I have to go to Jack."

"He's fine, he's sleeping, and we don't want to wake him."

"But...Jason, oh my God, what are we going to do?"

Pulling her through the door, he led her down the steps.

"There." Kara pointed toward a heap on the floor. "There she is. She's not moving; oh God, did I kill her?" Her hand flew to her mouth. "I killed her," Kara all but shrieked.

"Kara!" Holding up his hand to stop any further outburst. "Let me look."

Kneeling over the woman, Jason felt for a pulse. "Is she dead?" Kara whispered from behind.

Startled by her proximity, he stated more emphatically this time, "Kara stop."

A groan came from the heap on the floor. Kara could see the woman was struggling to sit up. Jason and Kara both backed away from her.

"Jason," Kara screamed, "be careful, she could be armed."

The woman, now in an upright position, her eyes darting between Kara and Jason, also backed away.

Jason looked at the woman and in a hoarse whisper said, "are you okay?"

Nodding, she continued to look from one to the other.

Jason stood slowly. "Kara come here," he indicated the back of the car.

Never taking her eyes off the woman, she inched her way to his other side. "What are you going to do with her?" she asked fearfully.

Pulling his keys from his pocket, he engaged the trunk open button.

Kara jumped at the motion. "You're not going to put her in the trunk?" Her eyes widened in surprise. "You can't do that, the police, call the police."

"No," Jason said, turning toward his wife, "I'm sorry Kara, but you're going in the trunk."

Astonished, Kara backed away. Unable to comprehend his words or what was happening, she whispered, "Jason?" That's when she noticed something glinting in his hand. "What...?" This was a dream, it had to be. Jason with a gun. Aimed at her.

"I'm sorry Kara, I didn't want it to happen this way. But you wouldn't give up, therapy, date nights. It's no good." Walking slowly toward her. "Get in the trunk Kara."

Her hands on her chest, "Jason, no, please don't do this. I don't understand. Please." Her voice was pleading: "the children, think of the children." Her back was against the wall. She could feel the knife handle against her spine, she'd forgotten about it.

Could she use it? Reaching around with one hand, she felt the handle under her waistband. How had this happened? Jason wanted out, how had she not seen it coming?

Jason raised the gun, "I'm not kidding Kara, get in the trunk." He pointed with the barrel. "Now."

Her heart beating wildly, she pushed herself off the wall, and took a tentative step forward. "Please." She pleaded.

He closed the gap between them, grabbed her by the arm and shoved her roughly toward the back of the car.

She stumbled against the bumper, and then righted herself. Jason was just about to push her again, when she spun around, her right hand wielding the knife.

"Jas," screamed the woman from the floor, "she has my knife."

Kara lunged at Jason, stabbing at him. He jumped back and took aim with the gun.

The sound of the shot was deafening as it pierced the air, the woman screamed again. Kara dropped the knife and grabbed her chest, waiting for the sticky liquid to tickle through her fingers. Jason slumped to the floor.

"Nobody move," boomed a voice from the stairs. Light flooded the garage. A cop stood at the top, still aiming his gun at Jason. Another cop was now standing over him, his gun also drawn.

"Mommy," Emily cried from behind the officer on the stairs, "Mommy, I'm so sorry." Pushing past the cop she ran to her mothers arms.

"Emily, my baby." She sobbed into her daughter's hair.

Sitting inside the ambulance, Kara numbly watched the paramedic remove the blood pressure cuff from her arm. Emily sat beside her, still sobbing. The female police officer stood outside the ambulance door, notepad in hand. "Go ahead, Emily, finish your story."

"She said she was our friend, daddy said not to tell you," she hung her head, not wanting to meet her mother's eyes. "I'm so sorry mommy. I went to her house tonight, I watched for you to come home and snuck out the back door. But she wasn't home. She left her cell phone behind; I thought if I looked through it I'd be able to find her."

The officer's hand was on Emily's knee. "It's okay, what happened then?"

Emily wiped her nose on her sleeve and looked at the officer, "She's been watching us," she looked up at her mother then, "she was going to hurt you. I got scared. I called the cops." A fresh wave of sobs racked her body, she slumped against her mother.

"I'm so sorry."

Kara gathered her into her arms, tears streaming down her face.

Neighbors had gathered on their lawns and the sidewalk. Jack and Ollie were tucked in with friends across the street. Kara and Harvey now stood outside the ambulance.

Through the open garage door she could see the paramedics had bandaged Jason's shoulder, his hands now cuffed behind him, the woman also cuffed, and they were being led to the police car waiting at the curb. He never looked up, just stared at the ground.

Kara took a hesitant step forward, "How could you do this to us?"

Jason paused and looked up.

"You haven't been listening to me," he said.

His eyes dropped to the ground and he fell back in step with the officer.

Kara felt Harvey's arm wrap around her, "come on, let's go get the kids, they need you."

THE HIT

by Patricia Kennedy

May 2013

Julia Garrett focused on the gunman at the end of the massive room. It really didn't matter how far away he was, being a professional, it was unlikely he would miss.

She felt a lump in her parched throat and tried unsuccessfully to swallow. The hit man adjusted his position. She wiped away beads of sweat from her forehead.

Julia looked through the dirty window of the abandoned structure. The building had once been a prestigious landmark housing a designer fashion studio and retail store. High-end clients, confident in their privilege, as well as regular shoppers, browsing but not buying, made it a favorite destination.

The waiting was the worst. How long had it been? How long would she have to continue to wait? Julia tried desperately to calm her shaking body. She was thankful to be sitting on the oak floor, as her legs felt like rubber and would not be able to hold her.

The gunman shifted his position again and looked directly at Julia. "He's a threat to national security."

Julia gave him an apprehensive look. "Why don't they just arrest him now that they have the opportunity?"

The gunman kept an eye on the street. "He's well-known internationally. At least his legend is well documented. The agency wants to avoid publicity. Details of his involvement with terrorist organizations can't be divulged to the public or in a courtroom. He could be released for a lack of evidence. That cannot happen. Don't be alarmed, it will soon be over." He smirked. "Nothing you do now can change the outcome."

"Nothing you do can change the outcome," Julia reiterated in her mind.

A tear escaped from Julia's eye and rolled down her cheek. Was she a murderer? Of course she was, even though her finger wasn't on the trigger. The remorse would no doubt haunt her until the day she died. Her body tensed, reminding her of why she had left the spy business.

"Don't feel badly. I give you credit for your courage in contacting authorities."

The sniper steadied his weapon and looked through the scope.

Julia repeated to herself over and over, almost as a mantra. "Nothing can change the outcome." Her split-second decision had changed everything. Had she made the right decision? Nothing can change the outcome. Indeed. Nothing.

Julia closed her eyes in anticipation of the initial shot from the powerful weapon. It would no doubt be loud, inflicting pain. Correction, not so loud with a silencer, however pain would inevitably follow. The suspense of waiting was almost as painful.

She spotted her target, entering the hotel across the street. "That's him," she informed her associate. The sharp-shooter held the automatic assault weapon with cool, experienced precision. Julia stood up and walked toward the exit of the building.

November 2001

Nathan Quinn rolled over, grabbed his mobile and checked the display.

"Quinn." He blinked, trying to focus and glanced at the time:

4:30 a.m. "Understood."

He pulled back the sheet, leaned over and kissed Julia's cheek, jumped up and grabbed his clothes. After a quick shower, he returned to the bedroom and switched on the bedside lamp.

Julia Garrett sat up, stretched her arms and yawned. "What's up?" She brushed back her short curly blonde hair with her fingers.

"It's time. We have to leave." After their late night, Quinn would have preferred to enjoy breakfast in bed as they had done many times, but lately Julia's casual attitude toward work was disturbing. Anyone could have an off day, but in their business a mistake could cost lives.

Julia made her way to the wing chair, picked up her leather bag, unzipped it and threw an energy bar to Quinn. "I'll be ready in ten." She disappeared into the bathroom.

Nat pulled back the curtains and looked out the hotel window. Another dull, rainy day, but that was to be expected in London this time of year. He secured his gun against his body and pulled on his jacket.

Nathan knew Jules would be ready in a couple of minutes. He liked that. Her perfume lingered and he breathed in the spicy scent. Quinn glanced around the hotel room thinking about their affair. If he were honest with himself, in the past year it had grown into passionate love.

Logically, he knew they wouldn't have a future. They had met in the complex and dangerous world of espionage. Julia had been a rookie field agent when she was assigned to his team. At first he felt the need to protect her, but soon realized she was more than capable of handling dangerous missions. He admired her intelligence, quick response, and how she obviously thrived in high-pressured situations.

But after 9/11 he noticed a change in Julia. She seemed less engaged and during one mission had hesitated slightly. A major concern.

Quinn and his team arrived at the upscale townhouse in Kensington just before daybreak. Intelligence sources had provided specifics about the kidnapping of an American diplomat being held inside the house. The three suspects were well trained in terrorism and committed to their cause.

After assessing the physical layout of the grounds, an agent disconnected the alarms on the security gate and the house. Two agents secured the front and rear exits of the townhouse, while the remaining members of the team entered. Quinn pointed at two agents instructing them to search the main and lower levels. Quinn, Julia and two additional agents ran up the staircase to the second level. They broke into pairs and proceeded in opposite directions to search the bedrooms.

Gunshots rang out at the far end of the hallway. Quinn and Julia looked at each other. So far there was no sign of either the kidnappers or the diplomat. Quinn pointed to a narrow stairwell leading to the third floor attic.

"They're up there, cover me." Quinn said.

"I've got you."

Quinn cautiously headed up the stairs, sensing Julia close behind him. At the top of the stairs he peered into a small room. The diplomat, gagged and blindfolded, was in the middle of the room, tied to a chair. Quinn slowly entered the room. He noticed an open window and pointed to it to alert Julia. The kidnapper had probably escaped onto the roof, but Quinn crept slowly to investigate.

Quinn heard footsteps behind him. He turned away from the window to see who it was. Julia rushed past him and headed for the diplomat. "What the hell are you doing? Stay down," Quinn whispered.

But Julia looked towards the window and yelled, "Quinn, look out!"

As he turned and pointed his gun, he saw a man standing on the roof outside the window. Just as Quinn fired his weapon, a sharp pain ripped through the side of his head, then through his chest. The last thing he remembered was hearing a scream and then the man disappearing from the window.

*   *   *

May 2013

Julia Garret left the abandoned building, crossed the street and approached the front door of the hotel. She smiled and nodded at the hotel doorman as he opened the 12-foot tall glass door.

Julia looked around the grand old lobby with its rich wood paneling, ornate carvings and antique tapestries hanging majestically from the mezzanine. Highly polished floors made an opulent statement, not to be ignored. Overstuffed beige leather sofas, red velvet and chintz covered wing chairs, brass lamps and imported Persian carpets offered intimate conversation areas. This was a luxurious hotel from a bygone era. Much too dark and heavy for her taste, Julia preferred a brighter, more colorful decor.

She hesitated at the lobby entrance, experiencing a myriad of emotions about this rendezvous. Although she looked forward to seeing her former partner, she was all too aware that controlling her emotions was absolutely essential.

When they were together it had been a different time, but she had a more purposeful mission to accomplish today. Julia didn't want her feelings to cloud her judgment or deter her from her goal. Events that had brought them together more than 12 years ago had been further complicated by their passionate love affair. Had they really been in love, or had it been just another façade in their complicated relationship. With the passing years she had become a very different person.

Julia glided across the lobby toward the dimly lit lounge where they had agreed to meet. She caught a glimpse of herself in a full length mirror before entering the bar. Her red silk blouse plunged revealing ample cleavage, and a black pencil skirt rested just below her thighs. The outfit hugged her body just enough to tease and black stiletto shoes accentuated her well-toned legs. Julia squeezed her red clutch bag, trying to calm her jagged nerves. Brushing back her long, straight blonde hair revealed perfectly applied makeup and enticing red lipstick. Memories flooded her thoughts and heightened her emotions. The four-inch heels helped her to project a confident six-foot height as she entered the lounge.

Julia glanced round. She knew from experience where Nathan Quinn would be seated, in the farthest corner, where he could observe everyone in the room. She walked towards him. His face lit up and he rose to greet her. He hadn't changed much. Nat was still as handsome as ever and her heart pounded with desire.

Their last encounter had quickly turned from passion to disaster. The connection they shared was unprecedented, at least in her life, but had ended abruptly on that fateful day. Her mistake almost cost Quinn his life.

The thought of their breakup jolted her back to reality. He had disappeared, with no explanation and no contact for more than a decade.

Rumors circulated and Intelligence confirmed. Quinn had expanded his professional career as a CIA agent to an espionage double agent, with connections to the Middle East. For the past year his activities had been closely monitored. A terrorist attack was imminent, but the CIA had recently discovered specifics on the target, location and probable timing. Quinn had eluded authorities and his exact location remained a mystery until last week. Right out of the blue Julia had run into Quinn at a party hosted by one of her prestigious clients. When Quinn asked if they could meet privately, she agreed.

As Julia walked through the lounge, her deliberate stride gave her confidence. He was hooked. Her plan was unfolding perfectly.

"Hello Jules." He put his arms around her and squeezed, lingering a bit too long. He pulled away and kissed her cheek, then gazed directly into her eyes. "You look magnificent." Nathan looked her up and down and sighed. "And, very, very sexy." He kept his arms around her, pressing his body against hers. "It's good to be with you."

Her stilettos provided the height to look directly into his eyes. "It's good to see you, Quinn," she purred. Julia took a small step away from him then touched his forehead with her fingertips. She brushed a lock of his jet black hair away from his face, noticing a distinguished bit of grey around his temples. He leaned closer once again, and his well-toned body brushed against hers. Julia ran her fingertip along the outer edge of his ear. Quinn's body shivered slightly.

They settled into the high-backed crimson velvet sofa. Julia slid to the center, putting some distance between them. She didn't want to continue the intimacy of a moment ago. For Julia to accomplish her goal, she needed a cool head while offering just the right amount of temptation.

He ran his fingers though his hair and took a deep breath, perhaps trying to control himself. He nodded towards the bar and moments later a waiter arrived with a medal stand holding an ice bucket. Cradled in the ice was a bottle. The waiter lifted the bottle of champagne and held it for them to see.

"Dom Pérignon. Perfect."

The waiter undid the wire, manipulating the cork loose with expert skill. He picked up each flute from the table and poured the liquid into the glasses. "Will there be anything else, sir?"

"Nothing, for now. Thank you Jimmy."

Julia smiled inwardly; noting Quinn still had the same infectious charm. Who would imagine how quickly his demeanor could change from charming to deadly.

Quinn raised his glass. "To the future."

Julia smiled and raised her glass. The familiar ping of the glasses caused goose bumps on her skin. She took a sip. The bubbles tickled her nose. The simple act of sharing a drink with Nathan brought back the familiar feelings she had suppressed for many years.

Nat retrieved an ice cube from the bucket and rubbed it on Julia's hand.

"Scoundrel," Julia whispered, remembering their past love-making.

"Thought you might need some ice to cool down." He smiled.

"That was long, long ago." She covered his hand with hers to brush away the melting cube.

Quinn placed his glass on the table and touched her hand. Removing the flute from her grasp, he set it on the table. He reached out his hand cupping her chin, and moved closer to her. Looking directly into her eyes, he inched his hand up her skirt, gently squeezing her upper thigh. Her senses heightened, and Julia summoned all of her restraint to remain focused on the real reason she was here.

"How are you, Jules? What have you been doing for the past ten years?"

"Twelve years, actually." Julia bit her tongue. Damn, she didn't want to reveal how much she had missed him and that she still cared.

He nodded. "Twelve."

"I'm still an agent," Julia whispered and grinned. "In real estate." Julia sensed disappointment on his face, but dismissed it.

"That's quite a change in professions." His stare was intense. "Doesn't sound quite as exciting as your former occupation."

"There are definite advantages and I love it. There's less danger and it provides me with a nice lifestyle now and for my future retirement."

"I'm also planning my retirement." Quinn smiled. "It's difficult to change when you grow accustomed to a certain lifestyle."

Julia looked down at her hands folded on her lap. By being a double agent? How could he? Was it all about the money? The Nathan that Julia knew and loved from years ago had turned into a different person. He had been the quintessential patriot and now he appeared to be selfish and without true morals. Did he even have a conscience?

Her heart sank. How could she ever have worked as a secret agent? She thought she'd possessed all the requirements for the job, but that was before she met Quinn. Maybe it was their romantic involvement that had created weakness within her. She had loved him dearly and was afraid of losing him. But her mistake almost cost him his life.

Quinn retrieved the champagne and filled their glasses. Julia took a sip and held onto the glass. Quinn swallowed several gulps and coughed when the bubbles caught in his throat.

He lightly touched Julia's hand. "I know it's been a long time. For what it's worth, I regret not contacting you."

"I understand, especially after I almost..." She looked away.

"Anyone can have an off-moment," he said, "don't give it a thought."

Julia took another sip of the champagne. "This brings back good memories of times we shared." She smiled at him.

"Jules, I've missed us," he said. "I enjoyed every minute we had together. I enjoyed our long talks, meals, and your laughter."

"Is that all you miss?" Julia grinned at him.

"I miss the intimacy and passion, of course. I've never felt the same since, and I think of you often."

Julia squeezed his hand, leaned close to Quinn and whispered in his ear. "I'm staying in this hotel."

"Do you have a suggestion?"

She looked into his eyes. "Why don't we go to my room, order another bottle of champagne, plenty of ice and chocolate covered strawberries."

They left the lounge together and entered the elevator. Julia repeated to herself, "Nothing can change the outcome." She smiled at Quinn as the elevator door opened to the floor of her room.

Quinn closed the hotel room door, removed his suit jacket and tie and unbuttoned his shirt. "I can't wait to be with you." He walked toward Julia.

Julia stood at the window and pulled back the sheer curtains, looked out and raised her face towards the sunlight. She hesitated for a moment, and then touched her ear.

A reassuring voice whispered in her ear. "Got him in sight," the hit man informed Julia.

Quinn's wide-eyed look confirmed it. "Why?" He reached out his hand to Julia as he fell to the floor.

"Mission completed," Julia confirmed. The hit was successful and she knew she had made the right decision

"Good job. With your help our country has one less terrorist."

End of the Relationship

by Ray Livingston

I preheated the oven to 350F and gathered all the ingredients for the lemon cake, the dessert for the home cooked meal that I promised Catherine. I wasn't much of a chef though. I bought a pre-cooked chicken and ready to serve potato wedges, both still needed to be warmed, and could be passed off as home-made. It was a small lie, but certainly not my biggest. Besides, I was making the cake, so it wasn't a complete lie.

Catherine had just lost her father a few days ago, and I thought it was just what she needed to get her through this tough time.

I took half a pound of unsalted butter and creamed it in a bowl using a mixer, adding two cups of granulated sugar until it was light and fluffy, adding four large eggs, and lemon zest

She was going to be here soon. I was so anxious to see her again. It had only been a month, but I already knew she was the one for me. I knew it the very first time I met her. It was under the most unusual of circumstances. I was waiting outside a diner for her father, a lawyer, when I saw her across the street. I didn't know she was his daughter at the time, and to be honest, it wouldn't have mattered.

She was beautiful, and I had to know her.

I was completely out of my element approaching her on the street. But I braved it all and walked up to her.

Right away, she knew I was nervous. She looked at me and my mouth opened, but no words escaped. I only managed an awkward smile. But she was kind.

"It takes courage to walk up to a woman," she said. "Not many are willing to brave the humiliation."

"Oh, am I about to be humiliated?" I asked.

"No, I would never be so cruel. You made it this far, so I just thought you were brave."

"I don't know about brave, but I think you're beautiful, and I would hate myself if I didn't say at least that."

"I hardly think I'm beautiful. My hair is a complete mess," she said running her hand through her jet black curls.

It looked like she just got of bed. "I didn't say it was your hair that made you beautiful."

She was caught off guard by what I said, but in a good way.

She held back a smile and shied away. "I don't even have any make up on."

She didn't have that model look, but I found her natural look refreshing. It made her seem carefree, normal. I needed normal. "A fact that would never take away from what makes you truly beautiful; your kind heart, the way you're so open and approachable."

It was cheesy, but she fell for it.

"My, name is Catherine," she said.

"Hi, I'm Richard." That was my real name. I didn't mean to, but I was struck dumb by her. It was too late to change it now, but to be honest, I was glad to tell it to someone. I was glad I told it to her.

We exchanged numbers after that and set a time to meet later for coffee. I gave an excuse and made a quick exit when I saw her father coming.

Only a month.

I sifted together three cups of flour, half a teaspoon of baking soda and salt, and in a separate bowl; I added ¾ cup lemon juice and buttermilk, and one teaspoon of vanilla. Bit by bit, I added everything to the batter, blending it all together, before pouring it into a pan.

I popped the cake into the oven and set the table complete with candles and fresh flowers. Almost forty-five minutes later and the doorbell rang.

Perfect timing. I was so happy to see her.

I took one last look around. Readjusted the flowers and lit both candles. I reached to open the door, but took one last second to fix my shirt. I breathed deeply then opened the door with a smile.

Right away I knew something was wrong.

Her arms were straight down at her side and clenched in a fist, her purse held tightly against her body. She looked away from me and walked by me. I've seen linebackers with a softer touch.

She was really close to her father. His death hit her hard, but this was something else.

"Is everything alright?" I asked.

"Why wouldn't it be?"

She answered a question with a question. That's never good.

Catherine walked almost to the other end of the room and looked out the window. She wasn't looking for anything in particular; at least I didn't think so. She was trying to build up her courage for something.

Is she breaking up with me?

"I came from the police station," she said before turning around.

"Oh, any leads on what happened to your father?"

"Oh, you mean, is there any leads on the man who murdered him?"

I answered slowly. "Yeah, did they find out who did it?"

"As a matter of fact, they managed to catch a glimpse of him." Her voice was raised.

I remained calm. "They did?"

Catherine reached into her purse and pulled out several photos and placed them down on the coffee table beside her.

She meant for me to come over and look at them. So I did. As I crossed the room though, she walked away, and moved to the other side of the room.

I was reluctant to look at the photos. Partly because I didn't want to see what I knew I would see and partly because I knew it would be the end of everything.

I had my back to her, but I glanced over my shoulder for an instant. I wanted to remember her like this; innocent.

I fingered through the photos. The first few were at a distance of a sniper perched on top of a rooftop where her father was killed. The face wasn't clear, but I knew it was mine.

The others showed a man coming out of the same building carrying a briefcase designed to carry a collapsible rifle.

It showed my face clearly.

I heard the slide being pulled back on Walther PPK handgun.

I turned around slowly. She was pointing it right at me.

She was breaking up with me.

"You killed my father," she said matter-of-factly.

I've had a gun pointed at me before, but this time was different. This time I was in love.

"I can explain," I said.

Worst line ever.

"Don't even. The police told me everything," she said.

The police? What could they possibly know about me? I've never made a mistake, not before now anyways, not before I met her.

"The police don't know everything. Your father, he was not a good man."

He was. He was a lawyer, the good kind, always going out of his way to defend the little guy. He volunteered in the community, even gave to charity.

Hell, I wish he was my father.

But he decided to go up against the wrong people, tried to bring a wrongful death lawsuit against a construction company. The owner had ties to organized crime and didn't think twice about sending a message to me.

"He was dirty and on the take," I said.

"Shut up. Don't say another word," Catherine yelled. The gun shook in her hand, emphasizing each word. "Everyone loved my father. He was a good man, a great man. And you killed him. Was it all just an act? Did any of this mean anything to you?"

She had told me to shut up, so I didn't say anything.

"Answer me," she said.

No answer would ever satisfy her, but a yes would make it easier for her to pull the trigger.

"No, it was not a lie," I said. "I didn't know who you were when I met you."

She lowered the gun slightly "And after? You knew he was my father. You knew how much I loved him, what it would do to me to lose him. He was my whole world, and you took him away from me."

Catherine raised the gun, steadying it with both hands. "You took his life. Now I'll take yours."

The oven timer went off and a bullet left the chamber. The gun shot was distinct, so loud that it sent a shiver down my spine.

I fell to my knees.

She slumped to the floor.

When I looked down, my compact Smith & Wesson revolver was in my hand. I didn't even remember drawing it. I didn't even remember firing it.

What had I done?

I looked across the room. She was still alive. I could still hear her breathing.

I dropped the gun and ran over to her.

The bullet hit her square in the chest. It was a fatal shot.

"I'm so sorry," I said, crouching down beside her.

She looked away from me, but not out of fear. Her hand desperately clawed for the gun that was just inches away from her fingertips.

Catherine didn't deserve this. If I could take it all back, I would. I should have walked away when I found out who she was. She would have mourned her father, but she would have lived, instead of lying here on the floor dying.

I should have let her kill me.

Her fingers managed to reach and pull the revolver close for her to grab a hold of.

She barely had the strength to lift it, but she tried.

I grabbed the hand that held the gun.

She looked at me, a tear streaming down her face, and fear in her eyes.

I adjusted the gun in her hand, and lifted it for her, aiming it at my heart.

I deserved to die. I could have walked away at any time, but I stayed. One way or the other it was coming down to this. At least she would have some peace before the end. At least I would.

Her hand went limp, and her eyes stared blankly at me.

She was gone.

No rest for the wicked? Maybe not.

Definitely none for the damned.

EASY TARGET

by Cindy Carroll

"Great job tonight, everyone! We'll practice highlighting tech-niques on Friday," the painting instructor said.

Mildred Buttons scraped the other side of her mountain onto the canvas with a palette knife. With a thick two-inch paint brush covered with Sap Green she dabbed at the mountain's base to cre-ate bushes. She hated to leave it unfinished but the seniors centre would be closing soon for the night and her friend Olga would be anxious to leave.

Mildred rubbed the brush against the screen immersed in sol-vent, back and forth until all traces of paint sank to the bottom. She took the brush out, shook it vigorously, and then wacked it a few times on the metal leg of her easel. Solvent spattered her black painting smock to join drops of a variety of colours. She wiped paint off her palette knife with a paper towel. The wax pa-per taped to a clipboard that she used as a palette would have to go in the garbage. At least she'd used almost every colour tonight. She removed the wax paper, folded it four times and shoved it in her smock's pocket.

She stood back, cocked her head to the right and looked at her painting with a critical eye. The rolling hills of the landscape, the peak of the mountain, the water all needed work. Some highlights perhaps, possibly a reflection in the water of the trees that lined the shore. Next class she could fix those items. The beauty of the wet on wet technique the class taught was that her painting would still be wet at the end of the week when class met again. Another benefit to the freestyle technique – she didn't need to have any artistic talent or a steady hand.

She never had learned how to properly hang a painting. As a result her living room walls remained sadly bare. The pile of family portraits, vacation pictures, framed postcards collected dust in the attic waiting for Bob to have the time to hang them. Or teach her to hang them. Neither of those things would happen now. Once she had perfected the painting she would enlist her neighbour's help in putting it up on the wall in the living room. Her kids would get a thrill seeing anything on the wall even one of her paintings.

She gathered her wet paint brushes with hands that shook like an 80-year-old with Parkinson's. She managed to get all of the brushes in the container without dropping any. Next she took her time putting the caps back on her oil paints. At her age she rushed nothing, taking the time to enjoy the moment because the next moment was never a guarantee. Her Bob knew that all too well.

"Okay, ladies, that's it for today! Be careful out there, make sure you buddy up on the trip home. Never make yourself an easy target," the painting instructor said. "If you're taking the shuttle it leaves in five minutes."

Olga shuffled over to her, valleys around her eyes revealed a life full of laughter but tonight worry lines creased her old friend's cheeks. At 70, Olga moved like a 60-year-old. If Mildred had kept up with the walking after the incident she might have been able to move a little easier now. Hmmph. None of that mattered. What was the rush? If you rushed through life you missed some of the best moments. She wished she could go back and relive some of her best moments. Trouble was when they're happening you don't know they're going to be one of your best moments.

"Let's hurry, Mildred. It's getting dark out there."

Mildred patted Olga's arm with a gnarled hand. "We'll be

okay."

"The paper said he killed someone else last week. I can't believe I let you talk me into continuing with these classes."

"I will not allow these ruffians to stop me from living," Mildred said. "And neither should you. We need to get out and experience life."

Olga pouted at the inference. "I experience life."

Mildred raised an eyebrow but said nothing. Since meeting Olga five weeks ago when she was signing up for class the woman had only left the house for these art classes. Every time Mildred called, tried to coax her out for lunch or an early dinner Olga refused. She'd tried to get her out to the seniors' bowling league with no luck. She even had groceries delivered.

Olga grabbed Mildred's easel with both hands and moved it to the back of the room to make space for tomorrow's class. Mildred smiled thanks when Olga took the container of paint brushes from her and put it on a table at the back by the easels. Mildred shuffled over with her selection of paints and placed them on the table beside the brushes cursing the cane she used to help her walk. Olga always jumped to help her because of the cane despite her protests that she didn't need help. Before the paints were down Olga grabbed her arm and dragged her away. The tubes of paint scattered, most of them hitting the can of brushes.

Mildred picked two up and placed them vertically on the table in front of the brushes. When she reached for two more tubes Olga grabbed her arm again.

"They're fine where they are. We need to get going."

Though she hated a chaotic table Mildred acquiesced. "All right then, let's go."

Olga walked three steps ahead of her turning around every few steps to urge her on. Mildred's cane made a soft "clump" noise as it hit the tiled floor with each step forward. All hallways not in use at night remained dark. Fluorescent lights in the main hallway guided them through the corridors and to the centre's lobby. If they made the shuttle it would take her ten minutes to get home. If they had to walk it would take fifty minutes, maybe more.

When they emerged from the seniors centre they saw the tail

lights of the shuttle as it slowed to turn right. Olga huffed. Mildred noticed her friend's trembling hand when Olga swiped at her bangs. Her friend's breathing quickened. Despite walking home without incident these past four weeks Olga still fretted every time they missed the shuttle.

"Sorry about that. I guess we have to walk."

"We always have to walk," Olga said.

"I know. I'm sorry. I can't move as fast as I used to." Mildred waved the cane to prove her point.

"Aren't you worried about walking alone at night?" Olga asked.

"I'll be walking with you."

"After that. My house is first. Aren't you worried?"

Mildred chuckled. "My, no. My Bob showed me how to look after myself. Everything will be fine. You'll see." Mildred patted Olga's arm. "Shall we?"

The wind came up a few minutes after they left the seniors centre. Mildred pulled her sweater tighter over her smock and did up the top button. Olga clutched her sweater closed at the neck, her friend's arthritic hands unable to sew on the missing top two buttons. They walked arm in arm along the sidewalk, staying as far away from any bushes or trees as possible.

With no moon to speak of the street lights provided the only illumination to break up the gloom of night. Shadows encroached on the sidewalk almost forcing them into the road if they wanted to stay in the light. Though the art classes were offered at various times during the day and an earlier evening class, Mildred had wanted to take the late class. They were less rushed being the last class of the day, allowing them to be more creative but the later class meant always walking home in the dark. In mid-fall the sun set at least a half hour before class ended.

When they rounded a corner strobing lights from a police car nearly blinded them. Two officers hunched over, talking to an old lady sitting in the back of a cruiser. Her hands shook as she dabbed her eyes with a tissue. Her hands flailed about as she told her story to them.

"So sad. What do you think happened," Mildred asked.

"I don't see a purse. I think she was mugged. She got away lucky."

"Yes, lucky," Mildred mumbled.

"I told you," Olga said nodding in the direction of the scene.

"She was alone. We have each other."

"Next time we're taking the day class," Olga said glancing around.

"The next class is your pick so whatever one you want."

"I am picking a day class."

She wished Olga would stop being so afraid. The purpose of getting out of the house, learning something new, having an adventure, was to live. Come out from the rock they'd been under and live a little. Have fun like two old gals can. You couldn't do all that if fear ran your life. Mildred sighed. Olga was right about one thing. The city wasn't safe anymore. But they shouldn't let that stop them from living. Then the ruffians won.

Gnarled naked tree branches rattled with a gust of wind that lifted the wet, dead leaves off the ground. Dust and dirt swirled on the street, blew across the sidewalk, encompassing them. A coughing fit seized Mildred as dust teased her nose. Unable to walk, she paused until the coughing stopped. Olga regarded at her with concern.

"I'm fine," she insisted.

"We should have taken the shuttle," Olga said.

"A walk will do us good. This is the only exercise I get, these trips to the centre."

Olga looped her arm through Mildred's again and they continued to walk. "Me too, I guess."

Mildred thought about steering them into the street where the light was better but though it wasn't busy a lonely car passed by every few minutes. They weren't as spry as they used to be. It would take too long to move out of the way, so they stayed on the sidewalk increasing their pace as much as possible.

Footsteps trudged behind them. Loud, pounding steps that grew louder no matter how fast they walked. Mildred's heart beat faster as she held her breath. Olga clutched her arm, Mildred clutched back. Did they dare risk a peek over their shoulders?

Mildred turned her head to look behind them. The shadows followed them, a dark, looming shadow barreled forward at full speed. As the shadow got closer Mildred discerned eyes, a nose, lips. The shadow coalesced into a man dressed in black, a snarl on his lips when he had to walk around the two shuffling old ladies.

Mildred watched him get swallowed by the darkness. "See, a young fellow out for a walk," she said.

Olga's smile was thin. "Let's hurry."

"Fine, we'll hurry. What would your husband say about your fears? Without me you'd never leave that house."

Olga shrugged frail shoulders. "I miss him. You're a good friend for making me go out more."

Fighting the brisk wind had lengthened their walk to forty minutes by the time they arrived at Olga's door. More powerful and frequent streetlights illuminated the street with a yellow glow. The porch light of Olga's house welcomed them. Olga walked up the ramp she had installed when her husband had the stroke and needed to use a wheel chair.

At the front door she turned to Mildred. "Do you want to come in for some tea?"

Mildred smiled. Despite the lateness of the hour Olga's manners would not allow her to just say good night. "No thank you, dear. It's getting very late."

"See you in glass on Friday, then."

Mildred waited for the kitchen light to pop on before she turned and ambled down the street. She had work to do if it wasn't too late. Her art nights were the only nights she was able to get her job done. She tried so hard to make Olga feel secure. Olga needed someone in her life to keep her safe. Mildred needed the mission of keeping her friend safe. The job was getting more demanding and more tiresome as the weeks went on. But she'd never been a quitter.

The street was deserted save for a lone cat that dashed across the road and into some bushes. A high pitched meow followed by a squeal rent the air as cats fought in the distance. Somewhere a dog barked.

These were the autumn nights she loved the most. Crisp with

a brisk wind not too cold to need a coat but not warm enough to go without a sweater. She and Bob would walk the neighborhood, pop in to see friends, stop at the corner store to pick up ice cream. Then continue home and watch late night talk shows. Back when you talked to your neighbors. Back when you could walk alone late at night and not be afraid. Back when the neighborhood was safe.

Mildred sighed. She shuffled along putting her weight on her cane, her hand shook, her lower back ached. A good stretch and a hot bath would work out the kinks. And a tea always helped what ailed you. Before returning home she had work to do.

At the end of Olga's street Mildred turned right onto a side street with fewer lights, more trees, more bushes, more places for someone to lurk in the darkness undetected. This part of the walk always made her heart race. She'd never been afraid of the dark, not really, especially not after her friend Linda locked her in the basement and turned off the light when she was 10. Back then she hadn't been able to make it to the top of the stairs to flip the switch back on again. It had been almost an hour before Linda's dad came home and heard Mildred yelling to be let out.

Linda had done her a favor. Now the unknown didn't bother her. She never jumped in the water before checking the temperature of course but she still jumped in. It was all about mitigating the risk, knowing as much as you could, controlling the situation if possible. Once the situation was under control the risks were calculated.

Mildred hunched into her sweater when the wind picked up again. The walk from the seniors centre got more dangerous every day. Olga wanted to quit, said learning to paint a mountain wasn't worth the risk but what kind of life was that? Risk held excitement, reward, sometimes danger. The ruffians could not be allowed to take over their neighbourhood unimpeded. That was the trouble with today's youth. A sense of entitlement coupled with no common sense in a world that provided instant gratification had turned a lot of the young in the neighborhood into trouble makers.

She paused to stretch her back and look around. Early

evening the street would have been teeming with people but now, after nine, most families sat around the television the kids already tucked into bed. Shadows to her right moved when she walked past. She froze. Another cat darted onto the sidewalk, saw her then dashed back behind a tree.

Headlights from a fast oncoming car momentarily blinded her. She backed away from the street, as far away as possible while staying on the sidewalk. As the car rumbled past her a loud pop filled the night air. She jumped, her heart raced. Despite the noise no one looked out their windows, no one opened their doors, no one cared.

Instinct told her to move faster but that wasn't an option. She kept her walk at a shuffle leaning on her cane more than usual. The squeak of her running shoes echoed, bouncing off the trees, houses and three storey apartment buildings. Before she reached the end of the side street plodding footsteps behind her joined the squeak.

Her heart pounded. The urge to flee grew stronger the closer the footsteps got. It might be someone out for a walk. She clutched her purse tighter to her body, tightened her grip on the handle of her cane. She stopped, turned around. The darkness revealed nothing. She pushed on, turning left at the end of the street instead of right. If someone was following her she didn't want them to know where she lived.

At the house with Hallowe'en lights glowing orange she paused. Was it that time of year already? She would need to buy candy next week. Bob always took care of that. Her first Hallowe'en without him explained why she'd felt the need to keep busier than usual. Realization of the route she'd taken donned and though she wanted to turn around she had set this path in motion and needed to see it through. Bob always said, "Follow your fear. That way it can't sneak up on you."

She kept walking until she came to the corner store where they used to buy ice cream. The one where Bob got mugged. The one she hadn't been to in almost a year because she couldn't bear to relive that night. She saw it happening all over again, ghost images flitting through her mind making her remember every detail.

The patch of blood that blossomed on Bob's shirt, the ice cream melting into the blood creating an eerie pink puddle while EMTs worked on him. Phantom pain throbbed in her hip. She'd been lucky. The bullet grazed her.

A month after it happened she wondered how she could live the rest of her life without him. The thought of giving up, letting the thugs win sounded easy and less painful than living without her soul mate. Bob wouldn't have wanted that. He would want her to fight. She hadn't been lying to Olga earlier. Bob had taught her how to take care of herself in case something ever happened to him. She found a mission and her mission was the only thing that got her moving in the morning.

Her pace slowed almost to a halt until stomping footsteps cut through the quiet. Her heart matched the beat of the steps. Sweat tickled as it trickled down her face. Muscles tense, hands shaking, she picked up her pace, making it to the end of the street in safety.

She let out a sigh, peeked over her shoulder trying to find anything moving in the shadows. If he was there he wouldn't let her see him. Not yet. This fox and hound game happened every time. And every time it did not end well. Though she hoped every day that the criminals would wake up and smell the freedom they continued to rob and rape and murder.

Tired, longing for a hot bath, Mildred stopped the game when she heard the footsteps again and kept walking. One of them had to give in or nothing would get accomplished.

"Hand it over granny," a deep voice said.

Mildred turned to face the ruffian that had passed her and Olga earlier. "I don't have anything of value," she said.

"I'll be the judge of that."

"I'm sorry. No you won't."

She straightened. The pain from hunching for over two hours started to subside. His eyes widened, a sneer curled his lips. Faster than she could think about it she whacked his legs with her cane, sweeping his feet out from under him. He hit the ground with a thud.

Taking advantage of his confusion she touched the button on

her cane that released the handle from the collar. Silence still filled the night air. She pulled the handle from the shaft of her cane and pointed the gun at the thug He brought his hands up in front of his face. They were tough until someone fought back. Bullies.

Mildred inched into the shadows kissing the sidewalk keeping her gaze on her would be attacker. Her black painting smock helped her blend into the darkness. When she thought she was safe she pulled the trigger three times. Each one hit its mark, the thug jerking with each bullet. It wasn't a powerful gun but at close range it was always deadly. She never missed.

Adrenaline kicked in. Her mouth dry, her hands steady, Mildred grabbed the man's hoodie and pulled. Every few inches she stopped to catch her breath, gather more strength and then she pulled again until he was positioned behind a bush. No telling how long it would take someone to find him. And she needed to be elsewhere when they did.

Her mission for the evening complete, Mildred hustled along the sidewalk, doubled back past the store. The game had gone on longer than she intended but she still took the long way home.

Though not needed, she used the cane as a walking stick but increased her pace from her earlier 80-year-old shuffle to a much faster walk. A car back firing and a gun going off might not have caused alarm for neighbourhood residents. But it might have. If you knew the sound of both you wouldn't mistake one for the other. Fortunately most people didn't.

She enjoyed the rest of her walk in peace and an hour and ten minutes after leaving the centre she arrived home.

The house was quiet, empty. She always felt that way when she returned home from anywhere. The lack of Bob's presence weighed on her. It didn't smell like him anymore either. At once sad and happy that she hadn't kept his cologne, she dropped her cane by the door then proceeded into the house flipping on switches as she went. A spot of tea would do nicely she thought, remembering Olga's question earlier that night. Mildred ventured into the kitchen, grabbed the kettle from the stove and filled it with water. Seeing her knobby wrinkled hand she put the kettle on the stove and turned the burner on then went into the bathroom to remove her makeup.

First she peeled off the old hand gloves. Once her hand was free from the foam latex glove she wiggled her sweaty smooth fingers. The gloves kept her hands very warm but they were a necessary evil on her mission to make the streets safe again. Now that her hands could breathe she removed the face makeup she applied every Tuesday and Friday before heading to the seniors centre. Her once wrinkled face once again looked 58.

The kettle whistled.

She dashed out of the bathroom, made a quick stop in the living room to turn on the television and change it to the local news then hurried into the kitchen to turn off the stove. With a steady hand she reached into the cupboard, withdrew a mug, dropped a tea bag inside then poured boiling water over it. She liked her tea to be tea and not dirty water so she let it sit for a few minutes while she tidied up the few dishes taking up space on the counter.

She added a generous amount of milk to her tea, scooped out the tea bag with a spoon and dropped it in the garbage. Then she went to the living room via the entry way so she could grab her cane.

Seated in her favourite chair, legs propped up, cane across her lap, she grabbed the small utility knife from the side table. After the set of four vertical notches with a fifth crossing through them she started another set with one notch.

When the news came on she turned up the television. The neutral, trustworthy face of the anchor soothed her after a long evening. In the top right corner of the screen a picture of the neighbourhood appeared.

"Breaking news tonight as another victim was found just minutes ago in the Highland Trails area. Shot three times at close range, this is the sixth murder victim in four weeks. In other news police say other violent crimes in the area are down. Those stories and more tonight on your eleven o'clock news."

YOUR NUMBER IS UP

by Karen Blake-Hall

"Bet you don't have the balls to do it."

I hated it when Ricky sneered at me. I'm trying so hard to fit into the in crowd. "That's not what your mama said last night," I said as I punched him in the arm, hoping he'd lighten up.

"My mama is only interested in real men, not chicken-shit like you."

Damn, I'd only made it worse, and now I'd have to steal the phone from the scary guy. Well he probably didn't scare Ricky but he sure as hell scared me. He was tall and old, I'd guess 30. But it was the stillness in his stance that really seemed threatening. I couldn't see his face because of his hoodie, but he seemed all muscle and I was, well a skinny 13-year-old. "You couldn't recognize chicken-shit if you slipped in it." I forced a laugh and pointed. "You meant that guy."

"Yeah, I want you to take that guy's cell and give it to me."

I shook my head. "No way. If I'm stealing it then I'm keeping it. If you want it, you take it."

"Chicken-shit."

"No I'm not. I'll take it, but I'm not going to give it to you." I took a step closer to the man standing across the noisy food court from us. "I'm taking his cell and I'm keeping it."

"Stop yapping and go get it," said Ricky.

The other guys laughed and I took a deep breath then walked through the scattered table and chairs. Old people and mothers with yelling brats were the only ones in the food court at this time of the day. And us. But we'd all left school before lunch to show what bad-asses we were.

My mom would ground me if she ever found out but she worked such long hours she'd never hear about it. As long as I was in bed before she got home, everything was cool.

I skirted around the outside of the pillars then stopped. The guy shifted his weight to the other foot and I froze. He was waiting for someone. If I wasn't careful, I could have to deal with two old dudes.

He pulled out his cellphone and this time I could see it. I'd never seen a cell like it. It was black, larger than most and yet very thin. The screen glowed greener then I'd ever seen. Great, it was a piece of junk and I was going to risk being tossed out of the mall permanently just to prove to Ricky I had balls. Why did I care about what Ricky and the other guys thought about me? But I did, and that was why I was here.

I watched the guy slide the cell back into his hoodie's pocket. I might be able to lift it before he noticed. My dad had taught me how to pickpocket but I'm not sure how good he was. After all, he's in prison and that was why my mom and me had such a hard time. But I was sure I was better than Ricky and the other guys.

I moved closer as he pulled out his cell again and scrutinized a picture on it. He looked at the man sitting on the bench by the fake palm tree all twinkly with the Christmas lights then he walked over to the man, and sat down beside him.

I looked over at Ricky and the guys. They were laughing at me but there was nothing I could do. You can't lift a cell from a guy sitting down.

He leaned towards the man beside him, extended his cell and took a picture of the two of them then stood and started walking as he slipped the cell back into his pocket.

I glanced at the guy on the bench. He was slumped against the bench, stoned or something.

For a moment I wasn't sure what I should do. Go and see if the man was all right or follow the dude with the phone. I glanced at the man on the bench. He didn't move, and the blank stare on his face creeped me out so I followed the phone. After all, the bet was for me to get the phone.

The guy quickly crossed the food court and headed down the hall toward the bus stop. He picked up his pace and it was all I could do to keep up without running after him. When he suddenly stopped, so did I. I didn't want to spook him and end up getting caught like my old man.

Then the hooded man started walking again and so did I. Somehow I had to get to his left side if I was going to score the cell. I would have to bump him then twist away and pocket the phone as I did it. It would have been easier if one of the guys was with me to set up a diversion, but I was solo today.

A fat woman barrelled down at both of us. I was one lucky bastard. Stepping sideways I bumped the guy, lifted the phone and took off. I'd done it. Now Ricky would have to shut up about me. I was now as much a member of the group as he was and he couldn't stop me.

I slowly worked my way back so it wasn't obvious I took the cell if the guy noticed it was missing. When I got to the food court, the mall security guys ran past me and I froze. Ricky and the guys were standing right where I had left them so I sauntered over to them, hoping the mall cops didn't notice me. "Got it."

"Shut up." Ricky glared at me. "What's wrong with you?"

"Nothing. What's wrong with you?" I punched him in the arm but this time I drove my fist into him as hard as I could. "I got the cell."

"Don't you see the cops?" He pointed toward the bench. "That guy just died."

"Who?" I turned around and saw security standing around the man slumped on the bench. I pulled the cell out of my pocket. "Hey, I got the last picture of him right here."

Ricky tried to grab the phone but I turned to block him and jammed it into my pocket. "Finders keepers."

"You'd better drop it so someone can find it. It's got incriminating evidence on it," Ricky said.

"Who do you think you are? Incriminating evidence." I looked at Simon and nodded in Ricky's direction. "Guess who watched CSI?"

"Keep your voice down. The mall cops might hear you."

"Even if they do, what are they going to do? I found a cell-phone? I'll tell them I found it in the washroom and all they will do is take it away from me."

Ricky raised his finger at me. "You lifted that phone from the hoodie guy."

"If you try to prove it, you're a snitch." I look at the other guys. ``Ricky's a snitch, Ricky's a snitch."

"Am not."

I poked him in the chest. "So, I found it." I looked at the guys and nodded my head. "Right guys."

Max, Jimar and Simon all nodded and for the first time in my life I felt like a winner. The old man's lecturing had finally paid off. I was a master pickpocket and the guys were in awe of me.

"Can you show me how to do it?" asked Simon, the eagerness on his face made me laugh.

"It takes years of practice to be able to do what I just did."

"Yeah, if that's true, who taught you?" challenged Ricky.

"My dad. I don't usually tell anyone this but he's in prison. The old man is a master thief."

"He wasn't that good if he got caught," sneered Ricky. God, I hated his superior attitude.

"Your old man just sells shoes, so who are you to talk." I turned to face the guys, making sure he was at my side. I stole the cell, not him. "My dad was in charge of a major theft ring." He wasn't. He was the chump that took the rap for the leader, but the guys didn't need to know that. "He's got millions stashed away so when he gets out, we're gonna live the high life."

I could tell by the way my friends' eyes widened they believed my story. It felt good to be looked up to.

"What ya gonna do when the guy finds you and demands his phone back?" Ricky refused to let me win.

I waved my hand, dismissing him. "He didn't even know I

took it."

"He knows you bumped into him and he'll notice his phone is missing. He'll put two and two together and beat the crap outta you."

Shrugging, I said, "You worry like my grandma." Looking over at the other guys I added. "Ricky is such an old woman." He tensed and I knew I'd just made an enemy but it didn't matter. The other guys saw me as a hero.

A cop came over to us. "You boys should go home now."

Taking the lead I nodded and said, "Yes, officer. We'll leave right now."

The guys looked at me and I knew I was now the group's leader. "Come on guys," I said as I headed down the hall leaving the food court. Max and Simon walked beside me but Jimar lingered with Ricky. I didn't trust either of them. It would be just like Ricky to tell the cops I lifted the guy's phone. With the picture of the dead guy and him on it, I'd get busted. "Look guys, I gotta take a piss, you guys leave and we'll meet up in the park by your houses."

They looked at one another, nodded and started to walk away. Now all I had to do was get into the bathroom and leave the phone on the sink counter. Someone else would take it and I wouldn't be connected to it anymore.

I slipped down the hall toward the washroom, glanced around and then ducked in. Taking the phone from my pocket I placed it on the water soaked counter.

"Hi." The guy had followed me into the bathroom.

"I didn't take it."

"What?"

"Your phone, I didn't take it. It was, on the counter when I walked in."

"Good, because you don't know what I would have to do to you if you took my phone."

"I didn't."

He reached out and snatched the phone from the counter, wiped it on his worn jeans and slipped it back into his pocket. "You should go home now. It's not your time."

"You don't have the right to tell me what to do. It's not like you're my old man or anything." I wanted to run past him but my legs were glued to the floor.

"Son, you don't want to fight with me. It's not your time, but things have a way of changing."

I tried to walk around him but he seemed to take up the whole space at the door. "What do you mean it's not my time?"

"Just that. It's not your time."

My heart raced, my palms sweated but I still couldn't move past him.

Son..."

I pointed at him. "I'm not your son. Just take your damn phone and leave me alone or I'm telling the cops."

"Telling them what?"

My fingers were shaking so badly that I jammed my fists into my jean pockets. "I saw you take that picture and then I saw the man die. You killed him. I saw the whole thing so leave me alone or I'm telling the cops."

"Son..."

"Don't call me that."

His phone rang and it was then that I noticed it in his hand. He didn't answer it. Now he was even creepier than he'd been before. He looked at me and I saw pity, not contempt. I was used to contempt, but pity was harder to deal with. "Answer it."

"I don't think you want me to do that."

"I told you to, didn't I?"

The thing glowed with an eerie green light. His phone was possessed. Who the hell had a possessed cell?

He raised it to his ear and I saw the pity drain from his face. I tried to get past him but it was like he had a force field that held me in place.

"Son, say cheese."

The flash of light was all I saw as I crumpled to the floor and heard him say, "Never tell the Grim Reaper to answer his phone. That means your number is up."

BBQ

by Rick Gustafson

We'd claimed it as road kill.

But the truth was we'd pinched it from beneath a balcony at the Beverly Crest Apartments on our way home from the bar, tossing the old barbecue grill into the rusty bed of my roommate's purple El Camino and making our getaway.

Inspired by our acquisition, me and Mickey decided to celebrate by holding the first ever Oktoberfest that night at our apartment, but there was already a hitch. We hadn't counted on the $25 deposit the clerk at the all-night gas station demanded for the propane tank. That left us $9, not enough for both a six pack and brats. We bought the beer.

Later, I purposefully made my way to the refrigerator case at the SuperMart, hoping my baggy coat wasn't too conspicuous. I snatched two packages of brats, slipping them into my oversized pockets just as another shopper rounded the corner from the snack-food aisle. Not waiting to see if she had seen, I stepped into the aisle behind me, snagging a jar of sauerkraut and dashed for Mickey's waiting El Camino.

All the way home, I watched the rear-view mirror for signs of pursuit, my stomach rumbling with hunger in anticipation of grilled brats and beer.

I breathed a sigh of relief as we reached the entrance to our apartment complex. But as we pulled into our parking spot, the El Camino's headlights flashed across the vacant spot previously occupied by our barbecue grill and propane tank.